ONE GAME AT A TIME

ONE GAME AT A TIME

GEORGE F. BROWN

First published 2023 by DB Publishing, an imprint of JMD Media Ltd,

Nottingham, United Kingdom.

ISBN 9781780916545

Printed in the UK

1

The boos started as soon as the final whistle blew. The tension had been building long before that. All four corners of Yewtree Lane were united in a cascade of anger and abuse, marked by row after row of snarling, reddened faces, all hurling insults towards the grass. Some had made their way down the stands to the Vanarama advertising boards that lined the borders of the pitch, arms outstretched and fingers pointed, to make sure their frustrations could be heard even clearer. A half-full coffee cup was launched into the air, landing to the left of the goal frame, the contents glazing the murky, green turf.

The Bucknall players made their ways to the changing rooms as quickly as they could. The manager, John Summers, shook the hand of his opposite number and offered a nod of congratulations, but could barely lift his head to fully acknowledge the animosity around him. He had heard the chants aimed at him, prompted by the concession of the third Yeovil goal: 'You're getting sacked in the morning!'; 'Fuck off, Summers. Fuck off.' The disconsolate expression that had settled on his face suggested he had already accepted his sentence. He put an arm around one of the younger members of his team and joined him in disappearing beneath the shelter of the tunnel.

Watching his manager's head duck out of view from his vantage point several rows above him stood Steven Rosser, Bucknall's owner and chairman. He was dressed the same as ever: tailored chequered trousers, stiff cotton shirt and then a waistcoat to add some panache to the look before the more traditional blazer on top. A matchday kit to match the players. His large sunglasses occupied most of his face, hiding the cold stare he held in his eyes. Some of the fans nearest to him in the Village Stand had begun to aim some of their frustrations in his direction. He wasn't intimidated by the abuse. He'd seen it all before. But one man did stand out, standing down to his left at one of the exits. He wasn't saying anything but the gesture said it all. Arms held aloft, his was expression not one of anger but of total bemusement. 'What are you going to do about this?' Rosser got the message. In his near four-year stint as chairman, it had surely never been this bad.

In the far-right corner of the ground, tucked in the Batter's End, the stand named for the local cricket pitch behind it, was the electronic scoreboard, which blinked out in shaky red font: Bucknall F.C 1, Yeovil Town 4. It was the Bucks' fifth game of the season and it left them propping up the National League with just the one point.

		Played	Points
20	Dover Athletic	5	3
21	Altrincham	5	3
22	Eastleigh	4	2
23	Gloucester City	4	1
24	Bucknall	5	1

The stadium began to empty. Flocks of fans filtered out into the lane that ran parallel to the main entrance. Some stuck together in their packs, still lamenting the events of the game and the general plight of their local side, heading to The Crawford, the nearest pub, to continue the inquest. Others began to disperse down different alleys, heading home for dinner. A few kids began kicking a ball down the street, bouncing it off curbs and bins as they ran alongside it. The procession of grey-and-black-striped shirts gradually being stretched across the town, like a mass of advancing television static.

Back in Yewtree Lane, the club stewards began to solemnly move throughout the stands, dressed in their fluorescent yellow jackets and wielding black bin bags and litter pickers, removing the significant debris that had been left behind. In the ticket office, the officials were starting to count the takings. A club representative went to retrieve the corner flags, carrying them under his arm, the flags flapping as he moved. The angry, sweary echo had drifted away and some kind of peace had returned.

In the home changing room, the players sat silently on the benches. They had taken their shirts off, throwing them in a large pile in the centre of room, most not managing to find the linen bag that was the intended target. Some sat slumped forwards, heads in their hands. Others sat back, looking expectantly towards the coaching staff to provide solace. One repeatedly thumped his fist against his locker, but no team-mate bothered to offer a calming word. Summers made his way slowly to the gap at the front of the room, where all his players could see him clearly. He took a deep breath and began what he knew would be his final speech to his team.

2

Before the final whistle had blown, Gifford had already reached the comfort of his Golf. He flicked the button on his keys and stepped in the driver's side, removing the black cap he had been wearing and discarding it on the passenger seat before running his hand through his dark brown hair, sweeping some of the sweat back to act as a kind of holding gel. The reason Gifford had left early was so he could escape the post-match rush and the subsequent traffic around Bucknall, but he figured he had at least a moment to himself, so he turned two knobs on the dashboard, granting himself a blast of air conditioning and of Smooth FM. The question flashed through his mind, 'Are you going to try and not think about it?' He shook his head in response and pulled the car out into the middle of the street, turning the wheel slowly, before heading away from Yewtree Lane and starting his journey home.

Once he had made his way out of the suburban area that he had used for free parking, Gifford's mind went into autopilot, such was his familiarity with the route out of the town centre. His hands moved between the wheel and the gear stick but his thoughts were back on the pitch, replaying the events of the game. The positioning of the left-back for the first goal, higher than the rest of the back four, pressing the Yeovil winger when he should have delegated to one of his midfielders. The striker exploiting the space vacated behind him to run in and nick it over the lunging keeper. The complete lack of imagination on goal kicks, straight up to the hapless Bucknall striker every time, despite the fact he didn't win a header for the entire game against their two brutes playing at centre-half. The left midfielder standing on the edge of the box when there was an ocean of space at the back post every time they went down Yeovil's right.

Gifford knew this was futile. He had struggled with the pointlessness of these exercises for some time, but like any addict, it would take immense effort to cut the habit and unlike other addicts, his particular vice wasn't doing him any severe harm. He moved the players around in his head like he was playing Subbuteo, dragging the centre-halves five yards higher and tucking the midfielders in tighter. Watching the analysis of pundits on shows like *Monday Night Football* had been a major discovery in his life, as he could now visualise moving the players in stationary images or drawing triangles on the pitch to show them where the space was. He had borrowed the interactive boards used by the likes of Jamie Carragher and had recreated one in his imagination. All to fix a game that had already finished and could not be changed. It happened pretty much every time he watched football, on television and when he went to games live, but when it was Bucknall it was ten times worse. It was accompanied by an ache in his stomach, a burning urge to make it OK. To make the result what he wanted it to be.

That ache was paired with an increasingly dry mouth. He needed a drink. He would have normally had a pint during the game but his choice to bring the car and the fear of drawing extra attention to himself prevented that. His days of drinking in The Crawford were long gone, his choice of pub now a more upmarket and quieter spot further out in the country: the Goose on the Water.

He reached the last roundabout, Bucknall's entrance and exit, and carried on past the industrial estate and the McDonald's and instead headed down a narrower road into greener, rural surroundings. There was a sense of satisfaction at the ease of the journey, vindicating his call to leave early, as he knew the roundabout would be significantly busier in no more than half an hour's time. The road narrowed again at a junction and he began to swerve the Golf around country lanes, admiring the fields and hills that briefly dipped into view between the hedges and the trees. The Goose came into view on his left, marked by a picturesque pond and a small, arched bridge over a stream. The car park was made up of white stones and the car shuddered as it drew to a stop. Gifford instinctively went to reach for his cap but paused, opting to leave without it. Surely no one would recognise him here, he thought.

3

Lee Chugwell arrived at the Goose on the Water about an hour later. He was in the passenger seat of an Audi A5 that parked up in the stony car park. He got out the car first, readjusting the buttons of his suit jacket as he stood up. He and his two companions headed towards the pub building.

'You guys get a seat, I'll get the first round,' he said.

'All right, Chuggy. Mine's an Amstel,' came the reply from Nick, the driver.

Chugwell was almost universally known as 'Chuggy', a nickname first bestowed on him in Sunday league changing rooms and one that had followed him into business. It was perhaps not a name befitting of a chief executive, but it was too late to do anything about that now. Nick was Bucknall's commercial exec and an old mate of Chugwell's from their days working in the city. The third of the party, Rez, didn't work for the club but was staying at Chugwell's house for the weekend and had therefore been subjected to watching the game as well. They did as instructed and grabbed a table in one of the corners of the pub, with a decent view of the wall-mounted TV that was showing a muted Jeff Stelling running through the major results of the day. Chugwell went straight to the bar and ordered two pints and a cider for Rez before joining them.

'So, John is gone then?' asked Nick.

Chugwell nodded as he took a sip out of his beer, 'Yeah, Steve's told him before he left the stadium. No pissing around.'

'Jesus.' Nick leant back in his chair. 'Mind you, I guess it was sort of inevitable. We had a one-way ticket to relegation I think.'

'Exactly, it's a shame because John's a top bloke, but we wouldn't be doing our job properly if we didn't act. That was a fucking shambles today.'

'I blame Rez,' said Nick, affectionately patting him on the back. 'We're normally brilliant when you're not there.'

'Somehow I doubt that,' said Rez, with a wink.

'Any idea who's next then, Chuggy?' asked Nick.

Chugwell paused. He didn't. Bucknall were now looking for their fourth manager in as many years. They had promoted the academy coach to take over first team duties at the start of last season but that had gone disastrously and he and Steven Rosser had panicked after Christmas and gone for a steady hand in John Summers with a proven track record in the division. That had worked as they avoided relegation, but Summers's brand of football was mind-numbing and he was never going to last long when the results stopped coming. Part of Chugwell's role as chief exec was to find the right man to move the club forward and eventually return them to the EFL. That looked like a fantasy at the present moment.

'The issue is attracting anyone of any quality down here. Most of the managers who make it in league football cut their teeth in non-league first. Which means that you never know if you've got a fucking Guardiola on your hands or an absolute clown.'

'There's talent in that squad. I'm telling you. That's not a bunch of no-hopers by any means,' said Nick. 'You get the right man. We could go places.'

Something caught Rez's eye. He was sitting in the seat that faced out into the rest of the room and he watched as a guy appeared from a seat out of view and walked purposefully to the toilet door.

'Shit,' he said. 'I think I've just seen Darren Gifford.'

Chugwell and Nick immediately turned in the direction he was looking. 'Darren Gifford? As in *the* Darren Gifford?' asked Nick.

'Yeah. I swear. He's just gone in the gents'.'

'No way. I didn't think he lived in the area any more. Do you think he was at the game?'

Chugwell shook his head. 'I doubt it. If any of the ex-players want to come to games, we get them tickets. They come and do talks in the bar and stuff.'

He returned to his pint but the other two stayed with their eyes fixed on the toilet door. When Gifford emerged, lightly brushing his hands down the front of his jeans, he was immediately aware of the blokes staring at him from across the room. He looked down and made his way out of the pub.

'Oh wow, it actually is. Shall I get him over?' asked Nick.

'No, leave the poor bloke alone,' said Chugwell.

Nick sat back, with an expression akin to a scolded child. Gifford had almost reached the bar and the exit when he made a last-ditch decision to ignore Chugwell's instruction.

'Giff! Darren! Over here.'

Gifford flinched when he heard his name. He paused but stayed facing the outside, considering ignoring whoever wanted his attention. He sighed but turned on his heel and strode over to his caller's table.

'All right lads? What can I do for you?'

Nick's words got caught in his throat, as if he hadn't planned for a scenario in which Gifford had actually responded. 'Um. Can we buy you a drink, mate?'

Gifford smiled with a closed mouth. 'I'm afraid I'm driving. Already had one.'

'How about a coke then?'

Gifford's eyes left Nick's excited expression for a second to glance around the rest of the table. Another guy was also smiling nervously at him, but the third offered a more reserved nod. Gifford recognised him.

'Go on then.'

He took the last remaining seat at the table as Nick rose to get another round of drinks in. Gifford continued to smile politely, unsure exactly what was required of him. Was it just some eager Bucknall fans who wanted to ask questions about his heyday? He doubted the current chief exec of the club was going to indulge in that.

Chugwell extended his hand. 'Hiya Darren. You might not recognise me, I'm Lee, people call me Chuggy. We met at the club dinner a couple of years ago.'

'Of course, Chuggy. Nice to see you.'

'This is my mate Rez. And the twat at the bar who has interrupted your afternoon is Nick.'

While shaking his hand, Rez said, 'Hi Darren. Big fan of yours back in the day. Did you watch the game?'

Gifford's face twitched. He could already feel himself being pulled into the one discussion he didn't want to have.

'Yeah. Yeah I did.'

Chugwell's eyes widened. 'You should have said you were coming. We'd have sorted you out.'

'It's OK. I was trying to keep a low profile, you know?'

His two new companions both nodded, realising the irony of them interrogating him now.

'So, what are you up to now?' asked Chugwell.

'Oh, you know. Bits and bobs.'

Nick returned with the drinks, finding the table at a moment of awkward silence. Gifford's fingers drummed softly against his thigh.

'So, what did you think of today then Giff? Not great, was it?' asked Nick, maintaining his enthusiasm.

'No, it wasn't great. They'll sort it out. I'm sure the manager knows what he's doing.'

There were several awkward glances around the table. Gifford noticed but didn't press further.

'It's just a shame we don't still have you out on that left flank, that's for sure,' said Nick.

Gifford took a sip out of his coke and smiled back at him.

'What do you think of young Lewitt? Chuggy reckons he's got something, don't you?'

Gifford couldn't resist any further. He put the coke back on the table and took the bait. 'Yeah, I like his balance. He moves with the ball nicely. But he can work on his positioning. That'll come with more games.'

'What do you mean?' asked Chugwell, leaning forwards in interest.

'Well. He has a tendency to come inside at the wrong times. If he stands out on the touchline, he'll drag their full-back out and leave space for someone to make a run into. It'll also give him that extra yard of space if he wants to face him up and go past him.'

There was a pause as the three men looked at him, their lack of response inviting him to carry on.

Gifford's arms instinctively reached out across the table. He took the salt and pepper shakers in his palms and positioned his glass of coke in the centre of the table. 'Right so my glass is the goal right? Well here's Lewitt.' He placed the salt a few inches to the left of the glass. 'And here's the full-back.' He placed the pepper down an inch in front of the salt.

'Now if he gets the ball here,' he continued, drawing an invisible line on the table to symbolise a ball played into the winger's feet. 'If he gets his first touch even slightly wrong, the defender will press him and nick it off him.' He then moved the salt to the far edge of the table. 'But if he gets it here, the defender's not gonna come right out to the touchline with him, so now when he gets it, he can get the touch out his feet and now he's got that yard to go and run at him.

'Plus, whoever's playing left-back can start underlapping in this space here.' He used a sachet of brown sauce this time to mark the new player's potential runs. 'The underlap isn't used often enough at this level and it's a good option to have.' He signalled the demonstration was over by taking the coke out of the goal position and returning it to his lips. 'Anyway.'

His audience were visibly impressed. Nick puffed out his cheeks and smiled. Rez nodded along. Chugwell kept his eyes on Gifford, evaluating him.

'You sound like you've done some coaching, Giff,' he said.

'I've done my badges. I only coach my son's team though. They're under-13s so it's not exactly the Champions League.'

Gifford stayed talking to his new fan club for a further hour. They talked through the tactics of the Yeovil game, potential signings the club should make, things he had learned from his own experiences at Bucknall and anything and everything in between. Nick and Rez continued with the questioning while Chugwell took a quieter observing role. He listened intently to the way Gifford spoke, the clarity and passion with which he expressed himself and the frantic energy he seemed to possess whenever something needed explaining. He seemed a reserved and quiet man who came alive with any mention of a classic game, player or pattern of play. As if football brought him to life.

Chugwell left to light a cigarette outside, leaving Gifford with Nick and Rez. Once he was in the beer garden, he seated himself on one of the benches that overlooked the pond and put a Marlborough Red to his lips. He took his phone out his pocket and found 'Steve Rosser' in his call history, before pressing the phone to his ear, cigarette still in his mouth. He lit it as the ringing started.

After a while, the familiar Cockney grumble answered. 'Steve. Yeah it's me. Listen, I've had an idea. Yeah, I don't think it can wait until Monday. It's about a new manager. Yeah. Now hear me out before you say anything. Do you remember Darren Gifford?'

Gifford eventually got home just after seven. The Golf eased on to the driveway of his detached house, located in a quiet and pretty street, a few minutes off one of the county's A-roads. He turned the engine off and stepped out of the car, greeted by a combination of tarpaulins and bin bags, filled with branches and rubbish from the house. He needed to take them to the tip the next day.

He walked around the back of the house, through the wooden gate that remained permanently open and had a peek into the garden to see if any of his family were still out playing. They weren't, but as he turned, he saw the welcome sight of his wife through the window. He had married Keira 15 years earlier and had not regretted that decision for a moment since. A kind of contentedness that he only felt upon arriving to the familiarity of his house and family brushed over him as he opened the conservatory door and called out.

'Hello.'

'Hello,' replied Keira from around the corner.

He walked through the house to find her, stood leaning against their kitchen island, fiddling with a pack of batteries in her hands. Gifford placed one hand on the edge of her hip and kissed her cheek affectionately. Her warm, brown eyes met his gaze, but her eyebrows were raised, gently accusing him.

'I thought you said you'd be back no later than six.'

'I know. I got caught by a couple of guys from the club in the Goose.'

Her eyes continued searching around his face, as if weighing him up, but she sighed softly and turned her face so he could peck her lips.

'You don't taste like beer at least.'

Gifford smiled. His favourite thing about his wife was the combination of softness and steel that marked her personality. She had shades of her mother, a strict and sharp Irish woman you didn't want to cross, but balanced that with a far calmer and kinder exterior that made her impossible not to like, or in his case, love. She had been very accepting of Saturday remaining a day dominated by football, long after he had stopped playing it himself.

'Where are the kids?' he asked as he passed her, his fingers running along the back of her cardigan.

'Should be in the living room. I think Danny's watching football but don't get too comfortable because you're still making dinner tonight, remember?'

'Yes ma'am,' replied Gifford with a smug grin, earning a shake of his head from his wife but also a smile she failed to repress.

He found Danny sat in the living room, stretched out on the sofa, eyes glued to the second half of Everton vs Aston Villa on their flatscreen TV. Gifford ruffled his hair as he came to sit beside him.

'All right, Danno?'

'Hi Dad. How was the Bucks' game?'

Gifford shrugged and replied glumly, 'Awful. They got battered again.'

Danny frowned but immediately turned back to the TV. Gifford knew his son's interest in Bucknall had dwindled a lot in recent years. He didn't blame him; it was difficult to follow the doldrums of the National League when all your friends were talking about the Premier League. There was a period where he would take Danny to games, but as he had reached secondary school, he was more interested in meeting his mates in town than he was seeing a Bucknall vs Dover shitfest on a Saturday afternoon.

As Gifford fidgeted to ease himself further into the sofa, a bundle of energy entered the room. His daughter, Orla, ran across the carpet and jumped, arms outstretched, to land on his lap. He just about had time to brace himself and catch her on impact.

'Hello, Daddy,' said the six-year-old.

'Hello, Princess, how are you?'

Orla's big, bright face beamed up at him. 'Good. I helped Mummy do the shopping and we bought some special lights for my room.'

'That's nice.'

'Mummy says you have to put them up for me.'

Gifford laughed. 'Did she now? Well don't worry, I'll put them up for you for sure.'

Orla repositioned herself on his lap, so that he faced out in the room, noticing the television.

'Who's playing football?'

'Well, the blue team is Everton and the team in the kind of purpley kit are called Aston Villa.'

'I like them. I didn't know football teams played in purple. It's pretty.'

Gifford laughed while Danny rolled his eyes. Orla always brought a unique insight to their endless football consumption.

The evening carried on in the ritualistic manner of most of their Saturdays. Gifford dragged himself away from the football to start cooking dinner, while Keira poured herself a glass of wine and enjoyed whatever was the family entertainment show of the moment with the kids. Gifford put on his apron, a Christmas present, and set about making a tomato and red pepper pasta sauce.

Cooking had come into his life late. Like most footballers, he had never truly progressed from a schoolchild in terms of his eating habits, reliant on what the club either fed him or told him to eat. Keira had always done the cooking when they had first got together, but when he had retired, he had found that he enjoyed the moments of peace he gained when alone in the kitchen. He had inevitably been unable to suppress his sportsman's instinct and had found himself taking the practise more and more seriously, watching clips of celebrity chefs on his phone and experimenting with seasoning until he got it just right.

The phone rang at about half past eight, just as he was bringing the sauce to the boil. He knew Keira would answer it and stayed focused on what he was doing. He heard her exchange a few murmurs from the other room but then she strode into the kitchen, a slightly confused expression on her face. She held the phone out to him.

'It's for you. It's Lee Chugwell. From Bucknall.'

Gifford frowned to indicate he was just as uncertain as to what this was regarding and wiped his hands on a tea towel hanging from a nearby drawer. He took the phone and held it to his ear.

'Hello, Chuggy? It's Giff, what can I do for you?

Chugwell's voice crackled down the phone. 'Hiya Giff. Sorry to bother you late on a Saturday. I just called to say that it was nice speaking with you today in the Goose. And that I, on behalf of Steve and the rest of the board, would like to invite you to come in for an interview on Monday morning.'

Gifford tensed his body instinctively. Keira stayed in the doorway, trying to gauge the details of the conversation from his reaction.

He managed to stutter out a retort, 'An interview? For what? I haven't applied for anything.'

He heard Chugwell chuckle on the other end, 'I know, Giff. We're not taking applications for this position. John Summers was let go after the game today. We're looking for someone to replace him as head coach.'

Gifford listened intently to the rest of what Chugwell had to say, letting go of the end of the spoon he had been using to stir the sauce and instead resting his hand on the side of the surface. Keira watched him intently throughout, the serious look on his face signalling that this was not an ordinary phone call. At the end, Gifford thanked Chugwell for the offer and said he would think about it, adding that he'd call him tomorrow to let him know if he would come in on Monday. He put the phone down and looked back at his wife, who was eagerly waiting for some kind of explanation.

'Well, what was that about?'

'You know I said I'd bumped into some guys at the pub? Well one of them was Lee Chugwell. He told me that they've sacked the manager of Bucknall and that they want me to come in and interview to be his replacement.'

Keira raised her eyebrows and opened her mouth wide, 'To be the coach? Of Bucknall? The first team?'

'That's right.'

'Shit. That's big.'

They decided to leave the rest of the conversation until after dinner and didn't mention it to the children. Gifford was almost entirely silent throughout, his mind not on the food or the conversation, but replaying Chugwell's words instead.

He began to fantasise, with specific images coming to his mind. He saw himself on the touchline, dressed in a suit, with the roar of the home crowd behind him. He saw himself conducting training sessions, but this time with professional players rather than clumsy kids. He even briefly saw himself with an unknown trophy in hand, with his players soaking him with champagne. That image caused a shiver to run down his skin, so he pushed it back from the front of his mind.

It was only when he climbed into bed with Keira that night, after Danny and Orla had gone to sleep, that he addressed the subject again. He didn't lie down fully but instead laid back into the headboard, wrapping both his arms behind his neck so his hands could hold the back of his head. Keira's fingers began to stroke up and down his arm, and it was she who spoke first.

'Well, do you want it?'

'I don't know,' replied Gifford, his eyes staring up at the ceiling but not focusing on anything in particular.

'Tell me what you're thinking,' said his wife, in a soft, half-whispered tone.

'I'm thinking a lot of things. It's just so out of nowhere. I mean I'm barely qualified, I've no idea if I'd even do a good job.'

'Well that's not a reason, that's just fear of getting it wrong. It'd be the same with any job.'

'But it's not just any job, is it?' he said, turning to face Keira, 'This is Bucknall. My club. I take it personally when they lose now, what do you think I'm going to be like when I'm the manager?'

Keira smiled warmly, 'Seems to me like you're cursed regardless, might as well see if you can do something about it.'

Gifford laughed and stooped to kiss her head, 'Are you just trying to get me out the house?'

'No. I just don't want you to miss out on an opportunity like this. It's not going to come around again.'

Gifford paused. He knew that was true. There was still one nagging thought on his mind. He had enjoyed retirement as it had taken him out of whatever limelight he had briefly experienced. Playing lower-division football didn't exactly change your life, but it did mean that fans would shout things out in the street. Being involved in football, in whatever small way, basically meant surrendering your right to be treated like a normal person. You were now responsible for thousands of people's weekends, for creating enjoyment and entertainment; you held the weight of a whole institution on your back.

'It's going to mean a different life for us. I won't be about as much, physically or even mentally. And I love the ways things are right now.'

'Listen to me,' said Keira, leaning into his face to emphasise what she was going to say. 'When I married you, I married football as well. And even when you stopped playing, it never left. It's still there constantly in this house, because it's always there in your mind. You know you can't run from it. So, when someone offers you the chance to finally make an impression, with the club you love the most no less, you want to make absolutely sure before you turn that down, because that will haunt you if you regret it.'

With that, she fidgeted and readjusted her position so she was now tucked more comfortably under the covers, leaving Gifford to ponder her words. He stared blankly for a few more seconds before he joined her, wrapping himself around her so his head was pressed next to her ear.

'I don't know why you bothered handing the phone to me you know. You've always been like my agent. Knowing what I want better than I do.'

'Is that a yes then?' asked Keira, as she secretly smiled ahead, knowing he couldn't see her.

'It's a yes,' replied Gifford.

5

It was not since his playing days that Darren Gifford had been to Yewtree Lane as often as twice in three days. Rather than parking on one of the side streets a walk away to avoid paying, he was given a designated bay to pull into just outside of the stadium. Rather than walking in undetected among hundreds of other fans, through the turnstiles and into the stands, he was met by an official, who opened the front gate to let him through. Rather than wearing a nondescript jacket and a cap to obscure his face, he was dressed in his nicest grey suit.

He was led up the stairs of the Village End into Bucknall's modest hospitality area. He walked down the corridor, its walls marked by photos of glory days gone by. He recognised team-mates and occasions he had been a part of. It was appreciated, giving him a little kick of confidence as he reached the club bar, The Players'. He was shown inside, where the bar was nearly empty, most of the tables and chairs folded away and stacked against the walls, except for a space in the centre, where Lee Chugwell and Steven Rosser were sat, facing him.

Chugwell got up to greet him, shaking his hand enthusiastically. Rosser remained seated but extended his hand when Gifford sat down himself in the vacant third chair.

'Hello, Darren. Thanks for coming in. Can we get you a coffee or anything?' asked Rosser.

'Yeah, sure. A coffee would be great.'

Rosser called out to the official who had led Gifford to The Players', 'Could we get some coffees please, Stu.'

The official was dispatched and shut the door behind him. Gifford composed himself as best as he could but could feel an obvious tension in his legs. Like Chugwell, Gifford had met Rosser before at a club event, but he didn't have the friendliness or warmth of the chief executive and was a much sterner and more intimidating individual.

The chairman began to speak, 'I appreciate this meeting has probably come out of the blue, Darren, and in fact, from our point of view, it's not our usual process for recruitment either, but after your chat with Chuggy after the game on Saturday, we believe there could be some common ground between us and yourself, and that common ground is restoring a little bit of pride and success back into Bucknall Football Club.'

Gifford nodded in response so Rosser continued, 'Now, as you know, we parted company with John Summers after the Yeovil game. That means we are looking for a new first team manager. Chuggy has told me that he thinks you might have some of the skills needed to fill that role and we are obviously both aware of the affection and relationship between yourself and the club from your esteemed playing days, so there are already some key building blocks in place, but we're here today to ask some questions and see how you see yourself fitting into the managerial position and your potential vision for the team going forward.'

He paused after he finished, allowing the first lull in the conversation. Gifford's mind was working fast; he couldn't quite believe the situation he had found himself in. He looked at Rosser's stern, judging expression and then across to Chugwell, who offered him a reassuring grin. He took a breath in through his nose and then leant forwards as he spoke, to express his readiness.

'OK. Well, fire away.'

Rosser nodded. Gifford thought to himself that this was a man for whom this gesture would be his reaction to news as varied as winning the lottery and upon hearing his mother had died.

'I'll start. Now we're currently bottom of the league. Therefore, while myself and Chuggy do of course have loftier ambitions for the club, there is no point ignoring the fact that your immediate target will be to move us clear of any relegation trouble,' said Rosser, adding, 'How do you plan to manage that?'

Gifford began, 'I agree that that should be the club's short-term goal. From watching the games this season, I think the players are clearly low on confidence. And you can see that because they won't try that key pass or play into midfield, because they're petrified of losing the ball. So, it's safer to hit the pass over the top into space or to play back to the defence, but you'll never hurt teams playing like that. I need to give them the confidence to play the riskier ball, even if it goes wrong.'

'Anything else?' said Rosser, face still fixed with the same unflinching expression.

'I would also change formation; 4-4-2 is killing the midfield, we're getting overrun constantly and the defence is conceding so many goals. So, I'd switch to five at the back.'

Gifford paused, trying to see if this prompted any notable reaction from his assessors. They remained attentive so he continued.

'Five-three-two to be precise. So, we get another body in the two key areas in which the side is struggling. Which should help plug some of the gaps, but it doesn't mean that we just shut up shop all game either. The common misconception with five at the back is that it is a negative formation. It's quite the opposite if you utilise the wing-backs correctly. Look at Conte's Chelsea or Sheffield United under Wilder, even England at the last couple of tournaments. If you have the extra man in midfield, it means that the wing-backs will feel more comfortable going forward, knowing there's protection behind them. And in a situation where one wing-back is crossing the ball, you want the other wing-back and one of your three midfielders to be arriving in the box to support your strikers. So, you essentially have at all times, five attackers and five defenders. Balance. Solidity. A structure to build from.'

Gifford finished speaking. This time he got a reaction. Chugwell's grin had widened and he nudged Rosser's arm, looking pleased with himself. Gifford noticed that Rosser's mouth curled into a smirk of its own. The door opened and Stu returned with the coffees, placing them in front of the three men. Gifford thanked him and brought the coffee to his lips; the warmth of the steam that brushed over his face was a welcome sensation.

Rosser took a sip of his own drink and then asked, 'OK, well, Darren, what I am interested to know then, what is your football philosophy? I was told by a fellow chairman that at this level, to quote him directly, "Non-league is the place where philosophies come to die." I don't share that sentiment. I believe that a football team, like any other team environment in any other business, needs to have an identity of some kind. So, I want to know, what is yours?'

Gifford didn't answer immediately, rolling the question around in his head for a few moments. He had been expected to be asked about formation and tactics, but this was more complicated and all-encompassing.

'I guess it's this,' he said. 'Football is a simple game, that people try to overcomplicate. If you manage to create a team that knows how to score goals and can keep them from going in the other end, you'll be fine. I've been a player in that dressing room and I can tell you that we don't respond well to fancy tactics and complicated ideas. Tell them simply how they can achieve something and they'll do it. And also, things are never as bad as they seem. Success and failure are on opposite ends of a seesaw and if you add too much or too little of something important, you'll find yourself falling or rising quickly. But by that same logic, it's never too difficult to adjust the weight again.'

There was another murmur of acknowledgement before Chugwell added, 'Well I hope you've got someone massive to sit at the success end, mate, because we're sinking into the floor on the failure side.'

Gifford offered a charitable chuckle. Rosser, as ever, remained unmoved.

Chugwell asked his first question, 'Questions will inevitably be asked about your lack of experience, Darren. Have you got anything to say to that?'

Gifford leant forwards slightly in his chair; he could feel the confidence building in his chest. 'That's a question for you, Chuggy. You approached me. I'd still be telling a bunch of 13-year-olds how to stay onside if it wasn't for you.'

Chugwell smirked but Gifford noticed that Rosser made a note down on the document he had open in front of him, so he felt compelled to add more, 'Look. Bucknall is my club. It always has been. I've been retired for five years and I still can't resist coming to games. It pains me to see where the club is at this moment in time and I promise you, you could get in a hundred managers more experienced than me, you could get Klopp or Mourinho even, but nobody, nobody will work harder and give more to this club than me.'

He sat back in his chair and breathed out. He felt slightly embarrassed; every one of his previous answers had been measured and articulate and the first time he had felt doubted, he had responded with an impetuous rant.

For the first time, his eyes drifted past his interviewers and into the space behind him. The large window that stretched across the whole of the back wall of The Players' offered a view of the pitch. Gifford couldn't see it all from his vantage point, but he caught a glimpse of the white paint of the penalty box. His mind flashed to a memory. One of his favourite goals, cutting in on his right against Peterborough, opening the side of his foot up and curling one into the far corner. He could recall the way the ball just pulled back at the last moment, darting away from its initial likely target of one of the pillars on the Neil Buckley Stand and clipping the post as it went in instead.

He knew every inch of that pitch. He knew you could see out into the countryside beyond the cricket pitch when you were near the halfway line on the left-hand side, a glimpse of the hills in the distance. He knew the feeling of taking a corner, where if you stood as far back as you could, you were within arm's reach of the fans screaming you on. He knew that if you fired a shot badly high over the Village End, one of the poor ballboys might spend half an hour trying to find it in one of the allotments or garages that lined the back of the stadium. He knew the smell of the tunnel, of decades of sweat and mud all permeating through the cracks of the tiles in the wall. It was something he wanted to smell again.

The interview lasted for another half an hour. Gifford answered every question and by the end it seemed as if they were no longer talking hypothetically but were actually putting plans in place. At the end, Rosser stood up and extended his hand once more, officially offering him the job. Rosser explained that they would now draw up a contract and that when all the formalities were agreed, the announcement would be the following day so that he could take training later that day, in preparation for the game on the coming weekend.

Gifford took his offer of a handshake and thanked him. Rosser leant in close to him and smiled fully for the first time in their interaction, muttering to him three, carefully chosen words.

'Welcome home, son.'

The next 24 hours were a blur. It seemed to Gifford like a whirlwind of handshakes, photos and signatures. There were moments that stood out. Raising a grey and black scarf over his head in the centre circle of the pitch, while the club's media team directed him around him like he was on a red carpet. Being shown to his office at the stadium, a small room that was closer to a cupboard than a working space with a whiteboard one side and a shelf that contained a few books on motivation and a half-empty bottle of Bell's on the other. He thought that said everything about the world he was entering into. And finally, his first press conference, where a smattering of journalists squeezed into Bucknall's tiny press room, ready to quiz the new boss.

'Darren, you were a player during Bucknall's best ever league finish, do you think the club can ever return to those heights?'

'How are you going to solve the side's defensive issues?'

'Have you spoken to any of your former managers for advice?'

'Is it true that you got the job in a pub?'

That afternoon, he had swapped his suit for a club tracksuit and drove the Golf straight from the stadium to the club's training ground, a sports centre about 15 minutes down the road called Withington Fields. He parked up next to the tall green fence of one of the pitches and went to get out of the car. He stopped himself.

It suddenly hit him that he was about to take the training of a professional football team, a team he held close to his heart. Nerves started to bubble in his stomach and he began to take a few deep breaths. This was a big step up from under-13s football. Negative thoughts began to creep into his mind: what if they didn't listen to him? What if they began questioning his lack of experience? He caught his own eye in the rear-view mirror and shook away the anxiety. It was time to step up.

Gifford strode out of the car park and past the nearest fence, adjacent to the main building of the centre. He kept walking along the perimeter of the first pitch, preparing himself for what he was going to say first. Eventually he reached a line of hedges with a sizeable and deliberate gap to walk through. He did so and when he emerged, he found the training pitch that Bucknall would use for the rest of the season under his management. Nothing special by any means but at least they had two full-sized pitches at their disposal. Gifford doubted every club at their level could say the same.

He saw an uneven mass of players embarked in a jog around one of the pitches, a blur of black and red tracksuits, moving like a shoal of fish along the touchline. Nearer to him were two men, stood still, both with arms symmetrically crossed. They were watching the players as well and didn't notice Gifford approach them.

'Afternoon,' he shouted upon reaching them.

They turned and he was able to see their faces for the first time. There was an obvious size difference, with the smaller man barely reaching the other's shoulder. The smaller man was rodent-like in appearance with a scrunched up and weathered face, the kind that had clearly stood on wet and windy touchlines for a good portion of its life. The taller man was better looking, with a strong jaw, but with kind eyes shining out of his clay-like skin.

'Ah here he is. Welcome, Gaffer,' said the smaller man, extending his gloved hand. 'I'm Martin Gough, your assistant coach, call me Goughy, every other fucker does.'

Gifford shook his hand and turned to the other man.

'Marcus Haines,' he said, shaking his hand as well. 'Do you know, we actually played against each other back in the day.'

'Oh yeah?' said Gifford, intrigued.

'I had a spell at Port Vale for a while and I think we played you boys at Vale Park. I would have been playing midfield so no doubt I kicked the shit out of you at some point.'

'I think I remember,' said Gifford. 'Nice to meet you now that you're not, hey?' Haines smiled back at him.

'So,' said Gough, drawing their attention back to the players who were now jogging along the nearest touchline to them, 'You think you can get that sorry lot into some kind of shape?'

'I'll certainly do my best,' said Gifford, instantly regretting his weak response and adding, 'I think there's enough there to turn the team around for sure.'

'We weren't sure what time you'd make your way here from the stadium, but we haven't given them any proper instructions, that's all up to you, Gaffer. We can do whatever you want to do.'

Gifford nodded and looked out at the players. He could see that all of them were taking it in turns to look him up and down. He could see a few chuckles and muttered words between groups of three and fours who were running together. One even raised an arm in his direction, as if to say hello, before he was reprimanded by one of his team-mates. Gifford pursed his lips and then muttered to Gough,

'All right. Call them in.'

Gough shouted at the players in a loud bark that seemed to cut through the wind, 'Oi! You lot! In! Now!'

The players' runs came to a staggered halt and they turned and made their way towards the three coaches. Gifford decided to meet them halfway and the other two joined him. The group came together just outside the penalty box on one side of the pitch. The players' breathing was still heavy enough to create a light current of heat that rose up above their heads. They were now silent; the muttering and laughter ceased. They seemed to Gifford not dissimilar in nature to his son's team, which comforted him as he began to speak.

'Right. I want to introduce myself, lads. I'm Darren. You can call me that if you like or you can stick to Gaffer if you prefer. I don't care either way. Now I will try to talk to you all individually today and over the coming days as well, but I'm afraid there isn't much more time to waste now. We've got a massive game on Saturday and not much time to prepare for it.'

He took a deliberate pause, making sure to make eye contact with as many of them as possible, 'Listen. We all know the scenario here. We're bottom of the league. But I promise you, I think there is enough talent in this squad to get out of trouble. We're gonna try a few things today in training that we might use at the weekend but I also don't want you to think of this as a complete 360 from what you boys know already. We're gonna make small changes, small adjustments. And that's how we're gonna improve and rise up the table. I'm gonna level with you, lads. I'm no fucking Houdini. But I care about this club and I think I've got what it takes to move it forward. You trust in me and respect me and I'll do the same for you. And then we'll be just fine.'

He finished speaking and continued looking around the group. There was a mixture of nods, smiles and blank faces, but no one looked as if they weren't impressed. He clapped his hands together and barked out his first instruction, 'Right, now get the balls out and zip it around in twos and threes, get your feet warm. We'll do the first drill in a second. Ryan, can I have a word please?'

He signalled to one of the taller guys in the group, who was wearing a tight-fitting beanie on his head. The others dispersed with Gough and Haines marching after them. Ryan Brook was the club's captain and premier centre-half. His stocky build was apparent as he came closer to Gifford.

'Nice to meet you,' said Gifford, greeting him. 'I just thought I'd kick things off with you first. You were the previous manager's captain and you'll be mine as well. I know you've struggled at times this season, but I just want to assure you that you'll always be the first name on my team sheet. In return, I expect you to be the leader in the dressing room and keep the boys in check when I'm not there. I've seen you play enough to know you're going to give me 100 per cent every game, I want you to make sure everyone else is doing the same.'

His words had the desired result. Brook looked genuinely lifted by the news and smiled back at Gifford, before jogging his legs up and down as if to signal his intent.

'Thank you, Gaffer. I won't let you down.'

'Good lad,' said Gifford. 'Now off you go,' and Brook departed back into the group once more.

The first drill Gifford started was in aid of encouraging the players to pass through the pitch more. He did this by having a series of four sets of cones spread in and around the halfway line, with the aim to be to complete a pass through one of the 'gates' created by the cones. It took the players a while to get to grips with it; Gifford doubted they had ever done anything remotely like it under John Summers, but eventually there were more and more successful passes made and the aim of the exercise, for the midfielders and attacking players to make good angles to receive the ball, was achieved.

He also noted down the players who seemed to excel at the drill most, as it showed they were the ones who were most comfortable on the ball. Conor Caldwell, a young right-back who the club had picked up from even lower down the footballing pyramid, showed promise while Sebastian D'Amato, a cultured midfielder who seemed to feel the need to illustrate this by sporting a headband that held his long hair in place, had a lovely touch and began to glide round the pitch as he got more confident, demanding and touching the ball more than anyone else.

They spent most of the next hour working on shape as Gifford sought to establish his promised five-man defence. This involved working through certain scenarios, like establishing when it was the wing-back's job to chase back with the ball or when it was to be covered by one of the wider centre-halves. He explained that without the ball, the five defenders needed to stay standing in almost a straight line, with the wing-backs only a matter of yards more advanced than the wide centre-backs. However, when they had the ball, he made sure the wing-backs, Caldwell and Nick Wrenshaw, were higher and as wide as possible, literally on each touchline at times, to ensure they always gave an option to the player in possession.

The players seemed to take to it relatively happily and a bonus was that Gifford identified that one of his centre-backs, a young academy product called Ardie Adomako, was good at driving into space and passing the ball incisively. He decided to make him the central centre-back for the upcoming game. Gifford watched as the players shuffled into and out of position as the ball was passed across the pitch, checking their distances and taking it in turns to press. He heard Brook shout at his midfielder and wing-back to drop back into the formation when the ball was overturned, which gave him a sense of satisfaction.

They finished with a small-sided game. Gifford decided to stop instructing at this point and came to stand beside Haines silently, leaving Gough to do most of the shouting and encouraging. The team's striker and top goalscorer, Kieran Dunne, turned Brook, sending him with a quick feint with his left leg before smashing a powerful shot past the goalkeeper. Gifford pursed his lips together as Haines raised his eyebrows at him. They recognised that as a genuine piece of quality. Gifford also noticed Dunne shouting some pointed words at Brook after the incident; the chirpy, Irish accent drawing laughs from his team-mates. He was back in the football world. And he felt remarkably comfortable.

7

Torquay United vs Bucknall
Plainmoor
20 September

Game day rolled around quickly. The night before, Gifford laid awake until the early hours of the morning, his mind spinning with a lethal combination of anxiety and excitement. He stared up at the ceiling, not even bothering to close his eyes, thinking about every possible change he might make and every one of his team's weaknesses that could be exploited.

He was up earlier than the rest of his family, with there still being an early morning chill in the misty air when he quietly stepped out of the house to get in the car. He picked up a coffee from the local garage on his way out and headed to the stadium to meet the rest of the team and board the coach down to Torquay. A difficult first game, away at a team currently occupying one of the play-off positions and who, much like Bucknall, were once an established EFL side and had designs on getting back there.

He swapped the driver's seat of the Golf for one of the front seats on the large coach that was waiting for them at Yewtree Lane. Haines sat next to him with Gough the row across from them. The players and rest of the staff took their places behind. There was a good atmosphere among the players which pleased Gifford. A silent coach was like a kiss of death for a football team. He heard laughter and banter for much of the duration of the trip down south, with some of the players playing cards or arguing over their fantasy teams. Others, like Ardie Adomako, sat quiet with headphones over their ears, preparing themselves. Gifford didn't mind that either. He and the other coaches talked over their planned tactics, about Torquay's main threats and then, when the traffic worsened, about what a pain it was to get down to Devon on a weekend.

When they did arrive, they left the coach and made their way through to the away dressing room. Haines and Gough led the warm-up on the pitch with Gifford observing, trying to gauge what state his players were in. They had worked extensively on their shape in the remainder of training that week while he knew that the higher intensity and possession-based approach he demanded was going to surprise Torquay, because it was such a change from the club's previous gameplans. Gifford had decided on the starting 11 after a couple of training sessions and had announced it the day before the game:

Finch (GK)

Caldwell Brook Adomako Warren-Smith Wrenshaw

Golding D'Amato Harrison

Gujar Dunne

When the players returned to the dressing room, it was time for Gifford to deliver his most important speech to them yet. He made his way to the front and stood in front of his team, puffing out his chest.

'Right, boys. Now I want to thank you all for your efforts in training this week. It's been a brilliant start from all of you as far as I'm concerned. But all of that effort will mean absolutely fuck all unless we execute what we've worked on and come away from here with three fucking points. This is where our season starts as far as I'm concerned.'

He looked around at the team. Ryan Brook was nodding along, his leg shaking in anticipation. Others had determined expressions on their face, teeth gritted and eyes bulging.

'Now, my last message to you is to be brave. I don't care if you lose the ball, you keep trying it. Keep playing into and through midfield. Defenders, look for Seba and Danny as much as you can. Conor and Nick, you hold your width all game, all right? That's how we make the pitch big and we tire them out. But most of all boys, I want intensity. They do not want this more than we do, do they? So go out and fucking prove it. Go out there and run them off their own fucking pitch.'

Gifford finished his speech but stayed still after his final words, holding the pose as his muscles shook with tension. He could feel saliva building up in his mouth and the blood thumping around his body. He continued to glare at his players, as if he could telepathically fill them with the same level of motivation that he was feeling. Then he turned away and nodded to Gough, who stood forward and yelled in his typical fashion,

'This is our fucking day, boys! Come on!'

The players roared in agreement and the starting 11 began to make their way to the door, led by Brook, who looked akin to a man possessed. Gifford followed them out on to the pitch, greeted by the roar of the Plainmoor crowd. He sought out the Torquay manager and shook his hand.

'Welcome to the slog, Darren,' were his rival's words of wisdom.

He looked over at the away end, at the hundreds of Bucknall fans, all gathered in a corner of the stadium, the familiar black and grey palette a welcome sight. They were chanting something in his direction but it was drowned out by the cries of the larger home crowd. He walked closer to them in his technical area and extended a hand to wave. That was greeted by an unmistakeable cheer, which gave him a warm pang in his chest.

He stayed standing as the whistle blew and Bucknall kicked off. Pacing up and down to match the position of the ball, Gifford lost himself totally in the game. Whenever it was switched to his side, he would mutter words of encouragement and animatedly point where the ball needed to go next. Occasionally, Gough would come and stand beside him and add to the instructions.

Bucknall started well. They managed to dominate the possession with the extra defender serving its purpose in terms of there always being a spare man to pass to. Sebastian D'Amato started to get lots of touches of the ball, just as he had done in the training drill, and began to dictate the pace of the game. The first 20 minutes or so went by without any major chances for either team, with the match mainly being contested in the midfield.

Then, as they approached the half-hour mark, the ball was passed infield to Ardie Adomako who received it under no pressure. He looked up instinctively but saw his two nearest passing options were blocked, so he began to edge forwards with the ball. Again, no one approached him, positioning themselves to block the passing lanes into midfield instead. So Adomako kept driving up the pitch uncontested, picking up pace as he did so.

'Keep going, Ardie!' yelled Gifford, seeing that space was starting to open up for him.

As Adomako approached the penalty area, one of the Torquay centre-halves decided he had to engage him now and stepped out of defence to block a potential shot. Sajja Gujar, the Bucks' second striker, came short for him and Adomako finally released the ball, slipping it to Gujar in the right-hand channel. Now the Torquay left-back had to go and press Gujar, which left Conor Caldwell completely free. Gujar saw him and passed the ball along, leaving Caldwell a clear run on the right. The Bucknall fans began to rise to their feet and Gifford felt a surge of excitement. This was a chance. Caldwell raced to the byline and smashed in a low cross, but a defender stuck a leg out and the ball ricocheted for a corner.

Gifford breathed out as the chance went by but then clapped his hands together as hard as he could to express his pleasure at the play. D'Amato jogged over to take the corner, his hair bouncing underneath the headband. The three centre-halves trotted up and began jostling with the Torquay players to try and get a yard in the box. Gifford fixed his eyes on the area, looking for the best places to aim the cross. D'Amato raised his hand and then swung his foot back, getting a lot under it as the ball went high into the air. It was as it dropped that Gifford realised what a good cross it was. Right on the penalty spot. He also saw Ryan Brook had not made his run too early and had been hanging on the edge of the box. He now had a run at the ball and a marker who couldn't match his height or power.

Gifford took a sharp intake of breath. The ball continued to drop and Brook rose to meet it, butting his forehead forwards. The ball flew off it and high past the keeper's reach and into the back of the Torquay net. Goal; 1-0.

Gifford was caught between two reactions. He clenched his fist and thrust it in the air instinctively, letting out a loud cry, but he also found himself turning towards his bench and his other coaches, wanting to share the moment with them. Gough met him halfway and jumped in his direction as the two of them celebrated wildly.

It was only when the moment passed and the ball was restored to the centre circle for a restart that Gifford was able to appreciate the goal as a piece of play and not just an exhilarating release. He even chuckled to himself under his breath. All those fancy tactics and your first goal is a centre-half heading home a corner, he thought.

Now there was real confidence among his players. Their passes were played with more conviction and they began to play in triangles on the pitch, zipping it around with one or two touches. The raised speed of the play caused Torquay more problems and more space became available. D'Amato tried an effort from outside the area which rose over the bar and Gujar had a strike deflected for another corner.

It could hardly have gone better, Gifford was thinking, and he found himself looking up at the scoreboard, seeing there were no more than a couple of minutes until half-time. It was as his eyes returned to the pitch that there was a turnover; Nick Wrenshaw's pass on the left was cut out and one of the Torquay strikers was released down the channel. He faced up Max Warren-Smith who was close enough to him not to allow a shot on goal, but the striker instead laid the ball off to an arriving midfielder, who had run clear of Stefon Harrison during the counterattack. He struck the ball low and it clattered into the shin of the diving Adomako, spinning cruelly in the opposite corner to the one in which it was originally heading. Finch had no chance; 1-1.

Gifford winced. That was unlucky. But he also couldn't help feeling it was his first managerial lesson. Never get too comfortable. He clapped his hands and urged his players on again, but there was no getting away from the fact that that was a killer right before half-time.

When they returned to the dressing room, the players were clearly feeling the effects. He allowed them to get their breath and patted a few of them on the back, praising their performances so far. He had already planned his words as he was walking back through the tunnel.

'I'm actually glad they scored,' Gifford said, pausing so the surprise of his words could effectively get their attention. 'You heard me. I'm glad. Because if we had come in here 1-0 up with you having played that well, there's hardly anything I could have said to motivate you to match that performance in the second half. But now … you have to. It's 1-1. You have to go again, boys. You have to keep up that intensity. You have to keep creating the same level of chances. You have to score another fucking goal, I'm afraid. Otherwise, we don't get our win.'

He didn't make any changes, sticking by his message that he was totally satisfied with the performance. The second half kicked off with Torquay more on the front foot, clearly buoyed by their late equaliser. His defensive shape seemed solid enough though, with the extra defender effectively cancelling out their strikers and restricting Torquay mainly to crossing from wide positions near the touchline.

And then it all went wrong. From their own goal kick. Matt Finch played the ball short, as he had been instructed to do on occasion, to Brook, on the edge of their penalty area. Caldwell instinctively shuffled nearer to him to make an angle but was pressed by their winger, which had not happened much in the first half. That then left Danny Golding free to come and receive the ball but that extra second of hesitation from Brook upon seeing Caldwell marked gave the striker more time to get across to him. Brook panicked slightly and misplaced the relatively simple pass into Golding, sending it his right. Golding slid in to nick it away but the ball bounced loose and fell kindly for the Torquay midfielder. The other two Bucknall centre-halves rushed in to cover, which left a completely free striker in the box. The ball was passed to him and he had time to take a touch before smashing it past Finch; 2-1 Torquay.

Gifford closed his eyes. That was an awful goal to concede. All of his late-night fears about their vulnerabilities when trying to play out from the back had been realised. Now they were chasing the game.

He made substitutions, sacrificing a midfielder to bring on Archie Lewitt, a winger. Now though, Torquay were happy for Bucknall to come on to them, sticking to their shape and challenging the Bucks to break them down. Next, Gifford took off Wrenshaw and put another attacker on, making Lewitt play as an attacking left wing-back. They had a couple of half chances, with the ball pinballing around the area. The best fell to Gujar, when a nice D'Amato flick left him free in the area. He shanked his shot horribly wide.

And then in the final minutes, with Gifford and Gough furiously shouting the team forwards and pleading with them to keep putting the ball in the box, there was a Torquay breakaway. Nearly the entire Bucknall team was in the Torquay half, which meant that when the ball was cleared, there was suddenly a three-on-one situation. Gifford ambled slowly in the direction of their goal, sensing the inevitable. The ball was passed to the free man and he slid it past Finch; 3-1. Game over.

The Torquay fans cheered their team loudly at the final whistle. Gifford shook hands with their staff and headed down the tunnel. That was a frustrating loss. They had played well for large parts of the game and there were signs his tactics were having a positive effect, but ultimately the result had been the same. He felt a familiar ache began to swell in his stomach and he felt his head drop, not wanting to meet people's eyes. He was off to a losing start.

Final score: Torquay United 3 Bucknall 1

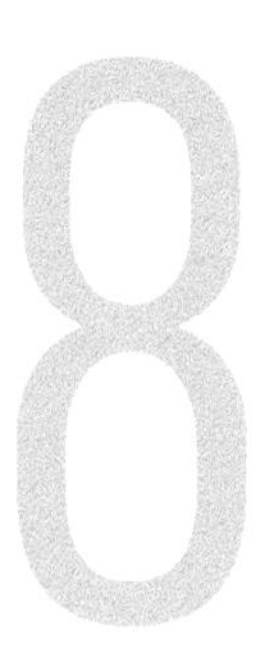

Gifford had to return to the pitch again, to conduct the post-match interview with the club's reporter: an eager and presentable young man with a distinctly private school appearance called Harry Latherfield. He positioned himself in front of the camera and waited for Latherfield to give him the all-clear for the recording to begin. Latherfield held the mic out in front of him while he asked the questions.

'Darren, disappointing start for you as manager. How did you see the game today?'

'Yeah, disappointing because I thought we were the better team for much of the game. I thought we kept the ball well and defended OK at times. The equaliser before half-time was obviously a blow, especially as it's a bit lucky for them. And then we give a silly goal away at the start of the second and that was really a killer for us today, with the boys' confidence as it is at the moment.'

Latherfield nodded along diligently and continued his questioning, 'Yeah it was notable that you wanted the team to play out from the back. Will the goal you conceded warn you against doing that in future?'

'Absolutely not. We won't abandon our plans because of mistakes like today. I've had less than a week to work with the team, so I've been impressed with how they've dealt with the changes so far and the more time we have to work on them, the better and more comfortable we'll be.'

'That's now five defeats in six for the Bucks to open the season, are you bracing yourself for a battle to avoid the drop?'

Gifford scowled at the reporter for the first time, but resisted saying something he'd regret, 'We're just going to take it game by game, this is only my first match in charge. Our only aim at this moment in time is getting that first win on the board and we will take it from there.'

Latherfield signalled and the cameraman lowered his camera, 'Thank you, Darren. That's everything. Hard luck on the result.'

The journey back to Bucknall wasn't as lively as the one on the way down. Gifford spoke to a few of the players on the journey, reassuring them that they'd played well and talking to them about little improvements they could make. He was beginning to get a feel for the different personalities in his squad. Some like Kieran Dunne seemed to be mainly unflappable, never appearing too down, while there were those like Ardie Adomako and Sajja Gujar who withdrew into themselves after a mistake and needed to be coaxed back. Ryan Brook had offered him an apology for the misplaced pass that led to the second goal but Gifford shrugged it off immediately,

'Forget about it. You were brilliant today.'

Gifford maintained the cheerful and positive façade right up until they returned to Yewtree Lane and all separated into their respective cars. He could feel the energy drain out of him as he drove home, the effort required in motivating and lifting the team had rendered him exhausted.

When he arrived and entered wearily through the front door, Keira greeted him with pity in her eyes.

She kissed him and said, 'I saw the result. Sorry, love.'

Gifford forced a smile to reassure her he was OK and then went to greet Danny and Orla. His dinner had been left on the side and he carried it into the living room on a tray and joined the rest of the family in watching TV. As he ate, he found his mind again drifting back to the match. Had he been too hesitant with his substitutions? Should he have been harder on them at half-time? Was 5-3-2 too restrictive in terms of creating chances? He could hear the kids laughing and Keira's occasional comments in the background, but it was as if they were much further away, their voices no more than echoes.

He helped put the kids to bed but then returned downstairs to watch *Match of the Day*. He told Keira he would be up shortly but after the show had finished, he found that there was a re-run of an earlier Bundesliga match on, between Eintracht Frankfurt and Mainz. He put it on at first to allow his mind to switch off, as if his lack of interest in the game would prepare him for sleep. However, he noticed that Frankfurt were playing five at the back and soon began noticing some of the ways they were using the wing-backs when in possession. Before he knew it, he was typing into the notes app on his phone, writing down passages of play he wanted to try out in training. When he did eventually crawl into bed, it was a way past midnight and Keira had long ago drifted into a deep sleep.

9

Training that week involved further developing some of the main ideas Gifford had introduced in his first few sessions. The five-at-the-back system had shown enough promise that Gifford had decided to persist with it, instead focusing on tweaking it slightly. This involved continuing to work on playing out from the back, as in light of Ryan Brook's mistake on Saturday, Gifford introduced an out-ball when the defenders' initial passing option was blocked. He instructed Sajja Gujar and Kieran Dunne to spin off their respective centre-halves and run in behind the right and left full-backs so that when Brook and Max Warren-Smith received the ball under pressure, they could hit a blind pass into space without the risk of a turnover in their final third. It gave them options, which was the byword that Gifford kept repeating throughout the week.

Midweek, he introduced an attacking exercise that he had used as his assessed piece in his most recent coaching course. It involved a slow progression of one-on-one attacking and defending, where initially the defender acted as a wall pass for the attacker to go and finish, before applying light pressure and then full-on game-pace defending. Dunne excelled, proving himself once again to be the best finisher in the side. Gifford knew that he was less good at the build-up side of the game so finding a way to create chances for him in and around the box was crucial.

He then introduced a third player to the exercise so it was now two v one, giving the man on the ball an option to pass to at all times. He was concerned with the lack of goals during this stage, with the defenders often coming out on top even though they were playing against the odds. He then introduced the intended coaching point of the session; instructing the second player to change his run and go in the opposite direction of the player with the ball.

This changed the angle and placed doubt in the defenders' mind. Gifford's hope was that this would subconsciously encourage the players to recreate this in the final third during the game at the weekend and ultimately create better chances to score.

After the session, when most of the players had already got into their cars to go home, Gifford realised he had left his jacket on the pitch with his car keys still inside. He jogged back through the gap in the hedge, finding Danny Golding and Conor Caldwell still knocking the ball around. He retrieved his jacket and put it on, feeling for the car keys in his pocket. As he approached them, Golding let the ball stop at his feet.

'All right, boys. What you doing?'

'Me and Con sometimes stay behind to practise various things. Is that all right, Gaffer?' said Golding, meekly.

'All right? Of course it's bloody all right. Do you mind if I join you for a bit? Don't worry, no coaching, we can just do what you usually do.'

'Sure.'

They started by taking it in turns to take shots from around the edge of the box. Gifford found himself smiling when he struck one sweetly and it clipped the underside of the bar as it went in. There were impressed murmurs from Golding and Caldwell immediately afterwards.

'You used to play for us, didn't you boss? Back in the League One days?' asked Golding.

'Yeah, left wing. Absolutely no pace but had a decent cross and shot on me.'

'Did you play in the play-off game?' asked Caldwell as he ran back from collecting a ball.

Gifford paused and nodded, 'Yeah I did. It was a great day. First time ever playing at Wembley and all that. Good game as well. Two-two. I made one of the goals actually. And before you accuse me, I was taken off in extra time so I didn't take a penalty.'

'I can't believe the club was a penalty shoot-out away from the Championship. And not even that long ago,' added Golding.

He was right. It wasn't that long ago. Gifford had only retired five years ago and the final had been two years before that. They had played Oxford United after finishing fourth in the League One table that season. It had been an exciting and even game with constant momentum shifts throughout. Gifford had enjoyed his battle with the young Oxford right-back, who he had seen had got a move to the Premier League recently. The game went to extra time and then to penalties, where Bucknall striker Dion Mackie missed the fifth penalty, sending Oxford to the Championship. Under the management of Martin Williams, it remained Bucknall's best ever league finish. Overspending to reach the elusive goal and the falling out of Williams with the board led to a dramatic plummet after that, with the club suffering back-to-back relegations out of the EFL and facing administration until Steven Rosser and his company came in to save it. That missed penalty and the dream of the second tier of English football had never seemed further away.

'Well, it's our job to start looking up again and not down, isn't it boys?' said Gifford, stopping himself from reliving the Wembley heartache. 'You two staying behind after training is exactly the kind of stuff that'll do that as well.'

He saw Golding and Caldwell exchange a smile. Caldwell then went out to the right-hand side and a mini drill was started which consisted of Golding hitting a switch and then racing in the box to join Gifford as Caldwell crossed the ball in. Gifford offered the wing-back some technical advice, suggesting he picked an area to hit rather than aiming for them each time.

'If it's in the right areas, it's down to the strikers to get on the end of it,' he said.

He stayed with them for another half an hour or so, only deciding to call it a day after attempting an extravagant overhead kick and missing the ball completely. He couldn't stop himself from laughing out loud, which encouraged the other two to join in. He bid them goodbye and walked back to his car with a giddy smile on his face. It was moments like that, he decided, which reminded him why he loved the game of football in the first place.

That evening, he met Gough and Haines for a pint in the Goose on the Water. Gifford had found himself enjoying their company immediately and was grateful for how they had treated him, considering they had been appointed under the previous managerial regime. There was a League Cup game on the TV which they half watched, occasionally commenting on a mistake or piece of excellence, but otherwise their conversation was entirely regarding their own side.

'Is there anything you think we need to look at changing?' Gifford asked, meeting their gaze to signal a more serious tone to the conversation.

'I think we need to find a way of getting Archie in the team,' said Haines, leaning back in his chair and crossing his arms. 'He's one of the few boys we've got with a bit of quality on his final ball.'

By Archie he had meant Archie Lewitt, the kid who Gifford had discussed in the same pub in the accidental meeting that had got him the job. He nodded along. Haines had a point. The only reason he hadn't started Lewitt so far was simply because there was no space for wingers in his current formation.

'Maybe try him off the front. Off Dunney,' said Gough. 'I'm not convinced by him and Saj playing together. They both want to play in the same spaces.'

'That's what we lack in my opinion. Our midfielders all do a job, but none of them have got that killer pass in them, to put Dunney through or whoever. A little bit of guile, you know? A little bit of flair even,' added Haines, 'Like … I don't know, a Lee Tomlin figure maybe. Or who's the fella who used to play up at Norwich? Hoolahan? Yeah, Hoolahan.'

Gifford agreed, 'I haven't asked about the transfers with Chuggy or anyone. I know there's not exactly loads of cash spare but if we could get someone in on a free or a loan, maybe even just to the end of the season. Just as a bit of surprise factor. Someone who might offer something a bit different.'

'I could see there was a massive improvement in the Torquay game,' said Gough, gesturing animatedly. 'We're not too far away from a proper performance and a win. I'm sure of it. Let's just hope it comes this fucking weekend, ey?'

Gifford smiled. That comment meant a lot, given that they had been partly responsible for the team's performances in the games before his appointment. He knew Gough was not the type to ever compliment him, or anyone, outright so that was as close to praise as he was going to get.

Haines, in his typically softer approach, asked, 'How have you found it then so far, Darren, honestly?'

Gifford took a sip and chuckled but gave an honest answer, 'I've enjoyed it. I like the players and I believe in them. It's just amazing how quickly it consumes you, you know? It's all I can think about. And I suppose I have nothing to refer to in terms of whether I'm having any kind of impact whatsoever.'

Gough and Haines looked at each other, as if silently communicating what to say next. Gough then took a sip of his pint and sighed, before leaning in closer to Gifford before he spoke.

'Look. Me and Hainesy have been here for the last two managers before you. And I can honestly say I believed in what they were trying to do as well and it made fuck all difference in the long run. But in this game, the second you doubt yourself, you're fucked. Back yourself, lad. You've got good ideas. We can all see that. And if you can completely back yourself, then we'll be right behind you all the way. We'll follow you into whatever shit is yet to come this season. You're the gaffer now. Start believing it.'

Gifford was touched by that. He smiled and held out his glass, prompting a cheers. When the glasses were returned to the table, there was a momentary silence, the kind that always follows a genuine moment of importance.

'Besides,' said Haines, filling the void, 'if the reaction you're gonna get at the Lane tomorrow doesn't make you feel like a manager, then nothing will.'

10

Bucknall vs FC Halifax Town
Yewtree Lane
27 September

Haines was right. The reception that Gifford got when he emerged from the tunnel at Yewtree Lane would stay with him for a long time. He could hear the levels of noise bubbling as he made his way down the narrow corridor, glimpsing the sun shining out of the gap at the end. When he came into view the crowd roared their approval. He stuck a hand in the air, as he had done the week before, only this time it was nearly 7,000 people and not a few hundred who gladly received his acknowledgment. A chant he hadn't heard since his last game for the club began, 'There's only one Darren Gifford. One Darren Giffordddd.' He could feel the hairs standing up on the edge of his arms and a tingle running throughout his body. The sensation was so strong that he felt a lump form in the back of his throat.

In truth, he hadn't been sure what to expect. He knew that he was held in high regard by the Bucknall fans thanks to his long-lasting contribution to the club's most successful ever side, but he was also an unproven and inexperienced manager tasked with piloting the Bucks out of stormy waters. He didn't anticipate any hostility, at least for the first game, but he hadn't planned for such a universally positive and ground-shaking response. He took his seat on the bench, which was welcome, as he could feel an unsteadiness vibrating in his legs.

The team was unchanged from the Torquay game. Gifford had discussed changes with Haines and Gough in the Goose, but they had decided the starting 11 had done enough in a tricky away game to merit another chance. Halifax were more favourable opponents, having had a modest start to the season, leaving them already stranded in mid-table. Put simply, this had become close to a must-win game for the Bucks.

In the minutes before the whistle blew, Gifford looked behind him into the Village End, searching for familiar faces. He found them soon enough, a few rows down from the back. Keira and his two children, all draped in Bucknall scarves. Keira had her hand over one of Orla's ears and had pressed her daughter close to her side. It seemed Orla wasn't as big a fan of the noise as her father. Gifford stuck out a hand to wave to his family and they excitedly waved back. He couldn't help but feel a swell of pride, followed swiftly by an even greater determination to win.

The game kicked off and another wave of cheers and shouts echoed around the old stadium. Halifax tried to keep the ball for the first few minutes, probably in an attempt to quieten the raucous crowd. Gifford had instructed his players to press hard and they followed his word, chasing down loose balls and charging at the opposing defenders. Every tackle or block was cheered on emphatically by the home crowd. The Bucknall fans were up for this one.

Stefon Harrison won a free kick just inside the Halifax half, nicking the ball in front of his opposite number and getting caught in the shin. This was their first chance to put a ball into the box. Ryan Brook and Ardie Adomako headed for the edge of it, ready to attack a deep cross. Kieran Dunne and Sajja Gujar made runs across the near post, offering the flick-on option. Sebastian D'Amato cut his foot across the ball, drilling it high towards the back post. A Halifax defender just got a flick of the ball which stopped Brook from smashing home another header. It came off the captain's shoulder instead and bounced just wide of the post. Another enthused roar. They had made the better start.

The game began to get scrappy, with niggly fouls and a succession of throw-ins breaking up its flow. Having three in midfield meant that Bucknall were competing better in the middle of the pitch, but D'Amato was being well marked and wasn't able to dictate things. Nearly half an hour had passed without a genuine chance for either side, when Matt Finch took a goal kick short to Brook. Gifford got off his chair and yelled at Dunne to make a run. Just as they had worked on, Brook took one look and hit the ball into the space behind the Halifax left-back. Dunne responded to Gifford's instruction and was already sprinting into the space. The assistant kept his flag down. It was the first time all game they had got in behind. Dunne charged forwards with the ball at his feet, the centre-halves retreating fast. Gujar had made an identical run on the opposite side and was ahead of the right-back.

'Square it, Dunney!' screamed Gifford, seeing the chance open up, with Gough charging past him in the technical area to shout the same thing.

Dunne looked up and saw his strike partner arriving in the box. He side-footed the cross, so that the ball began to curve into Gujar's path. It had become a one-on-one with Gujar free in the area. The crowd all rose to their feet in expectation.

'Finish!' yelled Gifford, his voice cracking in excitement.

Gujar chose to take the ball with his favoured right foot, even though it was settling perfectly in front of his left. This meant he arched his body slightly and struck the ball awkwardly. It bobbled into the side-netting and not the back of the net. Gifford turned away in frustration and the crowd let out a coordinated groan.

'Fucks sake, Saj,' yelled Gough, his face red with fury.

That was the best chance of the half. Gifford shook his head. He knew they had surprised Halifax with the quick pass over the top and that they wouldn't get caught out like that again. All the planning and preparation in the world couldn't legislate for poor finishing, unfortunately.

They returned to the dressing room with the score goalless. A couple of the boys muttered complaints in Gujar's direction. Brook heard them and shouted across.

'Forget that one, Saj. You'll take the next chance, hey?'

Gifford stepped forwards to address his team, 'Good half, boys. We'll take that. Now, listen to that crowd out there. I've not heard the Lane as loud as that for a good while. They are desperate for a goal and a win. And we're going to give it to them. Remember the drills from training. Make runs across each other. Change the angles. We will get chances. And we will take them.'

He saw Gujar had his head down, fiddling with his shin pads, 'Brooky's right, Saj. You can't do anything about the miss now, all you can do is bury the next one.'

The game restarted. There was notably more time on the ball for each side, with the respective midfielders able to take a touch and get their head up. Danny Golding hit a couple of switches to Conor Caldwell on the right, just as Gifford had seen them practise after training.

The ball was worked to Halifax's right-hand side just before the hour mark. They had a quick winger who was much talked about in the division and he received the ball in some space. Gifford sensed the danger and yelled at Nick Wrenshaw, who was now playing on his side, to close him down,

'Get tight. Nick. Don't let him run at you.'

It was a second or so too late. The winger took a touch out of his feet and faced up the left wing-back, shuffling the ball quickly from side-to-side. The jinking style worked as he turned Wrenshaw and strode past him on the wing. Wrenshaw was the club's longest-serving player and no longer had the pace to keep up with him, meaning his opponent burst into the box. Max Warren-Smith came across to cover but now the whole of the back line was running backwards. The winger cut the ball back to the edge of the box and there was a gasp around the stadium. The defenders desperately slid to the turf, knowing the ball was past them and they could only get a block in. An arriving Halifax midfielder got good contact on it and controlled his finish low into the corner of the net. Goal; 1-0 Halifax.

Gifford looked desolately at the floor. His reaction wasn't even one of anger. The way the winger had beaten Wrenshaw with ease merited more a reaction of pity. There was nothing that could be done about ageing legs. He could sense a level of hope and energy being sucked out of the stadium. It was as if the goal had briefly created a vacuum. As if time had briefly stopped.

He snapped himself out of it and urged his players forward, raising his arms and rotating them as if he was literally revving up the side's engine. He couldn't help but feel he was doing what he felt was expected of him, suddenly feeling the weight of thousands of eyes on his back. Brook shouted motivation from the back; Dunne slapped his forehead to demand more concentration and Warren-Smith patted Wrenshaw sympathetically on the back.

There was an unmistakeable lull in their play for the ten minutes after that. Gifford was learning fast about the fragile confidence of his side. Every goal that went against them seemed to increasingly chip away at their mentality. He knew a change was needed and introduced one of his youngest players, Manny Orize, who was a winger with genuine pace and power, but had only played a handful of games for the club before. Orize did exactly as instructed, in the way that only young players can, and ran again and again at the Halifax full-back.

This at least lifted the crowd, which was partly Gifford's reasoning for doing it. He knew from his playing days that there were some guarantees to generate more noise in a home crowd and a direct winger running with the ball was one of them. Golding made a good tackle on a Halifax midfielder and found Orize and he set off again. This time, Caldwell busted a gut to keep up with him and began to underlap the winger. Gifford could see what was needed.

'Get outside him, Conor. Change the angle!' he yelled.

Caldwell did so, arcing his run so he basically charged directly at Orize, before passing his right shoulder. Orize waited and then slipped him in, giving him plenty of space to get a cross in. Gifford muttered under his breath the advice he had given Caldwell after training,

'Hit an area.'

Caldwell opened his body up so that he was parallel to the byline and sent the ball into the corridor of uncertainty between the deepest centre-half and the goalkeeper. Dunne was bumped on his run through and couldn't get there in time, so the ball skidded off the surface and invitingly up into the air. Gujar, now playing on the left wing, was once again arriving at the back post and the ball was rising towards his head.

'Please,' whispered Gifford, his hope now creeping into desperation.

Gujar got too much on it and the ball went over the top. Now the atmosphere turned sour. The groans turned into frustrated shouts and a series of arms were thrown dramatically. Gifford became aware of what the supporters nearest him in the dugout were saying.

'Get him off! He's shit!'

'Fucking rubbish. Why's he still playing?'

He looked at Gough and Haines beside him. Their pained expressions said it all. He had to act. He instructed Archie Lewitt to get ready and told the fourth official of the planned substitution. When the numbers went up on the board, a chorus of boos passed around Yewtree Lane. Gifford reached out a comforting arm to Gujar, who took it but couldn't lift his head to meet his eye.

Into the last ten minutes, a ball was launched into the Bucknall area. Adomako didn't deal with it brilliantly and the ball began to be scrambled around the box. It fell to a Halifax striker whose shot was saved well by Finch but the ball still wasn't cleared. Gough became apoplectic on the sideline, bellowing instructions. It eventually was worked to the same winger who had skinned Wrenshaw for the first goal. He dummied well and sent the left-wing-back once again. He steadied himself and struck the ball, curling it off the far post, beyond both Finch and Brook, who had hurriedly positioned himself on the line; 2-0 Halifax.

Yewtree Lane began to empty. Fans started streaming towards the exits. They knew the game was up. Gifford couldn't help but look back towards his family. He could make out Keira's eyes among the commotion: a pitying, concerned expression reflected back at him. Danny had his head bowed, almost nestled in his scarf.

The added time was played out at testimonial pace. Gifford stopped focusing on the match, his mind spinning. He wasn't going to accept this. He couldn't. He decided that if there had been an easing in period, this was now well and truly over. Bucknall were about to lose their sixth game in seven and the first two under his management. Tough decisions needed to be made and they needed to start trying something, anything, that might make a difference and lift this squad. He began thinking about potential signings, about changes to his starting 11, about how he was going to handle dropping the players that now surely needed to be dropped.

When the final whistle blew, he had already mentally moved past the match it called to a halt. He shook a series of hands and walked out on to the pitch, his hands in his pockets and his head deep in thought. It simply had to get better from here.

Final score: Bucknall 0 FC Halifax Town 2

		Played	Points
20.	Bath City	7	7
21.	Weymouth	7	6
22.	Altrincham	7	6
23.	Gloucester City	7	4
24.	Bucknall	7	1

11

First thing Monday morning, Gifford met Steven Rosser and Lee Chugwell at the ground. This time, they spoke in Chugwell's office, a small room that overlooked the pitch. They placed three chairs around the desk and began their discussion.

Gifford started, 'I know that the first two results have not been promising, but I promise you that we are making progress. We just need a bit of extra help.'

Rosser's brow furrowed, 'What do you mean, "help"?'

'I believe we're missing a player in a key position. Someone to connect our attack and our midfield. A creator, if you will.'

Rosser and Chugwell shared a glance. Gifford had prepared extensively for their meeting the night before and was expecting some resistance and reluctance. He sat back and waited for the response.

Chugwell spoke next, 'You want to make a signing?'

'Yes.'

'The season's already started. We won't be able to go out and make a signing from any of our rivals in the division, not to mention that we've already spent the transfer budget this summer,' said Rosser, sternly.

Gifford nodded. 'I appreciate that and I would never ask you to spend above our budget or do anything that risks the club's financial future, especially after the last few years we've had. But I'm saying that if we don't do something, we would be risking our status in this division.'

He breathed out after he spoke, knowing he had essentially undermined his own ability to turn the team around. He had gone all in to try and force their hand. Rosser continued glaring at him, but Chugwell looked as if he was weighing it up in his mind.

'So, what do you suggest, Giff?' he asked.

Gifford smiled and said a name in response, 'Tommy Pearce.'

It was as if it took a second for the words to echo around the room. Chugwell broke into a half-laugh, half-smile hybrid. Rosser tutted under his breath.

'As in Bradford Tommy Pearce?'

'The very one. Not that he's Bradford Tommy Pearce any more. He's without a club altogether. Meaning he's available to approach and sign as a free agent.'

Rosser's voice rose above his normal monotone growl, 'There's a reason he's a fucking free agent! The bloke's a joker. He's a hooligan who just happened to be good enough to get on the pitch.'

'I agree he might be a little … high maintenance. But he's also good enough to play two, three divisions above this level and yet we might be able to get him.'

Rosser shook his head so Gifford continued his pitch.

'I played against him when he was just coming on the scene at Wycombe. He ran absolute rings around us. He's got that something different. A bit of maverick flair. That's what we need. And all right he's 32 and almost certainly not match fit but that doesn't matter. The other boys can do his running for him. He can go and win us games.'

Chugwell spoke directly to Rosser, 'I've seen him play a couple of times in the last year or so, Steve. He's still got it to be fair.'

Gifford smiled at him. He sensed that Chugwell was on his side now. Rosser started fiddling with his watch and running his fingers between each other, considering the proposal.

'We don't even know his situation properly. At the very least it's got to be worth giving him a call.' added Gifford.

'Yeah, I think I know who represents him. I've got the number somewhere,' said Chugwell.

'All right, all right,' said Rosser, irritated. 'You don't need to keep going on. We can give him a call. Go and see him. But I swear if he's in any kind of state, you do not even think about giving him a contract, you understand? The last thing we need is to give a fucking lunatic a wage to sit on his ass for the rest of the season.'

'Yeah, I understand,' said Gifford, getting up to leave the office. 'Thanks, Steve.'

He went to go to the door, with a smile forming on his lips. Rosser called out as he gripped the handle.

'Oh. And Darren, I appointed you because I believed you were the man to turn this club around. Now I'm supporting you wanting to make a risky signing. I hope you realise that if things don't start to improve, you won't find that I continue to back you quite so much,' said the chairman, his words calmly and slowly delivered, to emphasise the fact that he was issuing a thinly veiled threat.

12

Lee Chugwell phoned Tommy Pearce's agent and he and Gifford drove to the player's house in the chief executive's slick, black BMW. Chugwell drove how anyone would expect an owner of his car to do, hardly braking as he bullied cars out of the right-hand lane of the motorway.

'Don't worry about Steve, Giff. Even if he was happy with you, you would be getting the same treatment. He likes to keep people on edge, I think he thinks it raises standards,' he said to Gifford, who was stretched out in the passenger seat.

'It's really OK. I knew I was taking a bit of a punt. Thanks for backing me by the way.'

'Oh please. If we can't support you two games in, I figure there wasn't much in appointing you anyway,' he said, chuckling.

Gifford offered a weak laugh in response and turned to stare out the window, seeing a grey and murky morning, with rain beginning to spit against the glass. He was glad Chugwell had offered to drive, as he was finding himself increasingly exhausted and sluggish. He had stayed up late the last few nights, trying to create a new battle plan for the team and then finding that when he did go to bed, he couldn't sufficiently turn his mind off to get some sleep.

He had settled on Pearce as his number one target after researching nearly 100 players who he thought might fit the side's needs. Most of them were either happy at better-placed clubs or with their best days a way behind them. In terms of ability, Pearce was near the top of the list. It was his off-the-field antics and difficult reputation that provided the stumbling block. Gifford had decided to think of that as a positive. If Pearce was the model professional, there was absolutely no chance he would play for Bucknall. If they did sign him, they would be his tenth club in a professional career of just under 16 years,, a period that had also included a suspended prison sentence.

The journey took just over an hour, the BMW eventually pulling up on to a terraced close on the outskirts of Greater Manchester. Gifford and Chugwell jogged to the door of Pearce's house in order to spend as little time as possible in the now heavy rain. Chugwell rang the doorbell and they waited for the answer.

Chugwell winked at Gifford, 'Fingers crossed, ey?'

The door opened. Tommy Pearce answered. He hadn't dressed up for the meeting, wearing a pair of jeans and a plain T-shirt. Gifford noticed the tattoos that adorned both of his biceps, one running down to his forearm in a snake-like shape. Pearce had short hair pushed to the side with hair wax, with stubble covering most of his chin and cheeks.

'All right? Come in,' he muttered, in a gritty, northern accent.

'Thanks, Tommy,' said Chugwell as he and Gifford stepped inside.

Pearce led them into his living room: a dim and old-fashioned-looking space that didn't look like it had been redecorated for decades, except for the huge, wall-mounted TV. Gifford and Chugwell sat down in different armchairs and Pearce made himself comfortable on the sofa, raising one arm to rest on.

Gifford waited for Chugwell to speak first, instead watching Pearce closely, trying to work out his physical and mental condition as best he could. Now that Pearce was seated, Gifford could see there was a pouch of fat around his belly.

'Right, well Tommy. I guess we may as well get straight to it. I don't know what other offers you are considering at the moment, but I want to leave here with your signature on the contract that's currently in my bag. We want you to be a Bucknall player and we want to do it as soon as possible.'

Pearce didn't react to this with a change in expression. Instead, he just looked Chugwell up and down before he replied, 'You know, I remember playing against Bucknall. They were a decent side. And then I googled where you were after my agent told me about your call. Bottom of the Conference. That's rough.'

Chugwell shot a nervy look at Gifford, but responded, 'Yes, the club's endured a difficult few years and a similarly difficult start to the season. We're hoping your signing will act as a catalyst to start moving things in the right direction again.'

Pearce's face stiffened, 'You do realise I was playing in League Two last season. I'm too good to be a Conference player.'

Gifford spoke across the room before Chugwell could reply, 'I agree. And yet here we are, two months in the season and you're not playing in League Two, or anywhere else, for that matter.'

Pearce's face turned to meet Gifford's eye for the first time. He had the tough mannerisms of a bouncer or a boxer, not a footballer. Gifford doubted you wanted to bump into him in a dark alley, but he didn't let this show on his face. He knew that if he was going to have any hope of managing Pearce, he couldn't show any weakness to him.

'Tommy, this is our manager, Darren Gifford. Giff, Tommy,' said Chugwell, sarcastically.

'Nice to meet you, Tommy,' said Gifford, not averting his gaze.

It was Pearce who ended their impromptu staring contest to begin speaking to Chugwell again.

'Look. I'm 32 now. I know I don't have that long left in the game. People think I'm after money or whatever, but I'm not. I just want to play. Every game. I'm not coming to be a fucking sub. Everyone talks about the problems I've had at other clubs, but at Salford and Rotherham, the manager never even gave me a chance so what's the point in trying my heart out every training session and making sure I'm fit for each game when there's no chance I'll fucking play anyway.'

Gifford smiled, 'I can promise you, Tommy, you won't just start every game, you'll be the centre of the entire team. I don't want you to be tracking full-backs. I want your energy saved for the final part of the pitch.'

Pearce relaxed his stance a little. Clearly that had been what he was wanting to hear. Gifford was similarly enthused; one of his doubts had been whether Pearce even cared about the game any more, but even in his menacing scowls and ineloquent delivery, you could sense there was a passion and a drive, a will to win, which was something Bucknall badly needed.

Chugwell sensed this was the moment to progress the negotiations and reached into his briefcase to retrieve a series of documents, setting them down on the coffee table in front of Pearce.

'Now, we're offering you a short-term deal to the end of the season with an option to extend. Don't see it as a lack of faith, see it as giving the club and yourself a potential out. I'm also not going to lie to you, you're going to be on less than you were at Bradford. That's unavoidable when you drop down a tier, I'm afraid. But I promise you what we're offering you here still makes you one of the highest earners in the squad.'

Pearce flicked through the contract, his eyes scanning the pages as he went. Gifford and Chugwell sat patiently as he did so, exchanging infrequent hopeful looks. After a while, Pearce sat back and pushed the contract away.

'I guess you're going to send my agent a copy?' he asked.

'Of course,' said Chugwell, enthusiastically.

Pearce looked at Gifford once again. 'You best have meant what you said. I don't want to regret this.'

'I don't want to regret this either. You give your all for me out on that pitch and stay out of trouble off it and you'll have my total support. In everything. I think you could be the key to our whole season.'

Pearce nodded, 'All right then, I'll sign.'

Chugwell continued going through some of the formalities with Pearce, mentioning that they wanted to get him registered so he was eligible to play in the next game. Gifford stopped listening and began thinking ahead once again. He couldn't help but feel he made some kind of deal with the devil, taking on an extra amount of stress and trouble for a chance of better success. Except in this instance, the devil was a tattooed and temperamental Mancunian centre-forward with 63 league goals to his name.

13

Bucknall vs King's Lynn Town
Yewtree Lane
6 October

Tommy Pearce was registered in time for the Saturday game but, much as Gifford had expected, wasn't anywhere near fit enough to start. He was named on the bench, with Gifford making only the one change to his starting line-up. He had made the call to drop Nick Wrenshaw at left wing-back. It was a position that demanded a certain level of athleticism and in his mid-30s, this was asking a lot of Wrenshaw. Crucially, Gifford had decided that he didn't offer enough in the attacking third of the pitch and the mistakes he was making defensively meant he could no longer justify his selection. Throughout training that week, they had done defensive drills with Archie Lewitt, predominantly a winger, in his place. Wrenshaw, to his credit, had taken the decision as well as Gifford had expected from a tough, old-school pro. The team knew the line-up a way in advance of the King's Lynn game:

Finch (GK)

Caldwell Brook Adomako Warren-Smith Lewitt

Golding D'Amato Harrison

Gujar Dunne

Gifford felt the most nervous he had been since taking the job in the period before the match started. He knew the stakes had been raised, partly by himself. He found himself unable to sit still, constantly wandering around the dressing room, frantically chewing his way through a pack of gum. He kept checking with his players on individual duties, making sure they knew who they were picking up on corners and what their plans for goal kicks were. Out of the corner of his eye, he could see Haines watching him, with a knowing grin on his face. When the players were all gathered and ready for the kick-off, Gifford began his team talk.

'There's not going to be any motivational speeches today, boys,' he said. 'There doesn't need to be. We all know how big a game this is. And I don't know about you, but I'm fucking sick and tired of losing. So, I'm only going to say one word to you: quality. That's the key today. That's what we've been missing. In the final third, make sure you bring quality. Be that a cross or a shot or final pass, make it a fucking good one. Actually, better than that, make it a perfect one. 'Cos good isn't good enough any more.'

He paused for effect and made sure to cast his eyes around the whole room before breathing out and saying, 'All right. Let's go.'

When Gifford emerged out of the tunnel on the pitch, there was a more muted response than the game before. The crowd still cheered the team as they made their way out but it was obvious that some of the blind optimism of his first home game was already slipping away. He shook hands with the King's Lynn manager and some of his staff and then took his seat in the dugout, tapping his foot in nervous anticipation.

King's Lynn pressed them early. They had probably guessed that an early goal would kill the confidence of Bucknall and went straight for the kill, flying into challenges and earning a couple of early corners. Gifford began chewing his lip as well as his gum. They had to get through the first ten minutes. A ball into the box was only half cleared by Max Warren-Smith and a King's Lynn midfielder smashed a half volley out of the ground. A loud 'Wahey!' was chanted, but it was tinged with relief.

Slowly, Bucknall began to drag themselves into the game, with each player getting more touches of the ball. Gifford stepped out of the dugout to urge his players forward. They won the ball in the middle of the park and recycled it to the back, with the three centre-halves passing it among themselves. Gifford made a gesture with his hands, pointing them in opposite directions, indicating for the wing-backs to get higher and wider. A pass was made into midfield and Sebastian D'Amato was allowed to turn. Lewitt sensed an opportunity and burst past him on the left-hand side. D'Amato waited and timed the pass well, playing it in front of the youngster and taking two King's Lynn players out of the game. Lewitt now had time to cross.

'Quality!' bellowed Gifford, knowing Lewitt would barely be able to hear him on the far side.

Lewitt rolled the ball out in front of him with his studs and then curved his stance to get extra purchase on the ball. It was a lovely looking cross, aimed just outside the six-yard box. Gifford's eyes flashed straight to the middle, looking to see who got on the end of it. He saw that the first centre-half had misjudged it and it was dropping just over his head. Kieran Dunne made a trademark sharp sprint into the space behind him and got his head to the ball, which was straight at the keeper but came at him too fast to react and it smashed against his shoulder before bouncing into the back of the net. Yewtree Lane erupted; 1-0 Bucknall.

Gifford put his arms into the air but couldn't even a muster a cry of celebration. The goal had surprised him. It was basically their first attack of the game. He looked back at the bench, where the subs had run out and jumped in the air. Gough was pumping his fists wildly in his direction, a typically deranged look on his face. Gifford tensed his hand as well. He felt immediately vindicated in his decision to pick Lewitt. Dunne was cartwheeling away near the corner flag.

As the game restated, Gifford began exaggeratedly miming to his players deep breaths and gesturing his hands towards the floor. 'Calm' was the message. He caught Ryan Brook's eye and pointed to his head. Brook nodded and shouted at his fellow defenders to concentrate. The goal had startled King's Lynn and they were now giving passes away sloppily. Dunne laid one off for Stefon Harrison, whose bobbling shot was parried away by the goalkeeper, to more mass cheers from the home crowd. They sensed this could finally be the day for their beleaguered team.

Lewitt in particular seemed energised and was now beginning to run at the full-back. Gifford was delighted; Lewitt's major problem was his confidence and he had worried that playing him out of position would only worry him, but it was quite the opposite. If anything, playing further back was offering him more space.

When the half-time whistle went, the players were roared back to the dressing room. Gifford now had a new situation to face: he had never addressed the players when they were actually in front. His feeling was to keep the adrenaline high and not to offer too much praise, instructing Gough to deliver one of his explosive, expletive-filled speeches to keep them fired up. Gifford caught Tommy Pearce's eye, the new signing looked like he was enjoying being back in a dressing room once again.

As they returned for the second half, Gifford couldn't help but imagine the scenes if they saw it through. He found himself imagining the table when Bucknall had four points instead of one. He thought about the upcoming fixtures and how many more they would need to start moving out of the relegation zone. Just for a moment, he began to see hope for his side.

14

Mansfield Town vs Bucknall
Field Mill
9 October

Bucknall's next game was the first midweek fixture under Gifford's management. They only had one training session before it, but he could tell there was a notable difference in the players' body language now they had finally got their first win. The match itself could hardly have been more difficult. Mansfield were top of the division and were considered by many to be the strongest team playing at their level. Added to that, they had won every single game at their Field Mill home. Gifford knew that it was going to take a huge effort to get anything at all, let alone add another win on the board.

It was a truly horrible evening in the east Midlands, with rain lashing down from the dark and storm-struck skies and a harsh autumn wind sweeping across the pitch. Gifford threw a raincoat on top of his club tracksuit and sheltered himself under the dugout. He could barely see the ball when it went into the furthest corner from his viewpoint and his shouts and calls often got lost in the wind.

The game wasn't a great spectacle either. Mansfield were a direct team anyway and so hit plenty of long balls, aiming for their tall and bulky striker's head. They were also known to be potent from long throws so Gifford had been sure to do a drill on this the day before. The conditions dictated that Bucknall couldn't play much of a passing game either, with the ball slowing down in the mud patches forming quickly on the pitch. This led to a game of few chances, with Bucknall spending most of the opening half manfully defending their box, with the centre-halves making a series of courageous blocks.

When they did return to the dressing room, Gifford barely recognised his players. Their black and grey kits were now closer to brown and their normally slick and sharp haircuts were ruined; their hair stuck to their rain-streaked foreheads instead. Gifford gave them extra time to warm up and catch their breath, appreciating how difficult it was to play a game like they were experiencing.

'Right, boys. We knew how hard this was gonna be and the weather has meant it has got even tougher. So, this becomes a different kind of test. It's not of your skill or your composure, it's of your fucking mental strength. Stick together, keep making tackles, keep making blocks, keep running. You've been brilliant so far. But we've still got a half to go. And I promise you if we stay firm at the back, we will get a chance. They were expecting to walk over you lot before the game, let's show them what kind of fucking team we are now.'

The game kicked off again. It continued to be stop and start, with a series of fouls from both teams breaking up the flow. They managed to get to the hour with the scores still level and Gifford sent on another defender to essentially create a back six. Finally though, the Mansfield players were able to exchange a quick couple of passes and beat the first line of defence. They worked it wide to the right-hand side and their winger put in a scuffed cross. The fact it was under-hit surprised the Bucks' defenders as they had been marking their opponents tightly and competing in the air all game, which meant that this low, bobbling ball made its way across the six-yard box. Matt Finch dived forwards to try and get a touch on it but the ball zipped past him on the wet surface and made its way to the back post. A home player stuck out their studs and made contact and he, Conor Caldwell, and eventually the ball, all ended up in the back of the net; 1-0 Mansfield.

Gifford exchanged a pained glance with Haines but there was a look on both of their faces that suggested, 'What can you do about that?' Gifford stepped out into the downpour to clap his players and try and pick them back up. Internally, it was the least devastated he had been by conceding a goal. He wasn't going to say it but he'd probably have taken a 1-0 defeat. He looked to his bench and told Tommy Pearce and Manny Orize to warm up. Just one moment of magic, Pearcey, he thought to himself, that's all we need.

They went on with 20 minutes to go. The Bucknall players looked visibly tired, with the increased number of games in a week combined with the rigorous defensive effort clearly starting to weigh on their legs. They tried a few shots from outside the box, without properly testing the Mansfield goalkeeper. The fourth official told Gifford there would be four minutes of injury time. He shouted that on to his players, urging them to keep going until the end. A long diagonal by Brook broke to Archie Lewitt. It slowed on the pitch and he could barely drag the ball out of his feet. The nearest Mansfield player got close to him and nudged him in the back. Lewitt fell to the floor, water splashing up as he hit the turf. Free kick. Last chance.

Gifford watched on as Sebastian D'Amato ambled over to take it but saw that Pearce had grabbed the ball and was starting to place it down. D'Amato was normally the free-kick taker and so there was something of a discussion between them. Pearce clearly won as D'Amato walked away, looking totally exhausted, his long hair completely all over the place and his socks cut up, with the shin pads underneath visible through the holes created. It was a long way out on the left-hand side, closer to the touchline than the box, but Gifford guessed that Pearce hadn't gone over there so he could cross it.

Pearce settled over the ball and repeatedly wiped the rain out of his eyes. There was a five-man wall and every other Mansfield player back in the box. Pearce took a couple of steps and then ran hard at the ball, deliberately striking the bottom of it to lift it high into the stormy air. Gifford strained his eyes to see where it was heading. It beat every head in the box and began to head for the far post, dipping fast. It eventually clipped the bottom of the crossbar and the top of the right-hand post and bounced down into the goal; 1-1.

Gifford was off. He ran back along the touchline, screaming out. Gough ran out to greet him and the two men gripped each other, jumping up and down. Suddenly, he couldn't feel the rain on his face or the moisture slowly seeping through his layers of clothing. Instead it was like a bolt of electricity was passed through him and he was sparked into life. Pearce ran over and executed a knee slide, making it a fair distance before coming to a halt directly in front of the Mansfield fans. His team-mates had piled on top of him before he had time to hear the first of the insults thrown in his direction.

It was almost the last kick of the game. Gifford ran on to the pitch and made sure to congratulate every single one of his players. They had nicked a point they definitely didn't deserve. Away at the league leaders no less. It was the kind of battling, gritty performance that the players didn't seem capable of delivering only a week before.

Gifford marched into the dressing room and delivered a short and simple message, 'I've instructed the coach driver that we will be making a stop before we head back to Bucknall. I will personally be buying two 24 crates of San Miguel and I want them all to be drank before we get home. You've earned it, lads.'

The dressing room erupted. Kieran Dunne started miming the classic Paul Merson drinking celebration. Tommy Pearce started banging loudly on the lockers. Gifford smiled and let them enjoy it. He would have said before taking the job that he would never celebrate a draw, but he could tell that things were finally starting to move in the right direction. A team spirit was building and in Pearce, they had found one hell of a get-out-of-jail-free card. They might still have been bottom of the league but the atmosphere in the Mansfield away dressing room was as if they had just won it instead.

Final score: Mansfield Town 1 Bucknall 1

		Played	Points
20.	Weymouth	9	10
21.	Eastleigh	9	8
22.	Altrincham	9	7
23.	Gloucester City	9	5
24.	**Bucknall**	**9**	**5**

15

Bucknall vs Bromley
Yewtree Lane
13 October

Gifford woke up on Saturday morning with an unfamiliar feeling of confidence. He was upbeat as he helped Keira make breakfast for the kids, tickling and play-fighting with Orla and flirting with his wife. He blew them both kisses goodbye as he left for the game. When he arrived at the stadium, he could sense a different mood around the place. When he passed club officials or stewards, they would give him a smile and a nod or an encouraging word. He began to feel like he was being treated with a kind of reverence.

He had only made one change to the line-up, with it being an obvious one. Tommy Pearce was ready to make his first start after a full week of training and had more than earned it with his substitute performances. Gifford felt guilty about dropping Sajja Gujar but it was a swap that had to be made. Pearce responded by being more energetic and boisterous, with Gifford noticing that he and Kieran Dunne had formed a bond, both of them being two of the loudest voices in the dressing room.

Ryan Brook led the team on to the Yewtree Lane pitch, the coaching staff following behind. Gifford was beginning to feel at ease in his dugout now and shook the opposition's hands with greater intent. It was, thankfully, a much clearer day and he stood out on the touchline as the game kicked off, bellowing instructions to his team from the minute the whistle went.

Bucknall responded to his words of encouragement. They were playing with a high tempo, no longer afraid to hit their passes with pace and conviction and starting to move it around with one and two touches. They had officially eased into their new shape and worked it efficiently, with the wing-backs always offering themselves as the spare man. Another advantage of Pearce starting over Gujar was that he was more prone to dropping back into midfield, which meant at times they created a kind of diamond that outnumbered their Bromley counterparts.

Archie Lewitt received the ball in space just inside the Bromley half and Dunne made a run off the centre-back to show for the ball. Lewitt curled the ball into him and Dunne laid the ball off beautifully to Pearce, who took it in his stride. Dunne then darted into the space that had been vacated by the centre-back following him infield. Gifford pointed furiously, seeing the opening. Pearce side-footed the ball, weighting it perfectly so that it slowed just as Dunne caught up with it. The striker was one-on-one with the onrushing goalkeeper. The fans all rose to their feet and there was an audible gasp of excitement. Dunne opened up his body and slotted it into the corner confidently. Bucknall were off to a flyer; 1-0.

Gifford put his hands in the air and thumped them together to show his approval. That was a brilliant goal. Dunne and Pearce were clearly connecting just as well on the pitch as they were off it, and his team were playing the best football he had seen yet. He allowed himself a look across the touchline at the Bromley staff and saw the worried expressions on their faces and animated discussions between them. Gifford couldn't help but smirk. It was a cruel thought, but it was wonderful to see someone else experience the pain for a change.

Bucknall continued to dominate. Pearce in particular was now thoroughly enjoying himself, trying extravagant flicks and hitting champagne passes with both feet. Just as Gifford had hoped, he was a cut above everyone else on the pitch. Another opening was worked down the left, and Pearce turned away from the defender, shuffling the ball from left to right. As the crowd howled for him to shoot, he set his feet to do so but at the last second stopped his swing and scooped his foot under the ball instead, sending a delicate chip up and over the goalkeeper. The noise that followed was a rare one, as a unified moan normally heard in bedrooms burst out from the stands. The ball dipped but crashed on to the roof of the net and not quite under the bar. It was totally audacious. Gifford looked at Pearce's face and saw a mischievous look of joy etched across it.

Bucknall were playing well enough to more than merit a second goal and five minutes before half-time, it arrived. Once more they worked a triangle in midfield, with Sebastian D'Amato and Pearce working space for Danny Golding on the edge of the box. Golding dummied one arriving defender and unleashed a powerful shot, which took a nick off a Bromley centre-half's knee and flew past the keeper into the top right corner; 2-0.

Gifford jumped in the air. He was loving this. When the half-time whistle finally put Bromley out of their misery, the Bucks fans took to their feet, letting out a ripple of thunderous applause. It was the loudest Gifford had heard them. This was a reaction that went beyond just supporting the team, they were actively *enjoying* them as well. Gifford stood in front of the door to their dressing room and congratulated every single player as they made their way in. For Pearce, he just winked at the centre-forward, who responded with a now trademark smug grin.

Gifford let Gough do the team talk, his number two shouting into the players' faces, 'We do not let up, do you hear me? If you ease off and take it fucking easy for even a fucking second in the second half, you will be running fucking laps on Monday to make up for it. You don't win a game at half-time, so go out there and win the second half as well.'

As it transpired, the second half was as comfortable and enjoyable as Gifford could have hoped for. The Bromley manager had responded to the total dominance Bucknall had enjoyed in midfield by taking one of his strikers off to introduce another body in the centre, which had the side-effect of completely eradicating what little threat they had posed to the Bucks' defence. Instead, Gifford's players kept knocking the ball around, tiring their opposition further and further, no longer needing to force it to try and score a goal. The half passed almost entirely without incident, with Gifford even able to rest D'Amato, Pearce and Dunne with time to go.

And then as the game threatened to peter out, Conor Caldwell found space down the right-hand side and ran into it. The Bucknall players started to burst into the box. Caldwell's cross seemed to be a bad one at first, sailing over the heads of those in the middle. However, Archie Lewitt had made the late run to the back post, the exact run Gifford had noticed he wasn't making when he watched the disastrous Yeovil game. The ball dropped in front of him and Lewitt caught it sweetly on the volley, crashing the ball into the back of the net. It was a screamer. Wing-back to wing-back. Yewtree Lane erupted once again; 3-0.

The mood among the Bucknall staff and bench was euphoric. They were playing with flair and skill and confidence. They suddenly looked like a very decent side. The fans broke out into a chant of 'It's like watching Brazil'. Gifford found himself laughing. It had been a perfect performance.

When the game ended and Gifford went to shake the hand of the Bromley manager once more, the visiting boss muttered back, 'You've done a hell of a job with this lot.'

The smile that Gifford couldn't wipe from his face was still present when he met Harry Latherfield for the post-match interview. He beamed into the camera as the reporter began to ask him the questions.

'Well, Darren. What a week.'

'Yeah. We needed it. As I had said before, I felt that we weren't far away from getting some results, because our performances were promising. But yeah, seven points from three games, especially considering the fixtures we've had, is obviously very pleasing.'

'Do you think you and the players have now turned a corner and can you start looking up the table?'

'I think it's still probably too early to say that. We're still in the bottom four and we can't forget that. We've got to keep doing the things we've been doing and keep putting points on the board and then we can see where we can go from there. What I would say is that I think the players have started to play with confidence again and that has obviously made a big difference.'

'And we have to talk about the performances of Tommy Pearce. He lit up the Lane today, how pleased are you with your new signing.'

'Very pleased, yeah. The thing I never worried about with Tommy is his quality. That's never been in doubt, but I suppose there are always unknowns about how he will settle into the dressing room and fit into the team, but he's been a revelation. Just what we needed. And he seems to be really enjoying playing in front of the fans here.'

Latherfield concluded the interview and thanked and congratulated Gifford, who then travelled home and enjoyed his evening with his family, managing to not think about football for the first time since he had started the job. Danny told him after dinner that Archie Lewitt's goal was unbelievable. Gifford asked him how he had seen it and Danny told him that they put the National League highlights up on YouTube. He sat next to his dad on the sofa and found the video on his phone, holding it out so they both could see. It was the first time Gifford had watched his team back for pleasure and when he saw the moment Lewitt struck the ball again, his head over it and his leg tensed, he felt a rush of adrenaline pass through him. Danny rewound the clip and the two of them enjoyed Bucknall's win over and over again.

Final score: Bucknall 3 Bromley 0

16

That week, Gifford and Keira invited Gough and Haines to their house for dinner, along with their respective wives. It had, inevitably, been Keira's idea, as she had reprimanded Gifford for the fact she hadn't even met the colleagues he worked with every day. She sent him out to buy a few bottles of wine and ingredients for the meal and she had organised that Danny would stay at a friend's house and her mother would have Orla for the night. Gifford said he'd cook and decided that he would make a mushroom risotto.

Haines and his wife, Clarisse, arrived first. Keira welcomed then in and led to them to the dining table, which she had already laid and decorated with candles. Gifford had smirked and pointed out that their guests were football coaches and not aristocrats. Keira had ignored him. Gough and his wife, Mary, followed suit soon after. Upon seeing Gough, Gifford took a while to process that he was wearing a smart shirt and jumper, as if he was seeing him out of uniform. Gough was a man who could have been born wearing a club tracksuit, a raincoat and muddy boots.

The food wasn't ready immediately and so Keira opened the first bottle of wine and poured everyone a glass. The wives exchanged polite compliments about each other's outfits and about Keira and Gifford's home while Gough and Haines shouted abuse through to the kitchen at Gifford not being ready. Gifford added the butter and parsley to his dish and laughed it off. He took a teaspoon to his mouth and tasted the food, smiling at the result. He carried the dish through, and the evening properly began.

'I'm so impressed with your cooking, Darren. Martin can barely make beans on toast without my supervision,' said Mary.

'I never learned to cook. That's the problem with working in football your whole life, you spend your life in canteens and hotels,' replied Gough.

'I know. Darren was useless when he was younger. They ought to teach footballers some basic life skills at least, otherwise you're just not preparing them for the basics of everyday life. Away from the pitch, you're just producing one useless young man after the other,' said Keira, gesticulating with the wine glass in her hand.

'I guess the clubs aren't interested in giving them responsibility, it's in their interests that they dictate exactly when and what they eat, less can go wrong that way,' said Gifford.

'Yes, but what if they don't have a career in football. God knows not everyone does,' Keira replied.

'Yeah, and with the awful injuries these days,' added Clarisse, to a unified murmur of agreement around the table.

'Martin stopped playing because of your knees, didn't you?' said Mary, encouraging Gough to explain further.

'Yeah. Torn my cartilage twice.'

'Mine was quad and ankle. Probably cost me another couple of years or so,' said Haines.

'Darren?' asked Clarisse.

'I would say I was fairly lucky, but I did have pretty consistent hamstring problems.'

'Fairly lucky?' interrupted Keira. 'See, it never makes sense to me when you talk like that. You spent a lot of your time not being able to do your job, in almost any other role that wouldn't be very lucky at all.'

Gifford put his hand out to stroke her arm, 'That's the game, I guess.'

Haines spoke up, 'I think that's how they get us, isn't it? It's like the army or navy or whatever, it's a form of brainwashing or something. They make you think that your way of life is normal and then you don't know any different. And besides, who are we to moan about it? Us three idiots finished playing and still couldn't leave it alone!'

There was laughter at that. Gifford offered out the last of the risotto which Gough heartily accepted. Keira refilled the glasses of wine and went to get another bottle. When she returned, she asked a further question to Gough and Haines.

'So, are you two both football addicts as well?'

'I'm afraid so,' said Gough.

'Guilty as charged, ma'am,' added Haines.

'I'm glad they've got each other is all I can say. It means he doesn't need to talk to me!' exclaimed Mary.

There were more chuckles around the table, the wine causing the laughs to flow more comfortably.

'I can't get Darren to talk about anything else now. We could have a conversation about anything, shopping lists, the kids, sex! And all he's wondering is whether to play a front two or a front three,' said Keira.

'Are you thinking about a front three?' asked Gough suddenly.

Mary made a series of tuts that reminded her husband to save the football questions for the morning, much to everyone else's amusement.

'At least things are starting to go in the right direction at last.' said Clarisse, with a warm smile.

'Absolutely. To Bucknall FC. And to the coach.' said Haines, raising his glass and nodding at Gifford.

'To the coach,' added Gough with a grunt.

Gifford smiled but felt himself sliding back into his chair. He felt undeserving of the praise and uncomfortable being the centre of attention.

'Have you two ever considered being head coaches yourselves?' asked Keira.

'Why, are you trying to get your husband the sack?!' joked Gough.

'You know what she meant,' said Mary, smacking him on the forearm.

'Never. I love the training and working with the players but I've not got no interest in being the man who has to make the big decisions. Plus, I'd be shite at all the media and admin stuff.'

Haines had stayed quiet and Gifford noticed he had exchanged a look with Clarisse. Keira turned to him.

'Marcus?'

Haines paused and stuttered a bit in response, 'When I first got my pro licence, I started applying to a few jobs here and there. I had a few interviews, but nothing really came off. It felt a bit … um.'

He paused nervously. The mood of the table quietened and everyone looked away, as if to give him space. Keira eventually prompted him again.

'What?'

Haines kept his eyes down as he spoke, 'It felt as if giving me an interview was them ticking a box, if you know what I mean. I never felt like I actually had any chance of getting the job.'

Gifford stiffened in his seat. There were looks of sympathy from everyone at the table. Clarisse stroked her husband's hand. Gifford cleared his throat and decided to speak.

'That's awful, Hainesy. I had no idea.'

'Oh, don't worry. I'm very happy with the role I've got now. I don't feel any resentment, honestly.'

There was an undeniable awkward silence. Gifford couldn't help but feel incredibly guilty, as if he had been handed an opportunity that people like Haines could work for years towards and never get anywhere near.

Haines worked a smile and the familiar spark returned to his eyes, 'What's for dessert, Chef?'

The guests stayed for another hour or so, with more stories told and more jokes shared. It had been a hugely pleasant, and successful, evening. It furthered in Gifford's mind that Haines and Gough were not simply his assistants but also his friends. Everybody kissed Keira goodbye and then the two of them started to pack everything away. It was as Gifford was washing up some of the pans in the sink that Keira confronted him.

'You can talk to me about your job, you know,' she said, as if thinking aloud.

Gifford looked at her in confusion, 'What do you mean?'

'Mary said that Martin didn't speak to her about football, I'm not sure I want that. I know that you're not going to talk to me about the tactical side of it or anything but if you're feeling stressed or under pressure or anything, you can always talk to me. It just feels like you've retreated into your world recently and I don't want you to.'

Gifford stopped moving the sponge round the pan and said, 'I know I can talk to you. I'm sorry if I've seemed a bit distant. It's just I've been putting everything into it, you know?'

Keira smiled and came to kiss him on the cheek, 'I know. Dinner really was lovely by the way, thank you.'

Gifford watched her leave the kitchen and resumed the washing up. He thought about what she had said and if he had retreated from her in any way. He placed the pan into the drying rack slowly and pondered that if he had in some way lost himself in this new world of his, he wasn't sure if he could bring himself back.

17

October turned out to be a wonderful month for Bucknall. Momentum was like a holy grail for football teams and managers, something so important and coveted and yet intangible; you could spend whole weeks, months and seasons chasing it only to come up short. Once you did have it on your side, however, it seemed as if you'd somehow lowered the difficulty of the league you were playing in. The quality of training was higher, the games rolled around quicker and decisions made themselves. Bucknall had finally got on a roll.

Aldershot vs Bucknall
The EBB Stadium
20 October

Gifford had settled on a clear first-choice 11, with Archie Lewitt and Tommy Pearce now regulars in their respective positions.

		Finch (GK)		
Caldwell	Brook	Adomako	Warren-Smith	Lewitt
	Golding	D'Amato	Harrison	
	Pearce		Dunne	

Fresh from the comfortable Bromley win, Bucknall went straight at Aldershot from the first whistle, pressing intensely and forcing free kicks and carving out half chances. They had developed a nice and natural understanding down the left-hand side where Pearce would drift over to make a triangle with Stefon Harrison and Lewitt, creating a near constant overload. Around 25 minutes in, that combination worked space for the left wing-back to curve in another beautiful cross towards the back post where Dunne peeled off his marker and glanced home; 1-0 Bucknall.

They controlled the game until half-time, where Gifford's team talk was all about taking their chances, suggesting this was a game they would kick themselves over if they somehow didn't win. His pleas were answered five minutes into the second half when Harrison made a blindside run off Pearce, who slipped him in with trademark accuracy and the athletic midfielder got a toe on it to take it past the goalkeeper; 2-0. Gifford clenched his fist and gritted his teeth in celebration. His team responding directly to his instructions added an extra level of satisfaction on top of the feeling of scoring a goal.

Aldershot responded after the second goal, roared on by the enthusiastic home fans. They dominated the game for the next 20 minutes and deservedly struck back when they lashed in after a couple of blocked shots in the area. The familiar nerves crept into Gifford's mind and body and he started to wish for the final whistle. His team were not the same fragile side he had inherited though, and they took the game away once again when Pearce received a loose ball on the edge of the box and curled the ball into the far corner; 3-1.

Final score: Aldershot 1 Bucknall 3

Dagenham & Redbridge vs Bucknall
Victoria Road
23 October

A tricky-looking midweek clash with Dagenham & Redbridge followed shortly after. This was not the dominant performance they had managed a few days earlier with Dagenham definitely the better side for much of the game in London. The hosts took an early lead when Bucknall failed to properly clear a corner and the second ball was converted by a gangly centre-half. They had to fight to work their way into the game with the defence doing a good job of marking Pearce and Kieran Dunne and forcing the attacks wide. However, luck was very much on the Bucks' side as a routine Conor Caldwell cross was miskicked into his own net by a Dagenham's earlier goalscorer under no real pressure, adding one in the wrong end to his personal tally. They went in all square at half-time.

Gifford decided to gamble and took off Danny Golding in favour of Manny Orize to switch to a front three, leaving only Harrison and Sebastian D'Amato in midfield. The ploy was done to free up space for Pearce as much as to add another attacking option as he could now play in the left-hand channel rather than being isolated centrally. It looked to have backfired ten minutes into the second half when Dagenham scored again, when their striker, who was one of the league's top scorers, brought down a hopeful cross on his chest and half-volleyed the ball back where it came in stunning style. Gough whispered, 'You can't do anything about that,' in Gifford's ear.

Gifford even withdrew Dunne with ten minutes to go, with the striker totally ineffective against a packed defence. He threw on Sajja Gujar, the first time he had used him since dropping him for Pearce. The sub ran himself into the ground chasing lost causes and it was a ricochet off his shins that led to the ball nestling at Pearce's feet. Gifford instinctively rose from his feet, sensing what might happen. Pearce got the ball in front of him and faked to go left before working it on to his right with the outside of his foot. He struck the ball low and it beat the keeper; 2-2. Pearce sprinted past the goal and dived into the Bucknall away fans, who mobbed him. He had already achieved cult hero status among them and they sang his name all the way to the final whistle.

Final score: Dagenham & Redbridge 2 Bucknall 2

Bucknall vs Eastleigh
Yewtree Lane
26 October

Back at Yewtree Lane, Bucknall had a huge game against another early struggler, Eastleigh. Gifford knew that all the recent progress could be undone with a poor performance and result against a team they had to beat. He was more animated and deliberate than normal in his pre-match team talk, marching around the dressing room and leaning into certain players to emphasise points.

'We are better than them, boys. I'm sure of it. I've seen their games and they don't have anywhere near the quality that we have. So, if you don't win this game, you can only look at yourselves. It will mean you haven't matched their energy or their desire and that would be a fucking disgrace. If you match them in those areas and you compete for every ball and win every fucking challenge, you'll win this today. Don't come back into this dressing room unless you can say you've done that.'

His words seemed to have the desired effect. Bucknall were absolutely superb and were three up by the break. First D'Amato sent Dunne through one-on-one. The striker raced on to it but then slowed his movement as the goalkeeper approached, almost stumbling over the ball. Gifford briefly panicked that the chance had gone but Dunne shifted it to his right and smashed it under the goalkeeper to give them the lead. A couple of minutes later, a free kick was won on the edge of the box and Pearce stepped up and clipped it over the wall and into the top corner. To add further gloss to the scoreline, a fairly average corner from D'Amato was given a flick on at the near post by Max Warren-Smith and Dunne was left completely unmarked at the back post to poke into an empty net.

The third completely killed Eastleigh. Gifford could see it in their body language, their heads were down and they were breathing hard, unable to keep up with Bucknall's quick interchanges. The dominance continued in the second half with the possession being so far in Bucknall's favour that loud chants of 'ole!' echoed around the ground as the home side stroked the ball around under no pressure. Pearce added a fourth from a tap-in from a Lewitt cut-back. His fifth in fifth games, to add to six in six for Dunne. That was now eight in the four games they had started together. They had officially clicked better than Gifford could have ever imagined.

With Eastleigh out on their feet as the game ticked to a halt, Bucknall produced one more piece of magic. They worked it across the pitch and then as it came to Golding on the right-hand side, Caldwell made a powerful late run outside of him. Golding knocked him the ball and Caldwell slammed home a fifth. It reminded Gifford of one of the most famous goals in football history: Carlos Alberto running off Pelé to score the fourth in the 1970 World Cup Final. His team really were playing like Brazil.

Final score: Bucknall 5 Eastleigh 0

In the dressing room after the game, Steven Rosser made his way down to congratulate Gifford and the rest of the team. He shook all the coaches by hand and thanked the players for their efforts in turning the team around. As he turned to leave, he gave Gifford a nod of appreciation. It was the happiest Gifford assumed Rosser was capable of being. Pearce and Dunne, wearing nothing but matching pairs of underwear, led the whole team in a singalong. The spirit was continuing to grow and grow. Gifford got out his phone to quietly check the league table, admiring his team's rise up it.

		Played	Points
15.	Bucknall	13	15
16.	FC Halifax Town	13	14
17.	Aldershot	13	14
18.	King's Lynn Town	13	12
19.	Bath City	13	12

This sudden upturn also led to Gifford receiving praise and attention for the first time in his managerial career, culminating in him winning the manager of the month award. Lee Chugwell phoned him to tell him and he drove to the ground for a presentation from the National League and a photoshoot with the trophy. He clutched the transparent sphere and held it aloft, mustering a genuine and broad smile for the camera. When he got home, he showed Keira and Danny and they made a spot on the mantelpiece in the living room to display it proudly. Gifford stood back to admire it, the light catching the glass of the award and sending a glint towards him. He found himself smiling once more.

18

Gifford rewarded the players' recent performances by making an effort to make training more light-hearted, finishing a midweek session with a crossbar challenge, with forfeits on the line for the losers. It somehow ended up with Gifford himself having the last kick, needing to hit the crossbar in order to stop himself, Gough and Haines from running laps around the pitch. The players were ecstatic and gathered expectantly around him as he prepared to strike the ball from around 30 yards out. Kieran Dunne started sledging him in his chirpy Irish tone.

'You feelin' the pressure, Gaffer? Have you got the balls?'

Gifford smiled but took a deep breath to compose himself and took a couple of quick glances at his target, assessing the distance. He took a short step back and clipped the bottom of the ball as delicately as he could, controlling its ascent through the air. The fact it suddenly went silent was a good sign; it meant the shot had a chance. Gifford looked up and saw the ball drop suddenly as the pace came off it, clipping the front of the bar and bouncing straight back. He had absolutely nailed it. The players erupted and some collapsed to the ground. Gough started screaming in celebration and wrapped Sebastian D'Amato in a headlock. Gifford felt a bolt of confidence pass through him and he strutted towards a manically laughing Dunne, not needing to say anything. Dunne applauded him in response.

That ended training. Gifford made his way to the Golf, a bag of kit thrown over one of his arms. He put it in the boot and put his foot up to take his boots off, changing back in to trainers. He received a couple of beeps of the steering wheel as players drove past him as they left the complex. By the time he was completely ready to set off, his was one of the last cars left in the car park. He got in the car and started pulling away but as he turned the corner, he looked back at the view of their training pitch, wondering if any of the players had stayed behind. He could see one still there, juggling the ball half-heartedly across the pitch. Gifford noticed it was Danny Golding and looked to see if Conor Caldwell was with him as usual. He wasn't. Gifford was ready to continue driving home but a thought forged in the back of his mind, nagging away at him. He stopped the car where it was and jumped out, making his way back to the pitch.

Golding didn't look up, still kicking the ball with short touches, keeping it close to his feet. He only became aware of Gifford when he was no more than a couple of feet away. He reacted with surprise.

'You OK Gaffer?'

'Yeah I'm fine, Goldo. Con not with you today?'

'Nah, he said he had to go pick his sister up or something.'

Gifford noticed Golding wasn't properly meeting his gaze. His suspicions increased.

'You know I love the fact you stay after training, Danny. But it is also OK to go straight back home now and again, you've earned some rest. You've been class lately.'

'Cheers, boss.'

Gifford looked more intently at him. Golding was dragging his feet into the turf, like a child who had done something wrong.

'Are you sure you're all right? You can tell me anything, you know. That's what I'm here for.'

Golding finally looked up. He wasn't crying, but his face was screwed up as if to stop himself from doing so. His eyes looked red and puffy and he looked in genuine pain.

'I don't want to go home, boss. Not yet.'

Gifford came closer to him and put his arm on his player's shoulder.

'What is it?'

Golding choked on the words as he spoke, as if he was straining to force them out, 'It's nothing, it's just … I have a bit of a problem with … gambling.'

His head looked down once more. Gifford digested the information. He patted Golding's shoulder reassuringly and pressed him further.

'OK. As in an addiction? 'Cos that's very common, mate. Honestly.'

Golding breathed out in a sigh, 'Yeah, I think so. I just can't stop it. And I really, really fucking want to. But it's all right there on my phone, and every time I delete the apps, I just go and download them again. The only time I can forget about it is when I'm playing and my phone's left back in my car.'

Gifford nodded. This all made sense. The staying behind after training was as much to avoid going home as it was to continue practising. He thought about the burning question in his mind but took his time asking it.

'Right, and I'm guessing you've lost some money? Are you in any trouble?'

Golding shook his head frantically, 'I won't take any money off you, boss. I can't. I'll be fine, honestly.'

'I wasn't offering you money, Goldo. I just want to make sure you're all right. You've got a missus right? Does she know about this?

Golding shook his head once more. Gifford came to another realisation.

'Does anyone know about this … apart from me?'

'No.'

'Well that's got to change. You can't tackle this on your own, It's none of my business whether you want to tell your partner or not, but you need to tell somebody. Talk to Con or any of the boys in the team, they may be an odd bunch but they're your team-mates. They'll look out for you.'

'OK.'

Gifford paused his questioning. He could see the shame and guilt was eating away at Golding, who now resembled a ghost of a man, scared of his own shadow. Gifford felt a sense of responsibility for him, an emotion he could only liken to what he felt towards his own children.

'And I'm going to try and sort something for you, all right? If it's OK with you, I'm going to talk to Steven Rosser and Lee Chugwell and see if we can get you on some kind of course. I don't know what's available but I'm certain the club will sort it out for you. In fact I'll make sure they do. You're a member of the PFA right? We'll talk to them too. They'll help as well.'

Golding didn't respond, beyond mustering a weak smile.

Gifford added, 'You're not on your own, son. I promise you that, if nothing else.'

He walked Golding back to his car in cold silence. Golding thanked him and climbed into the drivers seat.

'If you're ever struggling with it, you call me OK? I'll only be fuming with you if I find out that you haven't,' said Gifford as he departed.

The joyful haze of training had officially left his body and his mind was once again turning quickly, running through a series of scenarios and trying to come up with solutions. He thought about Golding's behaviour, challenging himself on if he had missed clues that he may have been struggling. There were none he could think of. Golding was a quieter member of the team perhaps, but he was still involved in the banter and always eager to work hard and get involved. As Gifford sat down once more, he reflected that results may have been improving but he had other duties that he couldn't neglect. He started the ignition and finally headed home.

19

Bucknall vs Doncaster Rovers
Yewtree Lane
9 November
FA Cup first round

Bucknall's next game was their most exciting of the season so far. They had made it through to the first round proper of the FA Cup and had been handed a home tie against League One Doncaster Rovers. Gifford had watched the draw on TV as it happened and had smiled when their opponents were revealed. This was a chance to test themselves against an established EFL side. Then to add to the excitement, he received a phone call from Lee Chugwell, telling him that the game had been chosen to be televised by the BBC.

The club clicked into fever pitch. Steven Rosser and Chugwell saw to it that Yewtree Lane had never looked better, hiring extra cleaners to make the dressing rooms, tunnel and facilities as shiny and spotless as they had ever been. The corridors were given an extra lick of paint and everything from the scoreboard to the kegs of beer offered at The Players' were checked and double-checked. The game was a sell-out, a reminder to the club's beleaguered supporters of previous heady days. It was going to earn Bucknall around £30,000 thanks to the broadcast payment with another £40,000 on offer if they were able to make it through to the next round.

Gifford wore a suit for the game, with Keira laughing at him as she helped fix his tie in the morning.

'Good luck today, Mr Bond.'

'Fuck off.'

He arrived at the ground and was amazed at the extra buzz around the place. There were big television vans parked in the car park and extra cameras and sound equipment dotted around the pitch. He bumped into Nick, the commercial exec, who had been part of the pub party that helped him get the job.

'They want to do an interview before the game. Dion Dublin's here! It's mad!'

Gifford prepared himself. He wandered into his office and made some notes ahead of the game. An official came to get him and he was taken down to pitchside to conduct an interview with the BBC team, who had set up alongside a pop-up desk. He shook the hand of the reporter and with Dion Dublin, the legendary former Premier League and England striker.

'Hiya. Good luck today.'

Gifford tensed and swallowed. He was suddenly feeling very nervous. This was not the kind of profile he had been expecting when he took a job at the bottom of the National League.

The reporter put the microphone close to him and began her questioning, 'So, Darren. Your team has recently enjoyed a good spell of form in the league, are you hoping to carry that into today and cause an upset?'

Gifford took his time answering; he was surprised with how much the reporter knew about Bucknall, but he reminded himself that they'd have done their research, 'Yeah, of course. For us, this game and this occasion is a bonus. And that's how the boys need to approach it. The pressure's not on us, which is nice because we have been under big pressure these last few weeks. They can enjoy it today, and hopefully get the win.'

'Have you got any secret weapons that you think can cause Doncaster some problems?'

Gifford laughed, 'No, no, nothing like that. For us, it's all about playing our normal game.'

He concluded the interview and returned to the changing rooms. The boys were in high spirits, kicking a ball around and playing music. Gifford called for quiet and gathered them around to make his speech.

'OK, lads. Now, this is going to be a very different test today. These are a proper side. They play two divisions above us, that's a fact. Which means they're going to have more of the ball and they're going to try and dictate the pace of the game. It also means that your normal level, as good as it's been in recent weeks, isn't going to cut it today. They're a cut above who we've been playing. So, as ridiculous as it may seem, that means I'm asking you to give even more. To chase harder, to get to the ball quicker and when we do go get our chances, to be even more accurate and clinical. I've just been out there and told the BBC that we're just going to enjoy it today. Fuck that. This is still a game we want to win. And you've all watched the FA Cup over the years; if it wasn't possible, then why do I see giantkillings every single round, year in, year out. Let's join that fucking list.'

Gifford looked around, deliberately looking for Danny Golding. He caught the midfielder's eye and winked at him, clenching his fist in his direction to indicate to him to be strong. He had considered leaving Golding out but decided that would only crush the lad's spirits further. Besides, football was his escape from his demons. It would be counterproductive to deprive him of that.

The players made their way out on to the pitch, greeted by a typically rapturous welcome from the Yewtree Lane faithful. Gifford and his coaches exchanged the normal pre-match pleasantries and then took their seats on the bench. Gough was already vibrating as he sat down, filled with anticipation. Gifford breathed in quietly, bracing himself. He knew this was going to be a tough game and a tense watch.

The game kicked off. As expected, Doncaster did control the ball and it was plain to see that they had an extra portion of quality with how they used it. Fewer of their passes went astray and they moved it from one side of the pitch to the other much quicker than their National League equivalents. Gifford saw a few of his players breathing hard, not used to exerting this much energy just chasing the ball. Bucknall barely moved forwards for the first half an hour, camped in their own half. They were holding their shape nicely, with the five at the back keeping good distances from each other and the three midfielders sweeping up in front of them. Doncaster's best chances actually came from set pieces as they won a couple of headers from corners, one being cleared off the line by Archie Lewitt. Gifford made a note on this. He would be furious if they lost the game to a set piece.

Tommy Pearce and Kieran Dunne were left completely isolated up front and Pearce began to drop deeper and deeper to try and get a touch of the ball. He ended up trying to hit 40- and 50-yard passes over the top for Dunne to run on to, but the Donny defenders were too used to dealing with that and mopped it up easily. Gifford started to appreciate that this was going to be a one-goal game and that they needed to somehow find a way of creating a chance. He was already halfway down the tunnel when the half-time whistle blew, planning frenetically.

He waited for the players to arrive, having already set up some magnets on a tactics board. His team arrived, all still panting, most with their heads down. He gave them a minute to have a drink before he began.

'I don't want to see any heads dropping, that's a fucking great result that is. We knew they'd be decent boys, nothing I've seen out there has surprised me. But we have got to find a way of creating chances. Pearcey, I know you're just coming deep to try and help out but don't, you're only limiting the space even further. We're too boxed in to break out. The space is out wide, so Con and Archie, it's on you two to break out of the shape when we turnover the ball. If you two move five or ten yards further forward, you'll create space and the others will find you. And once we're there, that's when we can start moving forwards.'

Gifford spoke while moving the magnets around to illustrate his point, using his fingers to illustrate the areas where they were currently trying to play and the advantage of knocking it wide.

'And we're going to have to make the most of half chances. So, any free kick or corner, I want all three centre-halves going up for them. And go to the back post, which means I want all crosses hung up for them. We've got to try and physically outnumber them boys, they're the kind of small differences that will get us a goal. Understood?'

The players nodded their heads and murmured in response. Gifford suddenly wished that they were like the players he imagined in his head before he got the job, where he could physically drag them into the positions he wanted them to be in. He left them to it, reminding himself to have some faith in his team.

The second half started in much the same manner as the first had ended, with Doncaster pressing Bucknall to keep them stranded in their own half. A poor cross into the box was headed by Ardie Adomako to Stefon Harrison who completed a pass into Sebastian D'Amato. With a player on his back, D'Amato controlled the pass on his back foot, turning away smoothly. He then clipped a first-time diagonal over the Doncaster midfield and into space with Conor Caldwell running on to it. It was the first moment of genuine quality from the home team. And the crowd reacted as if it were a goal.

Caldwell was now running away into space. Left chasing lost causes for most of the match, Dunne was suddenly re-energised and began bursting a gut to get into the box. Caldwell was eventually closed down but not before he could get a cross in, which collided with the Doncaster full-back's outstretched leg and trickled away for a corner. Gifford stood up and loudly applauded his team. That was exactly what he was after. Now they had a chance.

D'Amato strode over to take the corner. The Bucknall players began to jog into the box. Gifford patrolled his technical area. D'Amato stepped back and crossed the ball, but it was badly under-hit and was cleared by the first man. Gifford swore furiously. What a waste. As he had turned to exclaim in his coaches' direction, he saw that Golding had recovered the ball and played a one-two with D'Amato who was coming back from the corner. Golding received the ball again and leant back, sending a floated, high cross back into the box. The centre-halves had stayed up and had attacked the far post as instructed. The ball dropped on to the head of Adomako, who was under pressure and could only head the ball down weakly. Then, out of nowhere, Ryan Brook stuck out one of his legs and the ball cannoned off his shin before it could hit the floor. It went straight into the back of the net; 1-0.

Yewtree Lane erupted. Gifford jumped in the air. The players chased Brook across the touchline, the nearest jumping on his back. They had done it. As scrappy a goal as they would ever score, but no one cared one bit. Gifford landed back on the ground and immediately looked at the clock. They probably had half an hour to hold on.

If they were playing cautiously before the goal, the style after it was straight out of the 'park the bus' manual. Gifford took Pearce off for another defender after another ten minutes had passed. They were no longer pressing the Doncaster defenders, allowing them to encroach to the halfway line. The League One side had clearly become more desperate, taking shots early and from positions they would never score from, each one greeted with a beautiful chorus of 'Wahey!' from the Bucknall supporters.

Into the last ten minutes, the tension and excitement rose further. Matt Finch flapped at a cross but the ball fell just the wrong side of the Doncaster player who would otherwise have had a tap-in. Gough nearly entered the pitch to yell at the goalkeeper. Doncaster worked it quickly around the edge of the box. One midfielder stopped when he received it, drawing Harrison in to him. It was a deliberate ploy as he laid the ball off to an approaching team-mate who now had extra space.

'Close him down!' screamed Gifford, sensing the danger.

The second player had time to take a touch and get it out of his feet. He changed his stance and wrapped his foot around the ball, curling it towards the far corner, Yewtree Lane gasped. The ball beat Finch but smashed against the top of the crossbar. There was an audible sigh of relief.

The Doncaster manager sent on another striker as they resorted to hitting balls into the box continuously. Brook had been magnificent, even aside from his goal, and courageously attacked a couple of them, clearing them away. The fans startled whistling, begging the referee to do the same. The Bucknall players tried time-wasting from a throw-in but Doncaster won it back. A long throw was next; they were trying everything they had in their arsenal. It bobbled around but Max Warren-Smith put his sizeable right foot on it and sent it back into the Doncaster half. The referee put his whistle to his lips. Gifford breathed out. It was over.

He made his way on to the pitch, patting his exhausted players on the back and picking a few of them off the turf. The atmosphere was electric. He could see fans hugging each other and jumping up and down. An optimistic few started singing, 'We're going to Wembley!' He stayed on the turf even after the players had disappeared down the tunnel, taking his time to applaud each corner of Yewtree Lane. The fans responded as the familiar and spine-tingling sound of 'There's only one Darren Gifford' entered his eardrums once more.

Final score: Bucknall 1 Doncaster Rovers 0

20

The day after the Doncaster win, Gifford went to watch his son Danny play for the team he used to manage, the Rushwood Town under-13s. He dropped Danny off early enough so that he could join the team for the pre-match warm-up but stayed in the car himself. He felt strange about being there at all and wanted to limit his involvement as much as possible. Firstly, this was a team he used to manage and knew incredibly well and his presence would surely only put added pressure on his replacement. Secondly, his natural shyness meant him reluctant to interact with the other parents as he knew he would be treated like a hero after Bucknall's recent run.

He went on his phone and replied to some emails at first, before going on the BBC Sport website. Curiosity got the better of him and he clicked on the FA Cup tab. There it was. The second article on the page. 'National League Bucknall shock League One Doncaster'. He clicked on the article and read it keenly. It caused a strange sensation to build in his stomach. The bit that stuck out to him most was the following,

'Bucknall, who have enjoyed a remarkable resurgence in recent weeks under the guidance of first-time manager and club legend Darren Gifford, scaled to new heights by adding an established EFL side to their list of scalps.'

Gifford read the sentence a few times. He couldn't help but feel a sense of intoxication when he did. He tried to add some logic to his thoughts, as he knew that there was still most of the season to go and they, and he personally, hadn't achieved anything yet. And that praise and attention ultimately meant nothing. It didn't work. He felt a sense of pride and satisfaction that he couldn't shake off.

He did finally leave the security of the Golf in time to catch the start of the game, nervously taking his place on the side of the pitch, next to a few of the dads he knew well. He greeted them and then turned his attention to the game. Danny was starting and playing in an attacking midfield role. Watching the game turned out to be an immensely therapeutic experience; it was the closest Gifford had been to football where he didn't feel personally responsible for the result since taking the Bucknall job. He tried to keep his shouting to a minimum but couldn't resist the occasional 'go on, Dan' or 'well done' as the match went on.

At half-time Rushwood were a couple of goals up. Gifford went with a couple of the other spectators to grab a tea from the van that was set up near the clubhouse. The inevitable questions and comments accompanied the stroll.

'You're doing so well, Darren. We're all so proud of you here.'

'What's Tommy Pearce like? Heard he's a bit of a nightmare.'

'I think that you should give that young winger a more of a go. He always looks like one of the best when you do put him on.'

'Do you think you'll be able to reach the play-offs?'

Gifford tried to answer and respond as best he could, taking sips of the steaming tea in between. They began to annoy him though. He couldn't shake the feeling that these dads weren't qualified enough to coach their sons' team and yet thought they had some insight in how to improve a National League side, who quite frankly, were doing just fine as they were at the moment. He began to long for Danny's game to restart.

In the second half, Gifford began to notice that Danny was starting to come deeper for the ball, often dropping back into the line of defence. This frustrated him as he knew his son did his best work at the other end of the pitch. In a break in play, he whispered to Danny and gestured for him to move further up the pitch. Danny had turned to face him and saw the instruction but he turned away without responding. The game started to slow and peter out and Danny was taken off just before the end.

Gifford waited in the car once more for his son to join him. Danny took his boots off and put them in the car before sitting in the passenger seat, with muddy legs and his socks now dropped around his ankles. The heat coming off him steamed up the windscreen and Gifford switched on the air conditioning.

'Well played, mate.'

'Thanks.'

'What's with the coming to the ball by the way? Remember I told you that sometimes the best thing to do is go and stand in space, as weird as that seems.'

Danny scowled, 'Coach told me to do it.'

Gifford bit his tongue and got ready to pull away, 'Ah right.'

A few seconds passed before Danny spoke again, 'You know you're not our coach any more, Dad. In fact, this was the first game you've come to since you started coaching Bucknall.'

Gifford was surprised at the outburst and looked at his son with concern. The words had stung him.

'I'm sorry. Would you like me to try and come more?'

Danny looked out of the window absently and said, 'I don't care.'

21

Woking vs Bucknall
Kingfield Stadium
12 November

Bucknall resumed their league campaign away at Woking on a Wednesday night. Winter was officially arriving fast, with the temperatures below zero and an icy wind blowing across the Surrey pitch. Gifford added a thermal, thick coat and a hat to his normal matchday attire. A few of the players were wearing gloves, which, after a moment's consideration, he decided to let slide. 'Modern game,' he told himself. He rotated the time slightly after the exertions of the weekend, giving Sebastian D'Amato, Stefon Harrison and Archie Lewitt rests. He found that a tactical pattern had developed where he would approach away games with caution, focusing his team talks in the days before on the strengths of the opposition, whereas for home matches it was more important to motivate his team and encourage them to be on the front foot.

Bucknall were coming to the crunch part of the season, where the fixtures began to pile up and the rest times decreased. This was apparent when Gifford received Woking's team sheet and saw that they were resting some key players as well. He gathered his players around him in the away dressing room and warned them of complacency.

'I've seen it a million fucking times lads. A team gets a big result like we had at the weekend and in the next game, they can't get themselves up for it. I won't accept that. This game is just as important as the Doncaster one. So, use your fucking imaginations and let's play as if the BBC cameras are here as well.'

Bracing himself within the dugout, feeling the cold start to sneak into his fingers and toes, Gifford watched the game kick off. It was a slow affair, with the changes disrupting both sides' rhythm, with a lot of misplaced passes, especially around either penalty box. This led to a complete lack of chances at either end. Halfway through, Gifford felt himself snap and burst from the dugout, screaming at his players to switch on and up the intensity. It was one of the only occasions he had been angered by their performance.

And then Bucknall managed to scrape a corner. Without D'Amato, Conor Caldwell ran over to the far side to take an in-swinger with his right foot. It was curved nicely to the near post where Max Warren-Smith was making his traditional run. It seemed to ricochet off his head via a Woking touch and looped up invitingly to the back post. Kieran Dunne had peeled off and stuck out a hopeful leg, getting a stud on the ball to poke it towards goal. The keeper scrambled desperately across and managed to get something on it, but even without goal-line technology, it was obvious the ball had crossed the line. Dunne was cartwheeling to the corner once again. Gifford deliberately didn't flinch, even as Gough gripped at his arm in celebration; 1-0 Bucknall.

At half-time Gifford slaughtered the players. He had thought about it for the ten minutes before half-time, deliberating whether it was the right thing to do. He eventually decided that at some point he needed to remind them of what was needed to keep their good run going.

'You're so lucky to be one up, it's unbelievable. I'm actually fuming that you've scored to be honest, because you didn't deserve to. You deserve fucking nothing from that first-half performance. No urgency, no pressing, no quality, nothing!' He banged his palm into a locker, sending a clang echoing around the room, 'Yes we've got a lead but as far as I'm concerned, you've got another half to convince me of your right to play the next game, because that was not good enough.'

It worked. Bucknall were much improved after the break. They controlled the game well, restricting Woking to few chances. The Woking manager threw on a few of his regular starters to try and save the game, but to no avail. The three-man defence of Ryan Brook, Ardie Adomako and Warren-Smith were now a well-oiled machine, knowing when to cover each other and doubling up on attacking players when necessary. Gifford was satisfied he had created a team that was finally hard to beat. For the final five minutes, his team kept the ball at the right end of the pitch, with Pearce winning a couple of fouls and throw-ins, to his obvious delight. Gifford stood at the door of the dressing room as the players returned to it, offering nothing more than an expressionless nod. They had got the job done again.

Final score: Woking 0 Bucknall 1

Bucknall vs Darlington
Yewtree Lane
15 November

Gifford turned up to the Saturday game in a quieter mood. He had asked Danny if he wanted to come and watch the game but his son had refused. Keira had offered him a sympathetic look but hadn't tried to persuade their son otherwise. Gifford had trudged to the car, battling with the feeling that his family weren't enjoying his recent success as much as he was. He found it a relief when he entered the dressing room at Yewtree Lane, feeling the same sense of comfort he had only ever previously experienced when arriving home.

Restoring the side to his first-choice 11, he sent them out with confidence. They were on a fantastic home run and they had rebuilt a fractured relationship with the home fans. You could no longer hear gasps of exasperation or moans when there were mistakes or lulls in play, the fans giving the team time to sustain attacks. Bucknall responded by being quick out the traps, sprinting into tackles and pressing the Darlington defence high. They were rewarded almost immediately when D'Amato scored one of their goals of the season, receiving the ball in space about 25 yards out and hitting a wonderful swerving strike that flew past the goalkeeper into the far corner. The ground was bouncing once more.

Bucknall kept the lead until half-time and in the second half, Gifford decided to try something. He had been impressed by the performances in training of one of the club's youngest players, an 18-year old called Jordan Cassidy. Around the 70-minute mark he threw Cassidy on for his debut, embracing Danny Golding as he came off. The fans applauded warmly as the kid ran on to the turf. He responded as young debutants always did, running around like manically, chasing every ball and throwing himself around. Gifford gestured him for to calm down during a break in play, as he could see Cassidy was already panting hard after a few minutes.

His moment arrived soon after. It was worked down Bucknall's excellent left-hand side, with Tommy Pearce dropping into a pocket to allow Lewitt to dash past him down the flank. He was played in and the low cross flashed across the six-yard box. A Darlington defender got something on it, taking it away from a sliding Dunne but it bobbled up in the box. Cassidy had arrived late and the defence parted in front of him, giving him a clear shot on goal.

'Go on, Jordan!' Gifford yelled.

The young midfielder focused on getting his foot on the ball, but had maybe gone too far, as his strike went straight down into the turf. Gifford looked up expectantly as the ball bounced up, deceiving the goalkeeper who dived underneath it and it drooped into the back of the net; 2-0.

It was a brilliant moment. The whole team started chasing Cassidy. The youngster seemed unsure what to do, changing direction a few times as if he was trying to evade a predator. Gifford eventually realised he was heading towards the bench and reacted by sprinting towards the substitute. He reached Cassidy and threw his arms round him on the edge of the touchline, enjoying a couple of seconds before he felt the rest of the bench and the team jump and climb on top of them. The bundle lasted a few seconds before breaking up with Gifford ruffling his hand through Cassidy's hair before pushing him back on to the pitch.

Final score: Bucknall 2 Darlington 0

Harrogate vs Bucknall
The EnviroVent Stadium
18 November

Harrogate away was always going to be Bucknall's toughest fixture of the month, with the Sulphurites one of the other in-form teams in the division who were aiming for promotion. In Monday's training session, Gifford tried a new drill he had researched the day before, after watching Harrogate's most recent games. He split his players into three teams of four, with one four being the defensive unit. The attacking teams took it in turns to pass the ball into one of two 'wide alleys' which the defenders weren't allowed to enter. This gave those players time to cross the ball, but it meant that instead the defenders had to focus on their positioning, making sure they had every possible target covered.

They were pressured early in the first half by Harrogate, with a lot of balls coming in from wide positions as Gifford had expected. His defenders coped well. They looked dangerous on the counterattack and after Stefon Harrison made a great challenge in midfield, the ball was worked to Tommy Pearce who ran to the left-hand side of the penalty area. Archie Lewitt instinctively ran outside him, which briefly drew the attention of the nearest Harrogate defender. Pearce used this distraction perfectly, quickly dummying the ball inside and striking the ball quickly, before he had properly worked it out of his feet. This meant the strike had no backlift and the shot was nestled into the far corner before the keeper could move; 1-0.

It was their only shot of the game so far. Harrogate responded again, forcing a couple of good saves from Matt Finch. Gifford was starting to pray for the half-time whistle when a simple clearance was launched upfield from one of his defenders. Dunne did brilliantly, judging the flight of the ball perfectly to cushion a knock-down into the feet of the arriving Pearce. Again, Pearce didn't hesitate, hitting across the ball as it bounced, despite the fact he was a fair distance out. The result was another strange-looking shot, as it seemed to be heading straight at the keeper before moving late to his left. He couldn't adjust in time and it bounced off the pitch and into the corner. Gifford raised his arms victoriously once again. Pearce was making the difference. They had now had another shot, and had scored another goal; 2-0.

Gifford spent the rest of the game reflecting on the strange nature of football. A couple of months ago his players could do everything right and still not win. Now they were winning games without being the better team. They were now ten unbeaten in all competitions, winning eight of those fixtures. They had kept five clean sheets in a row. On the coach back from Harrogate, one of Gifford's old team-mates sent him a clip on WhatsApp. It was from *Soccer Special*, with Jeff Stelling talking about Bucknall's remarkable turnaround in form and praising Gifford's efforts. He showed it to Haines and Gough as the three of them enjoyed a moment of shared pride.

Final score: Harrogate Town 0 Bucknall 2

		Played	Points
10.	Bucknall	16	24
11.	Yeovil Town	16	24
12.	Bromley	16	22
13.	Stockport County	16	22
14.	Woking	16	22

22

At the start of December, the club organised a Christmas party for the players. Lee Chugwell had spoken to Gifford about it once the results had started to pick up and they had decided that they deserved a reward. Chugwell booked out the entirety of a local bar, Atlas. It was an upmarket place, with disco-style fluorescent lighting and an illuminated bar with liquid concoctions with more resemblance to potions and decorations than drinks.

Gifford had been reluctant to go. He couldn't help but feel how he imagined teachers felt when supervising an after-school event. This was an opportunity for the players to cut loose and their manager being there wasn't exactly going to contribute to that. Keira had told him to cheer up and the two of them caught a taxi into town, with her having brought herself a new dress and matched it with hooped gold earrings for the occasions.

When they arrived, most of the others were already there and it seemed they had not waited to get the party started. Gifford could see Tommy Pearce with a series of shots, handing them to the nearest group of his team-mates gathered around. Ryan Brook was talking to Max Warren-Smith in the corner, two half-drunk pints of Amstel in their hands. Chugwell greeted them as they arrived, introducing himself to Keira and telling them to get whatever they wanted from the bar. Kieran Dunne ran over to also introduce himself to Keira.

'You didn't mention your wife was a good Irish woman, Gaffer?'

'That's right. Which means she won't be have any issue sorting out any nonsense from you lot. You behave yourself tonight, Dunney.'

'Of course, Gaffer! You know me.'

Gifford settled down on a table away from the bar and was joined by Nick, the commercial exec, and, after a period of mingling around the room, Chugwell. Keira saw

Clarisse and Mary and joined them for a catch-up. Gifford positioned himself so he could see out into the room, keeping an eye on everything. Nick resumed his part-time role as interviewer-cum-Gifford's biggest fan for the evening.

'You're doing a fantastic job, you know, Giff. Compared to what we were like at the start of the season, it's bordering on a miracle honestly.'

'Thanks mate.'

'Me and some of the boys in the ticket office were talking and we reckon we might get play-offs, is that what you're aiming for?'

Gifford caught Chugwell's eye, 'Uh, I think we're just taking it one game at a time. We've just managed to find some form, so it seems silly to think too far ahead.'

Chugwell leant forwards, 'But do you think the lads are capable of it, Giff? I mean we're not far off the play-off positions now and there's still plenty of games to play. I spoke to Steve and we were talking about that being a realistic target.'

Gifford was taken aback and couldn't hide the frown that sneaked on to his face, 'I thought the primary target was keeping us in the division?'

'Well obviously, but look at how well things are going! You're smashing it, it's only natural to start looking up.'

'Yeah and from what I've seen, we're better than a couple of the teams who are up there at the moment. Pearcey's the best player in the league hands down and our defence looks rock fucking solid right now,' added Nick.

Gifford nervously sipped his pint. He couldn't deny that he had allowed himself to consider what might be possible for his side this season, but it was one thing him thinking it, it was another his employers beginning to expect it. He felt a flutter of anxiety build up and lodge in his chest, but he gritted his teeth and smiled through it.

The night continued to descend into greater drunkenness and all the classic Christmas party hallmarks. The cheesy old tunes were pumped into the bar through a series of large speakers and as the players kept drinking, more and more of them started singing along. Gifford rejoined Keira and spent most of the evening with their previous dinner party group. He watched and smirked at a series of highlights: a brief dance-off which culminated in Kieran Dunne busting out an admittedly impressive worm; Tommy Pearce trying to prove he could down a pint using only his feet and proceeding to pour most of it over his face and chest and all of the players joining arm-in-arm to belt out 'Sweet Caroline'.

Gifford had kept an eye out for Danny Golding throughout. He had spoken to Chugwell previously and they had booked Golding into a gambling addiction course, which he attended twice a week. Gifford doubted that he had told any of his team-mates yet though and while he had joined in the celebrations, there were occasions when Gifford would see him looking absently into the middle distance, his mind removed from the bar and the action going on around him.

Just as he and Keira had begun discussing making a move back home, Chugwell stood on a chair and began to clang a pen on the side of his glass. The music was muted and a series of shushes echoed around the room, ending in an eventual silence.

Chugwell began to speak, 'Sorry to interrupt what has been a brilliant evening, but I just wanted to thank you all for coming and congratulate the players and the staff on a fantastic couple of months. As we all know the season doesn't end in December and so I want to say on behalf of the board and everyone else at the club that we're all behind you for what I'm sure is going to be an exciting finish. And finally, I want to say that there was a time not that long ago when it didn't look like we would be organising a Christmas party of any description, and that was because there was absolutely nothing to cheer. This club was in a bad place and we mainly have the efforts of one man to thank for turning that around. So, if I could ask you all to show your appreciation to our manager, a man who's truly one of our own, Mr Darren Gifford!'

The bar burst into applause from all corners. Some of the players put their fingers to their mouths to whistle loudly. Gifford was touched and felt a bolt of energy pass through him, but he also felt distinctly uncomfortable and self-aware. There were a few calls of 'speech!' and after he attempted to bat them away with an outstretched palm, Keira and Gough both began to poke and pull him to his feet.

Gifford took a deep breath and coughed before he spoke, 'Thank you everybody. That means a lot, but I really cannot take all the credit for what we've achieved. That's down to Goughy and Hainesy and the rest of the staff who work tirelessly day in, day out. And of course none of us are the ones who play on the pitch so I'd like to say a big thank you to the players for everything they've given me in the few months I've been here. And I'd like to warn them not to drink too much tonight because they've got a massive couple of games coming up! Anyway, here's to a good night and a good rest of the season.'

He raised his glass and watched as everyone in the room followed. Gough let out a loud 'hear, hear' and another wave of applause and cheers began to break out, but Chugwell reappeared on his chair, raising his glass as well.

'Here's to the play-offs!' he shouted and Gifford saw a kind of manic energy in his eyes.

'The play-offs!' shouted the players and the rest of the room.

Gifford sat back down and the anxiety returned to his chest. He looked at Keira, who looked at him uncertainly, assessing with her eyes what he was feeling. He tried to reassure her by winking, but he quickly turned away and stared out into space.

23

Bucknall vs Sutton United
Yewtree Lane
9 December

Bucknall's good form and unbeaten run had continued into December, with Lee Chugwell's slightly drunken speech at the Christmas party refocusing the group towards the target of reaching the play-offs. To do that, the lowest they could finish in the league was seventh and then they had to go through the lottery of quarter-finals and semi-finals in an attempt to rejoin the promised land of the EFL.

Sutton were a rival with a similar ambition and, all of a sudden, a game that Gifford wouldn't have considered particularly important a month or so ago was now a must-win. He instructed the players to enjoy the fact that they were now looking up the table rather than down it and reminded them not to lose sight of the efforts and tactics they had used to get this far. He was recognising that he was feeling more and more nervous on Saturday mornings when he woke up, with a tight ball of anxiety forming in his chest. He spent the entirety of his journey to the stadium trying to release that tension, breathing in and out slowly as he allowed the sounds of Smooth FM to wash over him.

He allowed Gough to do most of the talking pre-match, deciding it was an occasion where his one-note, crazed aggression was needed. The players seemed motivated enough and as Gifford oversaw the warm-up, he was pleased with the application and attitude. By the time the referee called them out from the dressing rooms, Gifford felt the ball of anxiety had dissipated and had instead dissolved into an energy that ran through his body and to the end of his limbs.

His team started well. They won the first few challenges and Kieran Dunne won a few flick-ons ahead of his opposing defenders. A series of quick and precise passes played in and around the Sutton penalty area led to Tommy Pearce laying the ball to Sebastian D'Amato, whose shot was deflected off a lunging defender's studs and bounced dangerously just over the bar, to a huge cheer of encouragement from the crowd.

And then Pearce dropped deep, almost back to the left wing-back position, and turned on the ball. Archie Lewitt executed an underlap, bombing inside the full-back and making a striker-like run into the box. Pearce feinted to pass infield to Stefon Harrison but instead dug his foot under the ball and played a hanging chip over the back line for Lewitt to run into. It dropped just in front of him and he stuck out a leg to try and control it. The full-back had panicked as the ball and Lewitt went past him and desperately tried to get back. He ran into Lewitt's planted back leg and the two of them collapsed to the ground.

'Penalty!' bellowed Gifford, sprinting to the edge of the technical area.

The referee gave nothing and the Sutton centre-half covered and cleared the ball. The Bucknall players had basically stopped in their tracks and Gifford noticed that even a few of the Sutton boys had looked straight at the ref, a surefire sign that it was a penalty. Gifford walked over to the fourth official and yelled at him,

'How the fuck is that not a penalty?!'

The game carried on. The decision seemed to throw Bucknall off their early momentum and Sutton began to have a spell of possession, killing some of the pace of the match. They still hadn't made Matt Finch make a save until ten minutes before half time when a hopeful and straightforward ball was aimed in between Ryan Brook and Ardie Adomako. Both players went to collect but neither seemed to fully commit, unsure of whether the other was dealing with it, and the ball slipped between the two of them and through for the Sutton striker. Finch ran out but the striker dinked the ball past him and into the net; 1-0 Sutton.

Giiford threw his water bottle on the floor. Gough ran out to scream at Brook and Adomako.

'What the fuck are you doing?! Talk to each other!'

In the end, they needed half-time. Gifford sent one last scowl in the fourth official's direction and marched down the tunnel. Gough was still furious and so he decided it was on him to provide a more measured speech once the players had returned to the dressing room.

'Right boys. Everybody relax. Get your breath. Get a drink. Take a minute to compose yourselves.'

He waited and glared around the room. The players looked back at him with blank and hopeful faces. They were looking to him for inspiration.

'Now we've had a setback. We should have had a penalty. I know that, you all know that. But we can't do anything about it now. That's football, lads. What I'm more pissed off about is the reaction we've had since that moment. We lost our shape, lost our press. Ryan and Ardie, when have you two made a mistake like that all season? Fucking communicate! This is the test now, yes we know we can piss it 5-0 against teams like Eastleigh but if we are going to aim higher this season, we need to prove we can face adversity against decent teams and come back and react! I tell you, this next half will tell me a lot about you lot and this team's chances this season.'

Gifford deliberately stood right on the touchline as the second half started, hoping his presence would further signal the importance to his players. They began as they had started the first half, forcing a series of half chances. Gifford sensed they were on the brink of something. From a throw-in on the left-hand side, Pearce dragged one of the centre-halves out of position to receive the throw from Lewitt. Harrison made the run into the vacated space and Lewitt knocked the ball first-time towards him. The other centre-half now needed to cover and managed to make a challenge, but the ball broke favourably and Harrison now slipped in a completely unmarked Dunne. The pass was a bit weak which meant Dunne had to wait for it to come across to his right foot but when it did, he got enough on it to beat the keeper; 1-1.

Gifford leapt in the air and roared with delight, sending a wadge of saliva flying on to the pitch. As he turned, he sent a second yell towards the crowd nearest to him, as if encouraging them as well. He had never done that before and he reminded himself to calm down as he rejoined the bench.

Bucknall were now fired up beyond belief and Sutton were on the ropes. Harrison crunched into another tackle, winning the ball back to another huge roar from the crowd. Yet again, it was worked down the left with Pearce getting the ball in the box near the touchline. He had a man on his back but executed a sharp Cruyff turn to make a yard of space. As he went to cross it, the full-back stretched out and tripped him. Gifford looked straight at the referee. Again, no penalty.

He went to talk to the fourth official but before he could, he watched as Gough sprinted past him in a blur of fury and screamed in the guy's face.

'Are you taking the fucking piss?! That's two stonewall fucking penalties! You're a bunch of dirty cheats, that's what you are. Dirty fucking cheats!'

When the ball went out of play, the referee did finally blow his whistle to stop the game but only to head over and speak to the fourth official. Gifford knew what was coming and sure enough, Gough was called over by the referee and with a point of his arm, was sent off from the dugout. Gough departed with a last mutter of his new motto, 'dirty fucking cheats'. Gifford made sure to call after the ref as he ran back to the centre of the pitch,

'You've missed two, ref, so remember that.'

Gifford turned to his bench as the game settled into another tense and even period. He decided to throw on Jordan Cassidy once more, hoping he would repeat his debut heroics. He withdrew D'Amato, opting for energy over technique and urged Cassidy to put his foot in. The youngster did as instructed, bouncing around the pitch. The ball took a couple of deflections and broke loose near the centre circle with Cassidy and a Sutton midfielder an equal distance from the ball. Cassidy lunged, leg outstretched, and managed to half control, half tread on the ball. He reached it no more than half a second before his opponent who slid in and caught his ankle and not the ball. Cassidy hit the floor and the ref blew for a foul, with Gifford looking away to focus on the position of the free kick.

Suddenly, he became aware that something was wrong. Cassidy had stayed down, which wasn't uncommon, but the position of his body looked wrong. It was too twisted, too contorted. There was a look of genuine pain on his face. Some of the nearest players from both sides began to gesture to the dugout for the medical staff to come on. Gifford felt his heart sink in his chest. This had to be a bad injury.

The crowd went silent, with only the odd mutter heard. Gifford called over to Conor Caldwell who was nearest to him.

'What is it, Con? Is it bad?'

Caldwell's face winced, 'It doesn't look good, Gaffer. His foot, it, it shouldn't look like that.'

After a few minutes, the group of players around the incident parted and Cassidy was carried off the pitch on a stretcher, his limbs held in place by straps. The medical staff headed past Gifford to go down the tunnel and so he was given a chance to look at his player. Cassidy had tears in his eyes as he saw Gifford, who patted him sympathetically.

'Sorry, Gaffer,' said Cassidy, as he departed.

The crowd applauded him off. Gifford had already got another sub, to replace his last sub, ready. He could feel the emotion building up inside of him. It was difficult not to feel responsible; he had put Cassidy on. He had told him 'to put a foot in'. Trying to shake himself out of the numbness he was experiencing, he thumped his hands together to try and wake up his players after a lengthy delay.

The game ticked into the final ten minutes and Sutton were once again the better team. Bucknall now had an inexperienced midfield that hadn't played together and Gifford recognised that they were being played through more easily now. Sutton worked it wide and their winger took on Lewitt, who tried to show him on to the outside and his weaker foot. He succeeded but the winger took a touch away from him, making Lewitt try and get his body across to ease him off making the cross. In doing so there was contact and the winger hit the floor. Gifford this time didn't look at the referee, but the sinking sensation told him what was about to happen. Now the referee pointed to the spot.

The Bucknall players surrounded the referee. It seemed incredibly soft. Gifford found that all he could muster was a sarcastic laugh and a knowing point in the fourth official's direction. He couldn't fight the immense sense of injustice that he was feeling. Everything had gone against his team, to the point that it felt like it had been somehow orchestrated from behind the scenes. He watched as Tommy Pearce got right in the referee's face, screaming obscenities. It didn't make a difference. The Sutton striker eventually got to take the penalty. Gifford tensed his wrists, wishing Matt Finch to save it. Finch dived the wrong way and the striker rolled it in the corner; 2-1 Sutton.

The frustration in the ground was at an all-time high. There were chants of 'the referee's a wanker' and any decision that was given against Bucknall after the penalty, be that a throw-in or a free kick, was greeted with boos and further abuse. The Bucknall players were also growing visibly more and more animated too, with the emotion of witnessing Cassidy off only fuelling their anger. Pearce tried a trick near the corner flag and was crowded out by Sutton players. He went down, expecting a free kick. Nothing came. One of the Sutton players then muttered something to him after the ball was cleared. Pearce responded by throwing an elbow wildly in his direction. The player went down. The referee once more jogged over. The red card was drawn. Pearce was off. It was all falling apart.

There were more boos. More complaints from the Bucknall players. Pearce briefly remonstrated himself before trudging dejectedly towards the tunnel. Gifford wanted to feel angry at Pearce, for producing the kind of petulant, brainless moment that had all but killed off his side's hope for getting a result. Instead, he offered a comforting outstretched arm as Pearce walked past him. In truth, he felt like throwing an elbow at somebody as well.

He finally snapped. Walking over to the fourth official, he felt a surge of adrenaline surge through his body; his mind was full with lots of different images, all at once. The two penalties not given, the one that was, Cassidy's stricken, apologetic face and now his best player taken from him for at least three games.

'You're a fucking disgrace, you know that? You're a fucking disgrace. You and him and the lot of you. Bet you've never kicked a fucking football in your life and here you are ruining the game for all of these people. I hope you watch this back and realise what a fucking shitshow you have all put on here today. I hope you're embarrassed by your performance. You should be. You should be fucking ashamed.'

Gifford marched back towards the dugout, with Haines putting an arm around him to both comfort and restrain him. The referee was clearly spoken to by the fourth official and made his way over to the touchline. He looked patronisingly at Gifford and pointed behind him.

'Go and join your assistant in the crowd. You're off.'

Gifford looked at him in the eye as more images flooded his mind. He considered all the ways he could hurt the man in front of him. His body itched for action. He managed to hold back that feeling and marched straight down the tunnel, not even bothering to reposition himself in the stands. He heard the final whistle as he stood outside the dressing room, still trembling with fury.

Final score: Bucknall 1 Sutton United 2

24

In the end, Gifford was handed a one-match ban. He accepted it without complaint and spent the days after the Sutton game dwelling on his actions, haunted and embarrassed by them. It was the kind of reaction he had sworn he would never give in to. The kind he had hated in other managers when he was playing. He had lost his head. Plain and simple. His response was to sulk and reflect, trying to escape his family as much as he could. He mowed the lawn on Sunday, stretching it out for as long as he could so he didn't have to focus on anything else.

When Monday rolled around, he drove to the hospital before training, going to visit Jordan Cassidy. Gifford had always hated hospitals; they reminded him of his own time spent in them nursing injuries and even the experience of walking through the corridors put him on edge. They made him feel unclean. After asking the nurse on reception, he worked his way through the wards to find Cassidy.

The boy's face lit up as he saw his manager. Cassidy was reclining in the bed, his leg raised high and coated in plaster. His face had the ashen and ghoulish look of someone who had recently had an operation. His bed was lined with cards and gifts, with Gifford noticing a package that had been sent by the team, organised by captain Ryan Brook. It was a nice touch. Gifford walked across the room and sat down in the chair next to the bed.

'Hello, mate. How are you doing?'

'Not bad, Gaffer. Not bad. I've had my op now and they've got me on some pretty sweet stuff so I'm feeling all right.'

'Yeah? You sure there's nothing I can do? Move your pillows or whatever, anything you need honestly.'

'Nah. It's good. My mum comes in about five or six times a day. She's been making a big fuss so I'm all sorted.'

The mention of Cassidy's mother made Gifford's stomach flinch. It reminded him just how young his player was, young enough to still be reliant on his parents. He couldn't help but feel his own sense of paternal guilt and responsibility.

'Not been a particularly fun weekend then hey? The boys are all thinking of you, mate. We were all worried sick.'

'Thanks, Gaffer. I appreciate it.'

Gifford paused before asking the question he knew he had to.

'So, what did the doctors say? What's the verdict?'

Cassidy fidgeted and looked away as he answered, 'Uhh, I've got a fracture in the tibia? It's basically the shin I think, They said it often looks and feels worse than it is, but yeah I'll be out for a while for sure.'

'How long?'

'Uh, the doc said most likely six months.'

Gifford nodded and forced himself to smile. In his mind, he had already worked out the maths. There was no way Cassidy would play again this season. His Bucknall career had been handed a devastating blow just a few games after it had started.

Gifford tried to offer encouragement, 'Right, well you just need to focus on your recovery. You have a good few weeks of rest, we'll make sure we get you to and from the games and everything and I'm going to keep you involved as much as possible. And I'll talk to the medical team about getting you on a plan when you can start training again.'

He paused briefly before looking Cassidy straight in the eye, 'You're not going to be forgotten, kid. I promise. As soon as you're ready to kick a ball again, you'll be back in the first team.'

That seemed to brighten Cassidy's face. Some of the life returned to his eyes and he nodded enthusiastically. Gifford stayed with him for a while, talking him through what happened in the game and explaining his own sending off and ban. He only left when Cassidy's mother, Nina, arrived. They walked together to get a tea from the machine in the corridor.

'I'm really sorry about what happened to Jordan. It's so unfortunate.'

Nina was a well-put-together woman with kind eyes and a welcoming smile. She put her hand on Gifford's arm as he waited for the tea to pour.

'You don't need to apologise, Mr Gifford. You gave him his chance. He was so happy that day he made his debut and scored. The whole family were. We have nothing but gratitude for you.'

Gifford gulped and smiled shyly, 'Thank you. He's a talented kid, he's going to do great things, I'm sure of it.'

'It was good of you to come.'

Gifford left the hospital and retreated to his car. He slumped in the driver's seat and took a second to recompose himself. It had been an emotionally exhausting few days and now he had to pick himself up to coach the players after a damaging loss. He rubbed his face with his palms roughly, enjoying the feeling of his skin catching on his facial hair. With the Christmas fixture list coming up, there wasn't any time for a rest. He was going to have to keep powering on.

25

Christmas Day rolled around as deceptively quickly as it always seemed to. In his years as a player, Gifford had got used to only being able to enjoy half a Christmas, having to leave to join up with the team or sometimes even train, before a game on Boxing Day. It had been one of his favourite things about retirement: being able to fully enjoy, and indulge in, Christmas. Unfortunately, Bucknall had been dealt an away game, up in York no less, and the club had organised a stay in a hotel the night before.

This had brought the Gifford family Christmas forward a few hours, which suited Orla perfectly, and she woke up her parents by running into their room and leaping up on to their bed, before the clock had ticked round to six o'clock in the morning. Keira brought her downstairs and Gifford went to wake Danny up. The kids were allowed to open their presents in their stockings first, before Keira made a breakfast of pancakes and various other pastries. Gifford found himself beaming as he sat back in a chair and watched his children rip into the wrapping paper excitedly. It was a moment of connection with his family that he felt he had sacrificed to some extent since taking over the Bucknall job.

After breakfast, they returned to the living room and Gifford put some Christmas music on faintly in the background and they all exchanged their 'main' gifts. Danny got a new pair of football boots, made from a vibrant orange fabric. Orla was bestowed with endless dolls and dresses and other various nicknacks, half of which Gifford knew wouldn't be played with again. He had brought Keira a scarf and a sketching book, to encourage her to get back into drawing, something she had always loved. He got a new beard trimmer and cookbook as well as a relaxing neck pillow that vibrated and could be heated. He was a little thrown when he opened it, prompting Keira to add,

'I thought it might help calm you down if you lose.'

Gifford smiled and nodded in response. The rest of the morning and the early afternoon continued in more traditional fashion. Orla played with her new gifts on a kind of rotation, Danny went into the garden to test out his new boots and Gifford watched him through the window, curling shots into the net. Keira had made a Christmas dinner, but Gifford made sure not to eat too much, knowing he had another dinner organised for later. He made an extra effort to be affectionate with his family, pulling Orla on to his lap and tickling her and letting Danny have a sip of his beer with dinner. He then quietly withdrew himself to pack his things and came down to kiss Keira and say goodbye to them as he made his way to the car.

He drove to Yewtree Lane where the coach was waiting. Some of the staff and players were there already, with an obvious air of merriment among them, some wearing tinsel around the necks or crowns taken from Christmas crackers. He wished a merry Christmas to all of them and they waited for the last remaining few to arrive. Some of the players were late, but Gifford decided not to mention it, accepting it was a day where many would struggle to pull themselves away from their families.

Finally, at about four o'clock, the coach left for York. It was always a good time to travel, with the motorway opening up in front of them. The coach driver even cranked up the radio and there was soon a whole-coach rendition of Wham!'s 'Last Christmas'. Gifford joined in and started the clap immediately afterwards. He was impressed with the player's spirits, considering the unusual nature of their day.

It was late in the evening when they reached the hotel but the players were told to check in to their rooms and then come immediately downstairs for a whole-squad Christmas dinner, laid on by the club. They did so and some of them dressed up for the occasion, sporting a series of jumpers and shirts that Gifford assumed were recent presents. They sat at a long table in the centre of one of the large and luxurious dining rooms of the hotel. There were a series of bangs as crackers were popped and there were murmurs and smatterings of laughter along the table. Gifford was seated near the head of it and after allowing a period of time for them to get stuck into the turkey, stuffing, Brussel sprouts, potatoes, carrots, pigs in blankets and cranberry sauce, he stood up to make a brief statement.

'Sorry to interrupt, boys. I'd just like to take a moment to say thank you to you all for being here. I appreciate that you might have wanted to stay and spend more time with your families and having made the same sacrifice myself, I know how difficult that can be. However, I hope that you appreciate that this team and this club is a family of its own and I for one am very happy to be spending my Christmas day with you ugly lot. Now, there is a reason why you're all drinking water instead of beer or wine and that's because we have a big game tomorrow. And if any of you were thinking of buying me a present, all I want for Christmas is three fucking points. Now, merry Christmas!'

The squad echoed the call and there were clinks of glasses meeting and pats on the back. They finished the dinner and then Ryan Brook stood up and suggested there would be an impromptu talent show. Everybody remained seated as various players took it in turns to stand up and perform.

Brook kicked festivities off himself with a decent, Michael Bublé-esque rendition of 'It's Beginning to Look a Lot Like Christmas' which drew plenty of excited gasps and applause. Then, Kieran Dunne attempted to juggle with different and increasingly difficult objects, starting with oranges and then working his way up to the candlesticks that were scattered along the table. He was not very good and after one of the candlesticks nearly took Max Warren-Smith's eye out, he was told to sit down, accompanied by a chorus of boos and heckles. Sebastian D'Amato briefly left the room, only to return with a guitar. Sitting himself down, his tied back hair and his open white shirt making him look like a bona fide rock star, he proceeded to play and sing along to 'Wonderwall', encouraging the rest of the room to join in. It was a fitting finale.

Gifford returned to the hotel room and collapsed on to the bed. He phoned home and Keira answered. He spoke to her about how things had gone and told her about the talent show and that the potatoes weren't as good as hers. He asked about the kids and Keira told him that they had all settled down to watch *Elf* and Orla had fallen asleep on Danny by the end. Gifford felt a tinge of pain at missing such a sweet moment and Keira continued,

'Takes me back this, phoning you on Christmas day.'

'I know. Still at least I don't have to worry about what I eat now.'

'True. Good luck tomorrow, I'll be keeping my eye on the result.'

'Thanks. When do your parents arrive?'

'Who knows, around midday?'

'OK, well I should be back in time for the evening. Give them my apologies.'

'They won't care. They know the deal now.'

'Yeah, that's what happens when their daughter gets stolen away by a footballer, hey?'

'Shut up.'

Keira giggled, which excited Gifford, reminding him of their early flirtations. She sighed and then said in a deliberately hushed and affectionate tone.

'Merry Christmas, Darren.'

'Merry Christmas, sweetheart.'

26

York City vs Bucknall
York Community Stadium
26 December

Gifford was serving his one-match touchline ban at York and was set to watch the game in the stands. He spoke to the officials and members of York's hospitality team and it was explained he had a seat prepared for him and that he was to make his way there ready for the start of the game. He, Gough and Haines had worked out how they were going to manage the unusual circumstances, with Gough essentially becoming coach on the touchline while Haines would use his mobile to communicate with Gifford and pass on messages.

After he had issued his instructions, Gifford followed a steward up and out of the dressing room area and up the steps into the terraces. He was led to a seat at the front of the back row, immediately after you emerged from the shadow of the steps. He even had a barrier to lean against. Thanking the steward, Gifford sat down and nodded a greeting to the York supporters who were going to be his companions for the rest of the game.

'Go easy on me today.'

'Ah you'll be all right. Just as long as the Minstermen batter your lot.'

Without Tommy Pearce, who was suspended, Gifford had decided to reshape the team. He had considered putting Sajja Gujar back in, but the striker still hadn't recovered his form and was still missing chances in training. Trying to replace the creativity Pearce offered, Gifford moved Archie Lewitt further forward and brought in Manny Orize as well, switching to a 5-2-3.

Finch (GK)

Caldwell Brook Adomako Warren-Smith Wrenshaw

Golding D'Amato

Orize Dunne Lewitt

The game began and Gifford was taken aback by the roar of the York fans that surrounded him, the noise coming in from every angle. He was in enemy territory. Things were made worse by the home team also making the better start. They played accurate, direct passes in behind the wide centre-backs, which Gifford knew was a weakness of his side, with neither Ryan Brook nor Max Warren-Smith possessing much pace. Matt Finch was forced to make a good early save at his near post, with more enthused cheers following.

Gifford sent his first text of the day to Haines.

'Tell Brooky and Max to DROP.'

His eyes left the pitch and drifted to the dugout, where he watched to see the reaction. It was a bizarre situation, having an idea and then watching to see it implemented. Gifford felt like he was playing God to a degree, high up in the Yorkshire air. After a few seconds, he saw Haines leave the dugout and tap Gough's shoulder, relaying the instruction. Gough began barking at the defence and to Gifford's immense relief, they started playing five yards deeper, restricting the opportunities that were being created with ease.

Bucknall improved. Gifford had instructed Lewitt and Orize to come into more central positions in the half-spaces between midfield and attack and they began to get on the ball more. Lewitt played a nice one-two with Dunne and got a shot away which the keeper had to push over. Gifford managed to restrain himself from his normal claps of enthusiasm but was pleased at the way they were playing themselves into the game.

'That boy Lewitt can play,' said the York fan next to him.

'Yeah, he's got good feet,' Gifford replied.

Half-time came and went without major incident, with the game threatening to pan out like a classic Boxing Day encounter where both teams weren't at their sharpest. Gifford had urged his team to up the energy and put the ball in earlier as Kieran Dunne thrived off first-time deliveries. He sent instructions to prepare the substitutes, including Gujar as he debated switching back to two up top.

'Tell the wing-backs to push up. Don't worry about their wingers, they'll have to go back with them,' he texted Haines.

Danny Golding mistimed a tackle around the 70-minute mark and York got a free kick in a decent position on the left-hand side, with the potential of an in-swinger into the six-yard box. The York crowd, who had been sufficiently quietened in the second half, found their voice again. Gifford tensed. He felt helpless. He couldn't send a text that would be implemented in time before the kick was taken.

The York player stood over the ball. The players jostled for space in the box. It was floated into the centre, with good pace on it. It beat Brook and Ardie Adomako, two of Bucknall's strongest players in the air, and dropped on to a York head. It wasn't the cleanest connection, but Finch had been anticipating it reaching the back post and was on his heels. The ball skidded underneath his body and into the net; 1-0. Disaster.

All around Gifford, the supporters rose to their feet in delight. He was the only one in the stand still in his seat, head bowed. It was a goal out of absolutely nothing. He was already texting Haines before the game had even restarted, instructing him to get Stefon Harrison and Gujar on and to push Lewitt back to a more attacking wing-back. They had to go for broke now, with less than 20 minutes left.

The York fans started chanting once again. The supporter closest to Gifford shrugged his shoulders at Gifford, a smug grin on his face. Gifford wasn't angry; he didn't begrudge them celebrating their team. And he certainly didn't need another ban.

He watched as Gough and Haines sent on the subs and waved their arms to encourage the team. York began to sit deeper, clearly content with the one-goal lead and Bucknall started to dominate possession, without creating too many chances. Just as Gifford had worried would happen, they were missing Pearce's creativity. It was a game crying out for somebody to take a chance and create something out of nothing.

It reached the last five minutes and was still 1-0. Bucknall were getting increasingly desperate and when D'Amato smashed a half-volley practically out of the stadium, that was Gifford's cue to frantically text Haines once more.

'Not creating anything. Tell Brooky to go up and aim crosses to the back post. LAST CHANCE SALOON.'

A few minutes of play passed and Brook left his defensive position and made his way forwards, with the wing-backs tucking in to make a back four. Conor Caldwell received the ball just inside the York half in acres of space and looked up. He cut his foot across the ball, aiming a deep cross at Brook's head. Brook got up early and above his marker but could only aim the ball back across goal and not towards it. Gifford couldn't help himself sliding excitedly out of his seat when he saw Gujar make a dash to meet it. Now was their chance.

Gujar met it and skied the ball desperately. Gifford turned his head to the skies and slumped backwards once more. That was that. He looked back at the surrounding York fans with a slight embarrassed look on his face. His nearest companion spoke up once more.

'I don't know how the fuck he's missed that.'

The referee blew his whistle and the fans roared in appreciation. Gifford offered handshakes to those nearest to him and a few muttered 'unlucky' to him in response. As quick as he could, he made his way out of the stands and back towards the dressing rooms, not needing to be immersed in the home team's celebrations. Bucknall's good run had officially hit a rut. Once again, he was going to have to find something to help turn it around.

Final score: York City 1 Bucknall 0

		Played	Points
10.	Harrogate Town	21	37
11.	Trosley United	21	36
12.	Bromley	21	33
13.	Bucknall	21	32
14.	York City	21	30

27

Gifford got the players in early on Monday morning for training. The break with the normal routine was deliberate; it was to indicate that they needed to make a change on the pitch. He had spent almost the entirety of the previous day debating whether or not a change in system was what was required. The conclusion he came to was that his 5-3-2 was still doing more good than bad on the whole and that the issue was with how they were implementing it.

He gathered the players around him, 'Right, boys. Now we all know our good run wasn't going to last forever and if anything, it's on me for not addressing some of the issues with our system earlier while we were still winning games. Now we've had a couple of setbacks and it's time to respond. So, we're going to work on our shape and on creating chances when we are in possession because it's become pretty fucking obvious that when Pearcey's not on the pitch, we don't have enough ways of creating chances and scoring goals.'

Haines had been busy setting up cones in one half of the training pitch while Gifford spoke, creating a grid-like structure. Gifford instructed his five-man defence to stand, each in their own coned-off square. He then took his starting midfield and attack and instructed them to spread themselves across the squares in a similar fashion.

Gifford shouted his instructions, turning his body to project his voice in both directions, 'Right the rules are simple. You can't have two attackers or two defenders in the same square. You can't pass the ball through more than one square at a time. And it's three touches maximum. Zip it around quickly. Defenders, stay in your squares as much as you can and restrict the attacking team's options. If you get it off them, the same rules apply to you. You can score at the other end but no clearances, build it with short passes.'

He blew his whistle to signal the start of the drill. Sometimes, Gifford was content for Gough and Haines to do more of the hands-on coaching during training, preferring to observe it from a distance. He was doing that here. He followed the ball as it was worked around the grid, breaking into a sprint to match the movement of the attackers and offering continual words of instruction.

'Stay there, Archie. Get tight to him.'

'Quicker, Seba, quicker!'

'Shot away!'

The players took a little while to get used to the format of the drill. At first, the defenders were on top, with the attacking players struggling to work out how to play it through the grids one-by-one. There was a middle third of the half pitch which was essentially a no man's land, with no player from either side starting within those squares. Whenever an attacker did venture into the area, the defender in the nearest adjacent square would join them to cut off their shooting and passing options. As it progressed, Gifford blew the whistle on moments where two attackers would instinctively come into the same square and offered analysis on how else they could create space. He was pleased to see them start to drag the defenders out of position, to create pockets of space for others to make runs into. Anytime an attacker received the ball in an empty square, he clapped his hands together and praised them, before turning his attention to the defenders.

After a while, Gifford changed it up slightly by allowing switches of play, encouraging the attackers to switch the ball across multiple squares, therefore making them hold their positions in wide areas. It gave the defenders something else to think about and also gave them more of an out ball when they did intercept and have their turn in possession. In one exchange, Danny Golding received the ball in the furthest-right square and played it to Kieran Dunne who sprinted into the square next to him, with Max Warren-Smith pursuing. Dunne controlled the ball and backed into Warren-Smith before laying it back to Golding who had made a shuttle run away from Archie Lewitt. Golding controlled it and then swept a high, floated pass right across to Stefon Harrison who had run into the far-left square and was all alone. Harrison controlled it perfectly, knocking the ball in front of his feet. He put his foot through the ball and his shot cannoned in off the crossbar.

Gifford couldn't contain his delight, 'Yes, Stef! Fucking brilliant that, that's what we're after lads!'

Eventually, Gifford withdrew the cones so the grid disappeared and allowed the players to play a more traditional five-a-side game. Satisfied with how the drill had gone, he let Haines and Gough take on a more vocal role once more, withdrawing to the side of the pitch to watch how the play developed. What he hoped for was that the defenders would automatically remember their distances even without the squares there and that the attackers would still play quickly with two and three touches. He had enjoyed the session immensely, feeling as if he had been able to engage in and enjoy the true 'coach' part of his job description.

When training finished, he decided to treat himself before heading home and picked up a coffee from a cafe tucked by a service station along one of the roads he took home. He headed in and made his order, aware that a few eyes were on him. He noted that when the server looked at him, there was a momentary pause of recognition before he spoke. As he passed the order on to his colleague, he spoke to Gifford,

'I don't need to ask your name. I know who you are.'

Gifford waited at the end of the counter and when he took the coffee, the same bright-eyed boy had another message.

'I'm a huge Bucks fan by the way. I can't wait for Saturday. It's the biggest game we've had in years.'

Gifford smiled and left the cafe, reflecting on the server's words. He could see why their next game had caught the imagination. They had another home tie in the FA Cup, and their opponents were Crystal Palace. Premier League Crystal Palace.

28

Bucknall vs Crystal Palace
Yewtree Lane
6 January
FA Cup third round

The day arrived. In truth, Gifford had managed to push it out of his mind in the weeks previous, managing to focus on Bucknall's league form instead. They had known who they were going to face for about a month, after managing to win away at a potential banana skin in Yate Town in the second round. The moment their name had been pulled out of the hat, followed by the reveal of Palace as their opponents, a wave of excitement had swept around the club. If there had been a sense of opportunity when they had faced League One Doncaster, then the chance to play, and potentially knock out, an established top-division side was quite literally a whole other level.

All the stats that were always banded around whenever such a mismatched cup tie was scheduled filtered through in the week leading up to Saturday's game. There were just the 97 league places between the two teams. Palace's new centre-forward cost more than the net worth of Yewtree Lane. The clubs had only faced off once before and that was close to 100 years previously. Bucknall had only ever advanced to the fourth round twice in their entire history; Palace had reached the final as recently as 2016.

Gifford was determined to enjoy the occasion. He had given the players the Friday off before the game and his message all week had been that there was no pressure or expectation on them. Lee Chugwell had privately suggested that if they could squeak a replay at Selhurst Park, the club might be able to earn close to an extra £200,000. 'Thanks for that, Chuggy,' Gifford had responded.

When he arrived at the ground, the buzz was palpable. The tie was a complete sell-out and was scheduled to be Bucknall's largest home attendance in over a decade. Gifford tried to speak to as many of the club officials as he could, chatting away to the stewards and ticket office staff before he caught a word with the groundsman.

'You're too good at your bloody job, you are. We'd have more chance if we were playing on a skip today,' he said with a smile.

In terms of his team selection, he had even deliberated with rotating his side, given that the amount of games they were playing was ramping up by the week, but he decided he couldn't justify that and that this was an occasion all of his players wanted to play in. Tommy Pearce was serving the last match of his three-match suspension and Gifford made sure to speak to him before kick-off, knowing he would be gutted. He shared his striker's disappointment; whatever little chance Bucknall had of beating Palace in the first place had been diminished even further by the absence of their best player.

Eventually, the players returned to the dressing room and Gifford had his chance to speak to them one last time. The noise of the crowd was so great that it echoed through the concrete of the stadium and reverberated around the room.

'Listen to that, boys. That's what it means to this club, to our fans, to this town. They're not going to let you down today, I promise you that. They are going to cheer you on from the first minute to the last. It is your job to ensure you return the favour. I am not interested in the fucking result, honestly I'm not. Our season is not going to be defined by what happens out there today. But what I do want to see is a team that I can be proud of. A team that takes on a fucking top-division side and doesn't back down from the challenge for a single fucking second. That's what I'm interested in.'

Gifford followed the players out on to the pitch. As the Palace side ran out, it was hard not to be intimidated by them. The tracksuit tops that covered their kits were pristine, each player's hair perfectly waxed and positioned into place. It was like the Bucks were playing a side generated on a computer game. Gifford felt a similar sense of inferiority when approaching the Palace manager, a giant of the game whose number of amassed matches was in the thousands; Gifford hadn't yet hit 30. The Palace boss extended his hand and offered a warm greeting.

'Good luck. You should be proud of your club, everything's been fantastic. Let's hope the game lives up to it, hey?'

Palace hadn't even picked their normal starting 11; like many Premier League sides, they were using a cup competition to give their fringe players some minutes. Gifford had hoped that might be in Bucknall's favour, with their opponents suffering from rustiness. His wish went emphatically unfulfilled.

Palace were two up in ten minutes. They played at a pace that Bucknall simply couldn't cope with. It wasn't that Gifford's players weren't competing – they were getting to every challenge, but every time they won a tackle, it seemed another Palace player was there to recover the ball and play it in the gap that was vacated. On top of that, the quality of their finishing was astonishingly good. They created two openings that would have been considered half chances at best in the National League and yet on both occasions the ball was struck past Matt Finch before he barely had a chance to move.

The Bucknall crowd was silenced before they even had a chance to catch their breath. Palace kept recycling the ball, moving it from side-to-side, the Bucknall boys desperately trying to keep up. Gifford wasn't upset at his players; he had known there was always a chance they were going to be in for a beating. After the second goal, Palace did at least retreat a little and Bucknall were able to muster a couple of corners and long throw-in attempts, which at least managed to briefly wake the crowd up again.

And then just before half-time, the Premier League team decided they wanted to score again. The striker came short to make a triangle in the midfield, sucking in Ardie Adomako. This enabled a Palace midfielder to glide effortlessly into the space behind Max Warren-Smith, with a perfectly weighted pass played into his path on the half-volley. Finch rushed out and the midfielder clipped it over him; 3-0. Gifford wasn't sure whether to shout at his defence or applaud their opponents.

Gough whispered in his ear, 'Fuck me, *that's* a goal.'

The half-time whistle blew and Bucknall were granted some relief from their misery. Gifford contemplated what his message was going to be in the dressing room. He wasn't sure whether to generate a Churchillian speech to try and create one of the all-time great cup comebacks or to beg his team not to embarrass themselves further.

He settled on a simple message, 'Let's try and get a goal, boys. That's all I want. One goal. Let's give our fans something to cheer. And if we get one, we'll see where we go from there. But that's your only job. I want you to go out there and prove that we can score against this side.'

Mercifully, Crystal Palace seemed to have also recognised that the game had already been decided and took their foot off the gas, with the manager even blooding some youngsters in the second half. This meant that Bucknall were given a half-hour reprieve, with the fans deciding they were going to cheer anything of any note. Kieran Dunne let a pass run through his legs, fooling the defender marking him and it was greeted as if he had just scored the winner.

Palace made it four with ten minutes to go, one of their new, nippy wingers getting in behind Archie Lewitt and pulling it back for the striker to smash into a mostly open goal. He didn't even celebrate, which summed up the whole apathy of the situation. Gifford smiled and offered his players empty words. He refused to let himself be too disappointed.

Bucknall's moment finally arrived a couple of minutes afterwards. A throw-in was deflected into Lewitt's path. He hit a half cross, half shot across the box that looped up and was palmed away by the Palace goalkeeper unconvincingly. It didn't quite make it out of the box and as all the players turned their heads to see where it was dropping and the Palace defence instinctively stuck out their legs to try and get a block in, Danny Golding arrived and smashed a sweet half volley into the net. The ground erupted. Gifford tensed his arm and went to punch the air, managing to stop himself just in time. It was beneath the club for him to celebrate a consolation; 4-1.

The crowd started singing 'We're gonna win 5-4' which made Gifford and the Palace manager share a laugh. Gifford started to reflect on the day as a whole, deciding that he was going to put it down as a rare example when football wasn't about winning or losing. And as he continued his philosophical musings on the beautiful game, the Palace striker held off Adomako and bent another belter of a shot into the bottom corner; 5-1.

'For fuck's sake.' he said, sighing defeatedly.

When the game ended, the Bucknall players were still applauded warmly by their supporters. A few of them asked the Palace counterparts for their shirts and the manager told Gifford he'd visit him for a drink in his office afterwards. Gifford took his turn applauding the fans and then trudged his way off the pitch. Their exciting little cup run was well and truly over, but it had provided a much-needed moment of hope and escapism for a while at least. Now they had only one thing left to focus on for the rest of the season and Gifford knew that the goodwill and sportsmanship that had lit up the dreary January afternoon wasn't going to continue. It was now all about the league.

Final score: Bucknall 1 Crystal Palace 5

29

After a training session that week, Gifford got back in the car and took his phone out of the glove box to check any missed messages, as had become his custom. He flicked through the notifications absentmindedly until he saw one that made his eyes narrow.

It was from Keira, 'Come home straight after training. Just had a call from Danny's school.'

Gifford did as instructed, starting the car immediately and driving away from the training complex without waving at the players he passed. His mind ticked over what might have happened and anxiety took a hold of him as he started to imagine all the worst possible outcomes. The fact Keira hadn't needed to tell him in the message suggested Danny couldn't have been in any danger, but he continued to fight a battle in his head as he drove the route home, foot locked on the accelerator.

When he pulled up on their drive, he went straight into the house, leaving his kit and equipment behind. Keira came to greet him as he walked through the front door and his outstretched arms and confused expression compelled her to explain.

'I just got a call. Danny was found with cigarettes in his bag.'

It was a simultaneous moment of relief and anger that washed over Gifford. The endless corridor of worse possibilities drifted from his brain but were replaced with a feeling of disappointment that manifested as an ache in his stomach.

He pondered over his reply before he gave it, 'What do you want to do?'

Keira's lips had pursed tight and her face had taken on a hard quality, as if her normally soft skin had been replaced by granite. She was looking on Gifford as if practising her stern look for her son.

'Well talk to him, obviously. There is no way this is happening again.'

'Yeah, OK. I agree.'

'I just don't understand. This is so not Danny, do you think he's got in with the wrong kids?'

'Maybe. I always thought the friends we had met were nice enough, from good families. It could just be a phase.'

'That makes it sound like it was always going to happen.'

'No, that's not what I mean. It's just we don't know the context here. Let's give him a chance to explain, yeah?'

Keira's eyes flashed with anger and suspicion as she studied her husband. Gifford approached her tentatively, but she allowed him to put her arms around her and pull her into his chest.

'It'll be OK.' said Gifford, blankly.

Danny returned home a few hours later. Gifford and Keira were both waiting for him in the living room and had left Orla playing upstairs. Danny walked in, dragging his school bag in one hand, with a despondent look on his face, his eyes rooted to the floor.

'Come and sit down,' said Keira, with a complete absence of her normal warm and welcoming tone.

Danny took a seat on the sofa, arching his body so he could sit as far from his parents as physically possible. He continued to make sure not to meet their eyes. Gifford leant forwards in his chair and fixed his son with as severe a look as he could muster.

'We're going to give you a chance to explain yourself, so do you want to tell us why you had a packet of cigarettes?'

Danny's expression didn't change. He ran his hand along his thigh, picking at imaginary fluff on his school trousers. He took a while to muster an answer.

'Does it matter?'

Keira's voice rose, 'Yes it does actually. We want to know if this is something you've been doing for a long time or if this in some way a one-time thing, an experiment perhaps.'

'They weren't just for me, if that's what you're worried about.'

Keira looked across at Gifford. He could see she was teetering on the edge of her emotions, only a moment away from screaming at her son or bursting into tears.

He took the hint to heighten the questioning, 'We're going to need a lot more than that, Dan. Look, you're in trouble anyway, you're not going to make it any worse by explaining everything.'

Danny's head rose for the first time and he fixed Gifford with a hateful scowl. His eyes were like dark slits and Gifford felt them bore into his skin.

'Fine. Me and a few friends chipped in to buy a packet the other day after school. I ended up being the one who had to keep them in my bag and one of the teachers saw as I opened it in my History lesson.' He paused and then sarcastically spat out another word, 'Happy?'

Gifford felt his body tense up and anger started to swell in his chest. He could feel himself being challenged by his son and clenched his fist as he rested it on the armchair.

Keira spoke once more, 'Right, well that's totally unacceptable. It's illegal for one thing as well as being incredibly dangerous. I just don't see why anyone your age would want to do it, given you know all the health risks. You're never going to be a footballer if you smoke, for one thing!'

Danny shouted across her, 'I don't want to be a footballer!'

That stabbed at Gifford. He had never heard Danny say that before. At that moment, Orla trotted into the room, holding a doll upside down. The voices were lowered as she came into everyone's view.

'Why is everyone shouting?'

'Don't worry, sweetheart. We're not shouting any more. Mummy's coming to play with you, I just need to have a talk with Danny.'

Keira began to walk her towards Orla, but she glared at Gifford as she passed, a glare that could easily be translated as 'you better deal with this'. She scooped Orla up and left the room, closing the door behind them.

Gifford let the silence hang in the air for a while before he attempted to speak. Danny's icy persona had shifted slightly and he had leant back on the sofa, his arms crossed in a protective stance. Gifford went and sat beside him.

'I don't want to argue with you, Dan. But I'm sure you understand that finding this out has worried your mum and me a lot.'

'I won't do it again. It's not like I'm addicted to it or anything. I didn't even like it.'

Gifford breathed out and nodded, 'OK. Well that doesn't mean you're not going to be punished for this. You've let us down. I expect so much more of you, Dan.'

Danny didn't respond. The scowl had returned to his face, as if turning his nose away from a bad smell.

Gifford continued, 'I think you owe an apology. Especially to your mum.'

'Fine,' Danny muttered. 'I'll apologise to mum.'

The last word was emphasised deliberately. Gifford felt a wave of confusion and guilt as to Danny's apparent antipathy towards him. He had always been a bit of a daddy's boy, something Gifford had revelled in. Now as they sat a few inches apart on the living room sofa, Gifford had never felt such a great distance between himself and his son.

30

Bucknall vs Stockport County
Yewtree Lane
13 January

The next game couldn't roll around quick enough. Gifford was desperate for an escape from thinking and worrying about Danny and matchday was the perfect excuse, while his team badly needed a win to break their recent dip in form. They were provided a lift due to the fact that Tommy Pearce had served his suspension and was once again eligible to play. Gifford selected him to start, reuniting him with Kieran Dunne up front. He had continued to work on the shape of his back line in training and had encouraged greater variety in attack.

Gifford let Gough and Haines do most of the talking pre-match, not feeling up to giving a motivational speech. Instead, he observed the attitude of his players, watching how they interacted and if they still possessed the same desperate longing for winning that had been there when they were fighting survival. Ryan Brook was still as animated as ever, his stocky chest puffed out and his face strained. The quieter types in the dressing room, like Ardie Adomako and Danny Golding, still seemed engaged and invigorated by the pre-match instructions. Gifford glanced at Pearce, who was as lively as he had ever seen him, chomping at the bit to play again, like an addict awaiting their next hit.

They made their way on to the pitch. Stockport were decent opponents but had nothing to really worry Bucknall. They played a classic 4-4-2 system, which suited

Gifford's preferred formation perfectly. It meant they always had an extra man: one of the three centre-halves would be free to push forward with the ball, when attacking the five stretched across the midfield would outnumber the opposing four and especially with Pearce dropping deeper, they would dominate possession in the middle third.

Bucknall began well and used that extra man to their advantage with Conor Caldwell and Archie Lewitt receiving the ball in space on their respective flanks. Adomako was also not being marked and was able to carry the ball deep into the Stockport half. At first, the visitors still mainly restricted them to hopeful crosses from wide positions, with Dunne struggling to get a touch. And then Pearce came to the fore.

He received the ball with a Stockport defender on his back, but used his body to lean back into him, keeping the ball away from him with the ends of his studs. He feigned a pass and turned him slightly, finding enough space to squeeze a pass into Dunne. His strike partner immediately knocked it back into his path and Pearce burst into space. As the ball settled in front of him, he opened his body up, using another defender as a guide, and curled the ball into the far corner of the net; 1-0. Pearce was back.

Bucknall continued to control the game to half-time. Gifford's defensive work was proving effective, with his three centre-halves all holding good positions and maintaining good distances, as if the practise grid was visible on the Yewtree pitch. In the second half, Caldwell hit a beautiful switch to Lewitt, who controlled it and faced up the full-back in his traditional manner. He then tried a slip pass into Pearce, but a defender stuck out a leg to block the route of the pass. It broke to Stefon Harrison, arriving on the edge of the box and as the crowd furiously urged him to shoot, he dummied the ball with his right foot, executing an inside cut, before putting his left foot through the ball, drilling it past the Stockport goalkeeper and into the far corner; 2-0.

Gifford didn't restrain his celebrations like he had done against Crystal Palace, madly punching the air and gritting his teeth to form a determined grin. He had needed a win, badly, both professionally and personally, and in truth he couldn't have asked for a better game in which to achieve it. His players saw out the remaining minutes comfortably, passing the ball around. Pearce even tried to set himself up for an overhead kick that dropped over the bar, mainly to keep the crowd invested. When the game ended, Gifford was delighted. It was a rare afternoon in which he could enjoy watching his team, with minimal stress involved.

He made his way to join Harry Latherfield by one of the goals for the post-match interview. The reporter greeted him with his trademark overbearing grin and Gifford put his hands in his pockets and coughed to clear his throat.

'Darren, congratulations on the victory. Was it a much-needed one after the recent run of results?' asked Latherfield.

'Yeah, thank you. I think so. I said when we were on our unbeaten run that it was not going to last forever and I guess perhaps it was inevitable that when it did end, we struggled to get that momentum back. But that is what it is going to be like until the end of the season. We're going to win games and lose games. We've got to make sure we keep putting in good performances and, especially at home, try and win as many as we can.'

'Was one of the keys to the win today the return of Tommy Pearce?'

'Yeah, Pearcey's obviously an important player for us, but it's important that he's not the only one we rely on. We've got other players in our team who are capable of making pivotal contributions to games and a few of them did that today. They need to make sure they all do that consistently, because it won't be enough for one or two players to turn up until the end of the season. We need all of them.'

'We're basically at the halfway point of the season now. How do you assess the first part of your tenure here and what do you think you need to change or improve as you go into the second half?'

'Well, I'm glad you've asked that question actually,' replied Gifford, and he saw Latherfield fail to repress his delight, beaming back at him, 'I want this to be a season of two halves. We spent the majority of the first part battling and scrapping to move away from relegation trouble and to a certain extent, we've achieved that. Now we can be satisfied with that and we can settle back into old habits and play in our flip-flops until the end of the season, or we can regroup and move forward and see how far we can push ourselves and what else we can achieve. Because I'm not settling for just surviving relegation and neither is anybody else at the top of the club. My boys should see this as half-time. And you don't win a game at half-time.'

Final score: Bucknall 2 Stockport County 0

31

Trosley United vs Bucknall
Mackledown Stadium
28 January

Bucknall visited Trosley United at the end of the month, a tricky-looking fixture with the Diamonds having obtained a league-wide reputation for being tough to beat at home. Nonetheless, Gifford was determined to keep the momentum after a few recent victories and prepared his players to expect a competitive and close-fought occasion.

There was a raucous atmosphere at the Mackledown Stadium as they left the dressing room, the noise meeting them before they even reached the pitch. Gifford, wearing a warm, heavily fleeced club jacket over his normal tracksuit to battle the Lancashire chill, could still fee a tension in his muscles as he stood on the touchline. He couldn't quite shake the feeling that something was about to go wrong. He couldn't explain it or define it, but he felt distinctly uncomfortable as he waited nervously for the game to begin.

Trosley were as combative as expected. Tommy Pearce was clattered twice in the opening five minutes, their opponents not allowing him any space to turn and kicking away at his ankles. Pearce responded angrily and squared up to the defender on the second occasion. Gifford rushed to the edge of his technical area, urging him to calm down. They couldn't afford to lose him to suspension again.

And then the atmosphere seemed to turn on an incredibly innocuous and seemingly irrelevant passage of play. Trosley played a direct ball into one of the corners, but Ardie Adomako, as he always did, covered in behind Ryan Brook and collected the loose ball near the far touchline, controlling it and rolling it back to Matt Finch to clear. Gifford was too far away to hear anything, but there was a change in the noise levels at that end of the ground, as if a murmur had broken out, immediately causing a few other grumbles to follow. After Finch had kicked the ball up the other end, Gifford watched as Brook went over and muttered something to Adomako before running quickly back into position. Gifford kept his eye on his central defender and Adomako certainly seemed troubled, his face taking on a fixed ashen expression.

In the next break of play when Bucknall won a throw-in, Gifford approached Archie Lewitt, the closest player to him, and tried to work out what had gone on.

'Everything all right, Arch? What's up with Ardie?'

'I'm not sure, Gaffer. I didn't hear anything but Brooky said that someone had just called Ardie the "n" word.'

Gifford's heart sank. A series of emotions filtered through him one after the other. He felt a sense of pain and upset for Adomako immediately, wanting desperately to protect his player. This was followed by a burning rage and he took a deep breath as he blinked away the thought of running across the pitch and confronting the perpetrator himself. This then caused a feeling of immense responsibility, as he knew he had to act accordingly. The game, in one moment, had ceased to be purely about the result.

He called Gough and Haines over to him and informed them, before the three of them agreed on the next step. Gifford had undergone some training in how to handle these kind of incidents when he took the job and even back when gaining his coaching badges, but he couldn't help but worry he was ill-equipped to deal with it in reality. He walked over to the fourth official and spoke to him in as measured a manner as he could manage.

'Just to inform you, we believe there's been an incident of racist abuse directed at one of our players. A couple of our players have heard and it seems to have come from the far corner of that stand there. I just wanted to make sure you were aware and wanted to check on the protocols from here.'

The fourth official's face dropped and his voice took on a sullen and serious tone, 'Thank you for bringing the matter to me. OK so the options from here are I can inform the stadium announcer to make an announcement warning the crowd about their behaviour. I'll also make the referee aware and if it continues, it is an option for you to take your team off the field.'

Gifford nodded and walked back to his area, chewing his lip. He tried to shake himself out of his unease by clapping his team on but couldn't help but feel it was an empty gesture given the circumstances. He also found himself repeatedly casting an eye back to Adomako, watching his movements and his body language.

The game continued and Bucknall started to dominate. They forced a couple of saves from the Trosley keeper, the latter of which led to a corner. Sebastian D'Amato put in a typically well-struck, swirling corner that brushed off a Trosley head, sending the ball to the edge of the box. Stefon Harrison found himself free and pulled his foot back high to meet the bounce of the ball. He struck through it and got decent contact on it. It took a slight nick off a closing defender and skidded into the corner of the net; 1-0.

Gifford found he didn't have the energy to celebrate, his mind still on Adomako. Harrison, though, was mobbed by his team-mates as he made his way towards the travelling Bucknall fans. Just as the players began to take up their positions for the restart, Harrison turned to shout something back in the direction of a separate glut of Trosley supporters. He stayed standing in front of them for a while and there were audible insults exchanged. Again, Gifford couldn't make out what was being said from his position, but as Pearce arrived to drag Harrison away, and shout some abuse himself, his anxiety only rose. Harrison was still gesticulating and furiously muttering to his team-mates and Brook jogged across the pitch to talk to the referee. There had now been several minutes since the goal had been scored and the game still hadn't been restarted, which caused a chorus of discontent to echo around the stadium.

After a while, it was the referee's turn to jog, making his way to the touchline and calling Gifford and his Trosley counterpart over.

He spoke quickly and panted for breath in between sentences, 'So I've been made aware there have now been separate incidents of racist abuse directed at Bucknall players. I can now stop the game for a moment and we can get the players back into the dressing rooms while we look into further measures, what do you think?'

Gifford and the Trosley manager looked at each other, neither looking like they were happy to go first.

'It should be up to Darren and his team. They're the victims here. We're happy to go on, but only if they are,' said the home boss.

Gifford swallowed hard and added, 'OK, let's play on for now. Can we try and identify the culprits at least?'

'I'm afraid that's down to the Trosley staff now,' said the ref.

He turned to run back to the centre circle and finally blew his whistle for the game to restart. The Trosley manager caught Gifford's arm and muttered an apology, saying he would see what he could do. Gifford thanked him but doubted how much he could help the situation. As the players began knocking the ball around once more, it was obvious that both sides were affected by the uncertainty and tension, with there being a clear drop in the pace of the passing, and no player from either team wanting to take a risk or force an opening. As Bucknall regained possession, it became apparent that Adomako and particularly Harrison were now being booed every time they touched it. Gifford felt his heart rate rocket up and his skin began to heat up in anger. He looked back at the fans seated behind the dugout, fixing them with a furious scowl.

The game continued for another lifeless ten minutes until Brook, under no pressure, took one touch and smashed the ball as far as he could off the pitch. He immediately raised his hand to get to the referee's attention and once more the game was halted and the fans' grievances started up again. Gifford felt a steely determination settle over him now and he found himself marching on to the pitch, his legs moving before he had had time to think about it. He waited to catch Brook's eye and through a simple exchange of nods, he was soon waving his arm to encourage his side to leave the pitch.

A Trosley player approached him, 'What are you doing? Let's get to half-time, for fuck's sake.'

Gifford looked him straight in the eye and snapped back at him, 'This is bigger than football, son. You're going to regret saying that.'

The crowd's boos were now so loud that they made Gifford's eardrums shake. He tried to hold his emotions in check as best as he could, knowing defiance was his best weapon. He waited for all of his players to go first down the tunnel, making sure he was the last one to leave the pitch.

When they were all gathered back in the dressing room, there was a dumbstruck silence in the air. Most of the players were looking at each other, desperately looking for someone to guide them. Adomako sat with his head bowed and his eyes glued to the tiled floor. Harrison angrily smashed the side of his fist into the locker behind him. Gifford stepped in front of them.

'Right. Now I appreciate that none of us were prepared for what had happened out there, but the first thing I want to say is that none of you are going to face this alone. We are a team. Always. It's one thing being a team through wins and losses, but this is something different. We will stand by each other. Now, you need to talk me through what has happened. Brooky?'

Brook spoke up, 'I heard some prick abuse Ardie early in the game. He definitely used racist language. And then when Stef scored, there was more racist language directed towards him and that continued afterwards.'

Gifford looked at Harrison, 'Stef?'

'A few of them were definitely shouting at me after I scored. They were saying you black this, you know. I'm not fucking taking it, man. This is professional fucking football!'

Tears came to Harrison's eyes and he was shaking in fury, his last words sounding more like sobs. Max Warren-Smith put his hand on his shoulder. Gifford felt a lump form in his own throat.

'OK, well none of us is going to take it or accept it either, Stef. If you don't want to go out on the pitch again, none of us will be either.'

Harrison sat forward and spoke loudly, 'Nah. Fuck that. I want to beat these bastards even more now. If we leave, they fucking win.'

Gifford looked at Adomako next, 'What about you, Ardie?'

Adomako spoke at a pitch just above a whisper, 'Yeah, I'm with Stef. We can't stop playing.'

'Are you sure? You know I want these people removed and punished just as much as you do, but I cannot guarantee that will happen if we go back out there.'

Adomako lifted his head for the first time, 'What else can we do, Gaffer? All we can do to show them is play.'

About 20 minutes passed as Gifford spoke with the Trosley dressing room and the refereeing team, discussing their decision. There was action taken and an extra police presence was called to the ground. Officials at Trosley were hugely apologetic and vowed to do everything they could to identify the culprits. When the game had restarted for the final five or so minutes before half-time, it had been played like a testimonial.

In the second half the atmosphere had quietened at least, with the announcements and the realisation of the circumstances causing most of the Trosley fans to adopt a quieter position. There were still smatterings of boos when Harrison and Adomako got the ball, but they were infrequent and died out far quicker than in the first half. Gifford found himself similarly muted after the interval, his limbs feeling weak and heavy and a numbness taking over him after the heightened emotions had passed. He barely reacted when Trosley scored a late equaliser, except to look down dejectedly at the muddy turf beneath his feet.

Final score: Trosley United 1 Bucknall 1

32

The fallout and aftermath of the Trosley game continued for several weeks. Suddenly, the club were now in the back and front pages of national newspapers and Gifford was being asked for interviews by some major media outlets. The FA launched an investigation into the game and ultimately decided to fine Trosley for failure to deal with their supporters' actions. Trosley in turn banned three supporters for life. Gifford was pleased when this was announced, but as he sat in his living room one evening, it was Ardie Adomako's closing words in the dressing room that were still on his mind, 'All we can do to show them is play.'

He had spoken to both Stefon Harrison and Adomako privately after the game, checking on them to make sure they were OK. They had also received similar offers to speak on the experience, but other than releasing statements on their Twitter accounts, neither wanted to drag the matter on further. Harrison even revealed that after his tweet, he had received further abuse in the comments. Gifford shook his head quickly in response, exasperated by the whole experience. He spoke with Keira and admitted he felt he had to do something to try and address the situation. His chosen response was to send an email back to a Sky Sports News reporter who had contacted him, agreeing to appear on the programme via a video call.

He took the call from his office at Yewtree Lane, his laptop set up facing him as he sat at his desk. The moments before the call was due to start were inevitably nerve-wracking. Gifford mused on the fact that he used to try and hide himself in the crowd at Bucknall games; now he was speaking on live TV to talk about the behaviour of crowds in general. He fidgeted in his chair and rubbed his face with the palms of his hands a few times, before an icon flashed on the computer screen and the ringing of a virtual call began. He clicked on the screen.

The reporter was sat in familiar-looking surroundings, the blue of the background visible behind their safe but sharp suit. Gifford had spent large sections of his life with that same image on in the background of his home. The reporter welcomed him and thanked him for his time, speaking in a clipped and overly eloquent tone.

'So, Darren, we now know that both the FA and Trosley have acted on the incidents that occurred during your recent game at the Mackledown Stadium, do you welcome this news?'

Gifford deliberately slowed his words, making sure he said everything he wanted to, 'I do welcome the news. It is important that the people responsible are brought to justice in some way. There is obviously no place for them in football and I'm pleased that they will never be in a stadium again. I'd like to thank Trosley for their efforts in particular and make it clear that the club and the clear majority of their supporters did no wrong during the game and have in fact done a lot of good in the time since.'

The reporter stared back at him, nodding politely throughout his reply, before asking his next question, 'Now, if we can go back to the game itself, Darren. Can you perhaps explain the effect that this abuse had on your players and on you and your staff?'

'Yes, well it was an incredibly traumatic experience for all of us involved but I don't want to compare what myself or most of my players suffered to what Stefon and Ardie went through. They are completely the victims here and for two brilliant, hard-working boys like those two are, and two genuine and fantastic people as well, to suffer the abuse that they had to endure is absolutely disgusting. All we could do at the time, and what we will continue to do as a club now, is stand by them and support them, because they're not alone in this.'

'Now I have to ask you then Darren, given that this isn't the first incident of racism in football recently, throughout all different levels of the game, do you think enough is being done to tackle and prevent this?'

Gifford paused and breathed in deeply. He had expected the question but still knew he was about to throw his opinion into a heated and important social debate, which was a significant step. He measured his reply once more,

'I think, like most people who I have heard speak about this recently, that the answer is no, unfortunately. I can only speak about my experiences and during the game, there was a great deal of uncertainty and apprehension about how to handle the situation. Obviously, the refereeing team dealt with it as well as they could and I'm not criticising them, but I think that they, as well as myself and the Trosley staff, were all looking at each other as to the best course of action. We don't know how to deal with it during the game and that's because there is not enough being done to stop it at source. And as for the players, well it seems that there is an acceptance that they have no choice but to get on with it.'

The reporter probed further, 'So you're saying that more needs to be done to protect the players during the games themselves?'

Gifford leant forwards so his face took up a greater portion of the camera and delivered his final message,

'I'm saying it cannot be good enough that the players feel all they can do is play on. And that attitude is due to a lack of faith in the system, right up to the very top. I'm certain that we won't be the last incident, we probably won't even be the last incident this season, and the fact that racism is still an issue we're dealing with on a regular basis is simply not acceptable in this day and age. We all have to do more.'

'Thank you for your time, Darren.'

Gifford closed his laptop and sat perfectly still for a moment, staring out into the emptiness of the room. He turned his eye to the side and looked at the shelves of his office, still sporting the bottle of Bell's and a couple of small glasses, left over from John Summers's occupation of the space. Gifford deliberated for a few seconds before finally succumbing and leaning forward to open the bottle for the first time.

33

The legendary Manchester United manager, Sir Alex Ferguson, was known to regularly comment that March was always the most important month in the season. For the titanic Scotsman, it was when things really started to heat up and where every game and every point began to matter a little bit more, whether your club was hunting the title, promotion or fighting against relegation. For Gifford, Ferguson was not far short of being a living deity and he certainly wasn't going to question his judgement on this matter. So, as Bucknall approached the third month of the year, Gifford looked at the fixtures on the calendar and knew that their play-off ambitions could either be cemented or destroyed by the time they were through them.

Bucknall vs Weymouth
Yewtree Lane
8 March

They began with a home game against struggling Weymouth. Gifford had a full-strength side to pick from and put out his regular first-choice 11. He kept his team talk minimalist, reminding the players of their superior league position to their opponents and playing up their strengths as a team. Stefon Harrison and Ardie Adomako had seemingly recovered from the trauma of the Trosley game, or at least had stopped referencing it, and there were no doubts over their selection. After a slight goal drought in the period when Tommy Pearce was suspended, Kieran Dunne was now firmly back in form and seemed desperate to get out on the pitch as he bounced around the dressing room.

Bucknall began with intensity, trying to capitalise on Weymouth's lack of confidence. Gifford knew the first goal against out-of-form teams was so important, recognising it from his own players back in the gloomy, relegation-threatened days in the autumn. It arrived on the 20-minute mark, Archie Lewitt playing a looping ball into the channel for Dunne to run on to. The keeper took a few tentative steps out of his goal and a covering defender approached but Dunne, with one classy touch, knocked the ball high into the air with the outside of his boot and it bounced under the crossbar; 1-0.

Dunne added a second a few minutes later, some nice interplay between Pearce and Danny Golding freeing Conor Caldwell on the right and he was able to enter the penalty area uncontested. Caldwell had time to get his head up and he wrapped his foot behind the ball to drag it back across the area for Dunne to run on to without breaking his stride and smash it into the corner. It was a free-flowing move and a very well-worked goal which pleased Gifford immensely. His team looked a level above their opponents; 2-0.

The second half prompted a fightback from Weymouth and they pulled a goal back ten minutes after the restart, which in turn caused Gifford to scream at his players to wake up, furious with the lack of concentration. To their credit, they did respond and Lewitt smashed a well-struck shot across the goalkeeper and into the corner to make it 3-1. Gifford decided to throw on young Manny Orize to exploit a tired defence and he won a penalty with a few minutes to go, a Weymouth defender resignedly bringing him down in the box. Dunne had a chance for a hat-trick and duly drilled the ball low to the keeper's left to complete it. He walked back into the dressing room as happy as he had left it, the only difference being the match ball tucked tightly under his arm.

Final score: Bucknall 4 Weymouth 1

Chester FC vs Bucknall
Deva Stadium
15 March

From playing a team at the bottom of the league, Bucknall's next assignment was to try and topple a side at the top. Chester had been the league's great success story of the season, coming from nowhere to become one of the main title contenders, hunting down Mansfield for the first promotion spot. Gifford had prepared by watching their last five games, an exercise that had only served to make him admire his team's next opponents and fear the damage they could cause them.

It was a game where Bucknall's formation needed to resemble a 5-3-2, rather than the occasions at home where it was a more attacking 3-5-2. They had worked intently in training on stopping Chester building and then sustaining attacks from the back, with Gifford stressing the areas of the pitch in which it was essential to press and then the areas where they could afford to drop off and allow them more space. It was a game where if Bucknall approached it with their normal high-energy, sometimes chaotic style, they would be pulled apart.

Much to Gifford's delight, it was his side who made the better start, winning tackles and making interceptions in midfield and trying to spring counterattacks. They even created a glorious chance ten minutes in, with Pearce making a blindside run off the back of Dunne, who in turn slipped him in. It seemed to open up perfectly for Pearce to curl it into the far corner with his cultured right foot, but he scuffed the shot and instead it bobbled into the keeper's midriff.

And all it served to do was wake Chester up. The hosts began to get more on the front foot and they created numerous opportunities, striking the inside of the post and causing Warren-Smith to desperately hack off the goal line. Gifford could feel that a goal was coming and hated the sensation of helplessness as he watched his defensive line be pulled around by Chester's crisp passing. They worked an opening where their striker ran in behind Warren-Smith and received a toe-poke of a pass, striking it emphatically it first-time into the corner; 1-0.

Gifford tried to instil fresh belief in his players at the interval, abandoning his previously strict, tactical instructions and prioritising man-management and motivation instead. It didn't work. Chester's manager had identified the areas in which Bucknall were pressing and trying to turn over the ball and instructed his defenders to bypass that area completely. They kept their wingers high and wide, which pinned back Lewitt and Caldwell at wing-back and gave Chester's full-backs acres of space as they received the ball consistently in Bucknall's half. The second goal came from an uncontested cross from their right-back, floating it deep towards the back post for a midfielder to arrive late and glance the ball past Finch.

At this point, Gifford reluctantly accepted defeat and took off his key players. He heard a few mumbles and groans from the travelling Bucks fans after Pearce was withdrawn and he decided not to look back in their direction for the rest of the game. He was thinking in his own mind the message of losing the battle to win the war. Chester added gloss to the score line by breaking through the Bucknall back line once more; Brook and Adomako attempting an ill-thought offside trap. One Chester striker squared for the other to pass it into the empty net. As Gifford shook hands with the Chester staff after the game, he tried to fight the thought that he didn't want to come up against them if Bucknall did manage to make the play-offs after all.

Final score: Chester FC 3 Bucknall 0

Dover Athletic vs Bucknall
Crabble Stadium
23 March

Finally, Bucknall headed to the coast of Kent to play against Dover Athletic. It was one of the more scenic grounds in the division and you could glimpse the coastal countryside from the away dugout. It was also a brightly sunny day and Gifford pondered that spring finally seemed to be emerging after what had felt like a particularly long winter. Dover put up a considerable fight in front of their passionate home fans and there were several tasty 50/50s in the first half, with Gifford wincing as D'Amato and Pearce were on the receiving end of some crunchers, thankfully both making it back to their feet.

It was as the game dragged on that Gifford became more aware of how lethargic his team were, growing more frustrated at the lapses in concentration or miscommunications. They were errors that only seemed to happen when the team weren't fully at the races. Dover scored from a free header at a corner a couple of moments before half-time, which really summed it all up. Gifford was apoplectic; it was one thing losing to Chester, it was another being outfought and outthought by a team in a relegation battle.

He hadn't managed to calm down by the time his players had returned to the dressing room. He picked up a water bottle and sipped it sourly, glaring at his team.

'Does someone want to tell me what the fuck that was?! Hey?! That was a fucking shambles! You couldn't make one fucking pass between the lot of you! Not one fucking pass! I can only assume you don't want to make the play-offs, because based on that performance you aren't going to get anywhere fucking near them. Dover are in the relegation zone and you're making them look like fucking Barcelona!'

He couldn't stop himself from throwing the bottle at the floor in anger. It bounced and made a puncture sound as it collided with the tiles on the floor. Gifford hadn't tightened the cap properly either and water was sent splashing across the dressing room, some of it spraying into the faces of Brook and Caldwell. Gifford looked at them for a second, without softening his furious, pained expression and neither player so much as flinched.

'Go out there early and sort it out among yourselves, because quite frankly I'm sick of looking at you,' he said, and raised an arm to point at the door. The players were passing the ball around to warm-up for over five minutes before Dover returned, Gifford just about slowing his heart rate by the time the game restarted.

Bucknall improved slowly, gradually earning more possession and building regular attacks. Dover reacted by dropping deeper, though they managed to continue to restrict the visitors to half chances and long-distance efforts from outside the box. Gifford had instructed all of his substitutes to warm up, as another reminder to the players on the pitch to step it up. He then spent the middle period of the half frantically debating when to make a change. Gough muttered that he needed to throw another attacker on, but Gifford waited still, praying they could get an equaliser first.

Bucknall were now camped on the edge of the Dover penalty area, but couldn't fashion enough space to get a shot away. The ball was worked side-to-side with Caldwell getting a cross in, but it was poor and missed the men in the middle. Pearce controlled it well on the edge of the box and suddenly Gifford sensed an opportunity. The Dover wide midfielder had gone into the box when the Caldwell cross had come in, rather than staying with Lewitt. This left the left wing-back free to make a run. Pearce waited an extra second as more players approached to close him down and then slipped a blind pass into Lewitt's path. The ball was zipped across the six-yard box and Dunne, in trademark style, stuck out a toe to divert it in; 1-1. Gifford roared triumphantly and nearly pushed Gough over such was his excitement. Game on.

Now he threw the subs on, making a rare triple change, completely changing the formation to something resembling a 2-1-4-3 with only Brook and Adomako back, basically marking no one. The remaining minutes were a total onslaught with ball after ball tossed into the area for one of Pearce, Dunne or Sajja Gujar to attack. Dover were now desperately hanging on to their point. Bucknall forced a corner and the away fans let out a manic echo of encouragement. Even Matt Finch went to go up for the corner, with Gifford and Haines frantically yelling at him to get back in goal. D'Amato swung it in and a Dover head at the front post deflected the ball to the edge of the box. Caldwell, who always stayed back on corners ran on to it and Gifford saw that he was shaping to shoot. The clock had now gone past the allotted minutes of injury time. Caldwell struck it well but it stayed low and it crashed into the thigh of a defender. The ball spun up and nestled into the corner; 2-1. They had done it.

The players jumped on Caldwell and a huge bundle occurred on the touchline. Gifford found himself joining them, madly grabbing and patting his players in delight. When the pile dispersed, his hair was creased into his face and his eyes were moist. The referee blew the whistle seconds later.

Final score: Dover Athletic 1 Bucknall 2

Gifford checked the rest of the league's results on the coach home and saw that Harrogate had been beaten. He flicked the touchscreen on his phone to change the list of fixtures to the league table and saw that Bucknall now occupied the final play-off position. They had put themselves in contention for a thrilling end to the season and as he stared out the window of the team coach, he couldn't help but feel a swell of excitement and anticipation rise to his throat.

		Played	Points
5.	Woking	34	52
6.	Sutton United	34	52
7.	Bucknall	34	50
8.	Harrogate Town	34	49
9.	Torquay United	34	49

34

Gifford came downstairs in his tracksuit, ready for training, to find Danny sat on the sofa, staring blankly at the TV. He always started training after Danny had left for school and was taken aback by his son's presence.

'What you doing, Dan? Why aren't you at school?'

'It's a TD day,' replied Danny, without shifting his gaze.

'And you're just gonna spend it watching TV all day?'

Danny shrugged in response. Gifford had an idea. He approached Danny so he could make his pitch more effectively.

'You can come training with me if you want. It's a chance to play with some pros.'

Now Danny looked at him. His change in expression told Gifford he was both surprised and maybe even pleased by the offer. He was assessing Gifford's face to judge if the offer was genuine.

'Really?'

'Yeah, but you've got to go get changed right now. I need to leave in five.'

Danny moved immediately, springing from the sofa and jogging past his dad to find and get into his football kit. He didn't move quickly enough to prevent Gifford noticing the smile that flashed across his face.

When they were driving to the leisure complex, Danny stayed as uncommunicative as he had been in the recent months, but Gifford was content to enjoy the comfortable silence between them this time. They listened to the radio and both faced forwards. It was only as Gifford parked up that he offered any words of advice.

'Don't hold back, OK? Show the boys what you can do. They'll look after you.'

Danny nodded and opened the car door. He walked slightly behind Gifford, cowering behind the outline of his body as he used to do when he was a kid. Gifford strode through the gap in the hedge and on to the pitch, greeting Gough and Haines as he always did.

'Who's this little whippersnapper then? New signing, Giff?' said Gough, sending a mock look of threat at Danny.

'Thought I'd make today bring-your-boy-to-work-day, see how he shapes up against our lot.'

Haines, as ever, took a softer approach, 'Ignore everything they tell you, Danny. You're gonna be fine.'

Gifford called the players in once everyone had arrived and they huddled round the centre of the pitch.

'Right, boys. Big win last time out, but don't think I've forgotten how shit you were in the first half. We'll start with some rondos and some two-touch games, see if you can keep the ball any better than you did on Saturday. Oh, and this here is my son, Danny. He's going to be joining in so I don't want to see any of you going easy on him. Mind you, if any of you injure him, you might as well walk straight off and head home 'cos you won't be playing again this season. Understand? Right get into groups then.'

The group dispersed and Gifford nodded at Danny to indicate for him to follow them. Ryan Brook came over and put his arm round Danny, leading him over to join their circle. Gifford sat on the edge of the pitch, muttering with Haines, as he watched the players pass the ball quickly, the couple in the middle chasing furiously as it was flicked and switched around them. Danny's first few touches were solid enough and when he did have to go in the middle, he slid in to make a block on Kieran Dunne, drawing huge cheers. Dunne picked him and ruffled his hair and Gifford chuckled from afar.

As he made sure to check in on his all the players, his eyes darting from one to the other, Gifford became aware they were missing somebody. When he realised it was Danny Golding, he felt a wave of concern pass through him. Approaching one of the rondos, he called Conor Caldwell over discretely and spoke into his ear.

'Goldo's not here, Con. Did he mention anything to you?'

'No, boss. I haven't heard from him.'

Gifford sent Caldwell back to the drill and talked himself out of stressing further. It was possible that Golding was just unwell. Players missed training all the time. Gifford clapped his hands and shifted training to its next stage, with Gough and Haines setting up a narrow pitch with cones and mini goals at either end. It was one of Gifford's favourite exercises, with neither team allowed to score until a certain number of passes had been met and with the two-touch limit essentially restricting the players to controlling and moving the ball, meaning it forced teamwork.

They finished training with a small-sided game, with Danny making up the numbers. Gifford let Gough and Haines referee these affairs and would only throw in the odd word of instruction and praise. Danny got involved as much as he could and didn't look out of place, his technique and balance as he received the ball drawing attention.

'He can play you know, your boy,' said Haines as he passed Gifford.

The play was switched to the left-hand of Danny's side's defence and he was isolated in space in front of Max Warren-Smith. Gifford waited patiently to see what unfolded. Danny went to make a run towards the defender but stopped himself and instead held his position behind the opposition. Warren-Smith advanced into the space that he had left available, drawing a player towards him. Danny then called for the ball and it was passed to him. He took a touch out of his feet and hit a curling shot into the back of the net. Warren-Smith picked him up and carried him back into their half for the restart. Danny was laughing and smiling, his cheeks having obtained a deep red colour. Gifford turned away so he could hide his delight. He mused that there didn't need to be a moment of reconciliation between him and his son. Scoring one in the top corner, in front of your dad, would always do the trick.

35

Gifford had gone to sleep happy that night, untroubled by the normal nagging thoughts that occupied his mind. He had settled into such a deep slumber that when he was awakened by the phone ringing, it took him a few seconds to work out that he wasn't still dreaming. Keira's lethargic palm on his bicep eventually shook him into action and he stumbled into the hallway, like a drunk tramp on a high street.

He caught the phone on its last ring and brought it to his ear, still blinking the sleep out of his eyes.

'Hello,' he muttered.

The voice that trembled back down the line sounded fragile, 'Boss. It's Danny. I'm so sorry to call you like this.'

Gifford's mind briefly flicked to his son Danny, before he spoke his realisation out loud, 'Danny Golding? You all right mate?'

The voice broke out into a half sob, 'No, uh not really. My girlfriend. She – she found out about my gambling and the debt and she's thrown me out of the house. I've got nowhere to go, boss.'

Gifford felt his pupils coming into focus once more and the tired haze that had gripped his muscles was now washed away with a burst of tension.

'Oh god. OK. Where are you now? Can you not stay with a friend? Or a hotel even?'

Golding paused, clearly struggling to form the words in his throat, 'I've got nothing, boss. I lost it all. They won't accept my card. And I can't – I can't go to anyone else.'

'OK, right well you've done the right thing. You get yourself over to my house right now, I'll text you my address on this number, all right?'

He paused and added a quick follow-up, 'Have you got petrol in the car? I can come and pick you up if not.'

'No it's OK. I'll make it,' replied Golding. 'Thank you so much, Gaffer. I just didn't know what else to do.'

Gifford could tell that Golding was crying and he could feel his own emotions starting to get on top of him. His heart was bleeding for his player.

'You've done the right thing. We'll have a bed made up for you when you arrive.'

Gifford put the phone down and stood in the darkness of the hallway for a second, allowing the events of the previous minutes to properly sink in. Then he walked back into his bedroom and woke Keira up, explaining the situation.

'Is it all right? He's honestly got nowhere else to go.'

His wife responded as warmly as he knew she would, 'Of course! I'll go sort the spare room out now.'

'Thank you, sweetheart.'

Gifford went downstairs to make three cups of tea and stared out the window, waiting for the flash of a headlight to signal Golding's arrival. All he could think about was how it could have come to this, while he wrestled with his own guilt and culpability in the situation. How had he not picked up on more signals or clues? Why hadn't he done more to help?

Keira came down after a while and took her tea.

'It's all set up. I'm gonna go back to bed, Darren. I won't go to sleep just in case, but I don't think I should be here when he arrives. He's probably ashamed enough as it is. You need to talk to him by yourself.'

Gifford nodded and gave her a kiss on the cheek, holding on to her fingers softly as she left his side. He felt a huge amount of admiration for his wife. She hadn't even blinked in response; her generosity had come shining through.

Golding's car pulled up quietly not long after, the hum of the engine gently coming to a stop. Gifford went to the front door and opened it before he had the chance to knock, gesturing for him to come inside. He led Golding into the living room, where the teas were waiting for them, and let him get comfortable for a couple of minutes before he spoke.

'You're very welcome here, Goldo. I don't want you to think or worry about anything else at this moment.'

The soft light of one lamp was enough for Gifford to see the state of Golding's face. His skin looked like it had been pulled tight against his cheekbones and was red and patchy, with his eyes looking dry and wrinkled, apart from the layer of moisture that was provided by the leftover tears. His hair, normally styled so precisely, was matted against his forehead and looked greasy and tangled.

'Thanks boss. I'm so sorry to have done this to you.'

'Hey, I said don't worry about it.'

Golding collapsed into a sob again and put his tea on the side so he could hold his face in his hands. Gifford felt another lump in his throat and went over to put an arm on his shoulder.

'Come on, son. Why don't you tell what's happened?'

After a few moments, Golding eventually managed to sit back and began to speak, breathing out through his teeth in between words, 'OK. Well I had been really trying, boss. I promise. But I just can't seem to beat it. I've been going to the course and everything and that has helped but every time I'm left on my own, I'm just not strong enough. I have to bet. And once I've placed one, I just keep going and going.'

Gifford nodded along as he continued, 'Holly; that's my girlfriend. She began to suspect something, but I just couldn't admit to her the truth. I said I had it under control. And then I went and spent our rent money for this month to try and chase my losses. I've got nothing. And she went mad at me. She wants nothing to do with me. I can't even blame her. The truth is she's better off.'

'Why didn't you say something sooner? We've had given you more help if you needed it.'

'How could I? After everything you've done for me already, boss. I just keeping letting people down.'

Golding collapsed forwards again, as if he couldn't support the weight of his own head. Gifford stayed where he was on the sofa, his mind clicking through all the possibilities he could think of to try and help.

'Goldo. Danny. You have not let anyone down, you hear me? It's a disease, mate. You're addicted. That's not your fault.'

'I want it to stop. So badly. It eats me up inside.'

'Well, that's the first step already then. Look, I know some ex-players who have suffered with the same thing. I bet there's tons of support out there, specifically for footballers. I'll make a few calls. In the meantime, you need to focus on getting yourself right mentally. Have a few weeks off from training. We can say you've had an injury. And then when you've got your life a bit more settled, I promise you, I'll put you straight back in the side again.'

Golding bowed his head in response, 'OK, I promise I'll be out of your house as soon as I can. You've already done far too much.'

'You can stay for as long as you need. I mean it.'

Gifford quietly showed Golding up the stairs and pointed him to the spare room, telling him just to ask if he needed anything. Golding thanked him over and over, which Gifford waved away. He returned to his room, with Keira sitting up, disinterestedly flicking through a book. He clambered in beside her.

'Everything all right?' she asked.

'I think so, for now. Poor kid, he's in a really bad way.'

'I hope you told me he can stay as long as he needs.'

'Of course.'

Keira slid down the bed and laid her head on Gifford's arm, 'You've done a good thing, Darren.'

'Do you think? I just can't help thinking that I've let him down. I think I was the only one he told before Christmas. It feels like I spend my whole time thinking of them all as my players, I'm not sure I've done enough for them as people.'

'You've done more than most would.'

Keira turned back on her side and sunk further into the pillow to try and get some sleep. Gifford stayed facing straight ahead, knowing he had given up on further rest for the night.

36

Bucknall vs Dagenham & Redbridge
Yewtree Lane
8 April

Danny Golding's first missed game was a home clash with Dagenham & Redbridge, who sat three places above Bucknall in the league table. If the Bucks won, they could start thinking about challenging their opponents for an automatic play-off semi-final berth; if they lost it looked like they would be battling just to stay in contention.

It had become clear that the mood had changed in the dressing room before games. The players hadn't returned to the near-silence of the early, relegation-threatened days where fear and anxiety seemed to be the dominant emotion, but there was no longer the carefree, laughter-filled atmosphere either. The squad knew every game counted and Gifford started to see that reflected in their uncertain expressions and forced, stunted words of motivation to each other.

He sent them out on to the pitch with as much energy and enthusiasm as he could muster, though he was aware that his own preparation for the game had been interrupted by other distractions, like the Golding situation. The weather remained lovely, bright sunshine beamed down the Yewtree Lane pitch. It was a fantastic day for football. Gifford just hoped he and his team would be the ones to enjoy it.

The start was lively enough, with both teams working openings at either end. With both being nearer the division's summit than its base, there was notable confidence in each side's play. Gifford knew that Bucknall were going to miss Golding's energy in midfield and urged the three he had selected to prioritise their structure and positioning over exuberance and pressing, as he didn't want the game to turn into a contest that greater resembled basketball than football. As the first 15 minutes ticked by, he was quietly satisfied with how his team were matching up. And then a long ball was launched upfield by the Dagenham goalkeeper.

There seemed to be no danger whatsoever. Max Warren-Smith won the ball in the air and was under such little pressure that he was even able to turn his head and cushion it back towards Ardie Adomako to start a Bucknall attack. Such was the perceived calmness in the moment that Adomako didn't even go for the ball and instead watched it bounce over his head, allowing it to dribble back into the box for Matt Finch to come and pick it up. However, the Dagenham striker sensed an opening and made a dash in behind so that when Adomako left it, he was suddenly left one-on-one. The crowd broke out into desperate cries. The panic was so great that Gifford heard a few voices crack in the stands behind him. It was too late and by the time the defence had recovered, the striker had controlled the ball and smashed his shot into the ground, sending it bobbling over Finch and into the net; 1-0 Dagenham.

Now the fans went ballistic. Gifford put his hands over his face, praying he hadn't just seen what had occurred. It was a catastrophe of a goal to give away and the kind that Bucknall's defence hadn't looked like gifting at any other point all season. Gifford put his hands together and gradually smatterings of applause started to take over the groans as the ball was punted back angrily to the centre circle. Tommy Pearce was berating his defence and Warren-Smith and Adomako were arguing between themselves.

It was an error they didn't recover from. Feeding off the anxiety of the crowd, Bucknall endured a miserable end to the half, snatching at every half chance and rushing passes. The team began to moan at each other for mistakes and on two occasions, the ball was kicked forwards to nobody, after the runner changed his direction. Suddenly nothing was clicking. Dagenham took advantage and pushed hard for the second goal. A cross from the left was only half cleared and as the Bucknall defence tried to push out of the box, the ball was returned, and the same Dagenham striker was left completely free to head home from no more than six yards out; 2-0.

There were boos at half-time and Gifford knew they were merited. His team looked like they had mentally fallen apart. Gough wanted to scream at the team to wake up, but Gifford had advised against it, fearing it would only add to the tension. He took some deep breaths as he headed down the tunnel, trying to transform his own frustration into a calmer, more methodical line of thinking. His players needed some guidance badly.

When he did walk into the changing room, he found Pearce and Warren-Smith pressed up against each other, both with a grip around the other's shirt and screaming intently. Ryan Brook tried to prise them apart as others piled in. Eventually, the scuffle was over and both took a seat on opposite sides of the changing room. Gifford looked at the mess his team were in and held his arms out, urging the players to calm down and listen.

'Enough, enough. Everybody sit down right now. All we're going to do is relax. OK, you heard me. I want you all to take this time to get your heads right. No tactical instruction, no coaching, nothing. You're losing the game because you're losing your heads out there. All of you. Yes, it was a mistake for the first goal. So what? All we've done is since then is compound that by making even more. That's what I'm angry about. So, all of you, use this time we've been given to calm down and recharge. You can't change what's happened so far, but you've still got plenty of time to turn this around.'

He looked around the room. Pearce's face had shifted into a shade of scarlet, and he shook his head furiously, swearing to himself. Adomako still looked shell-shocked and was desperately trying to avoid anyone else's eyes. Even Kieran Dunne had lost that near-permanent smirk on his face, replacing it with a confused and pained expression of his own. Gifford let the players get on with their own half-time rituals without interruption. He couldn't help feeling this was a case where they had to sort it out themselves.

They returned for the second half. Gifford took a further series of deep breaths, preparing himself. The crowd found its voice again and some much-needed energy was injected into the ground. Gradually, Bucknall began to move the ball more efficiently across the pitch and won a few 50/50 tackles. Pearce smashed a powerful effort from distance that the keeper tipped over. They were starting to get back into it.

The Daggers' manager responded to the change in the momentum and readied a substitute. Gifford recognised the imposing, muscular figure who made his way to the touchline as their new loan signing, borrowed from Championship side Millwall. He made sure to get Ryan Brook's attention and pointed at him as he came on, instructing his captain to stay close to the sub.

Bucknall crafted their best chance of the game a couple of minutes later; Pearce and Archie Lewitt combining to send a floated ball towards Dunne. He had time to bring it down and had a free shot on goal. Gifford was almost celebrating before he had struck it. Dunne snatched at the shot and the ball was blazed over. There was an obvious gasp around the ground.

'He's not missed one of those all fucking season!' yelled Gough in Gifford's direction.

Gifford started to get the nagging sensation that this was not going to be their day.

Another long ball was played in behind Bucknall's defence and the substitute striker ran on to it. His pace put him ahead of Brook, but Adomako frantically dropped to try and recover it. Matt Finch also recognised the danger and ran to the edge of the box. The three of them seemed to reach the ball simultaneously and after a couple of bounces between them, it was the young striker who emerged, leaving Adomako and Finch in a heap on the floor. He walked the ball into the back of the net; 3-0.

This killed Bucknall's resurgence in one moment. Once more, the pace of their play dropped dramatically and the mistakes crept in again. The Dagenham fans started to cheer every pass their team made and a few of their players started to showboat, every flick seemingly coming off. Gifford stayed standing, refusing to move. He knew he had to stay strong and resolute, despite the battering his team were getting. The ball was put through for the substitute again and he faced up Brook and knocked it past him. The angle seemed too tight, but he stuck out his left leg and drilled it into the bottom corner; 4-0. It was the cue for hundreds of Bucknall fans to get to their feet and make their way out of the ground.

The last few minutes were played in near-total silence and when the final whistle put Bucknall out of their misery, the boos from half-time returned. Gifford shook the hands of the opposition and looked around at his demoralised team. This was the worst defeat of his tenure. In fact, it was Bucknall's biggest league defeat of the season, even worse than the disastrous games before Gifford took over. They seemed to be running out of steam at the very worst moment.

Gifford was in a desolate mood when he was informed he needed to conduct the post-match interview. He sighed and rolled his eyes but made his way back on to the pitch to meet Harry Latherfield and his cameraman. He couldn't even muster his usual polite smile to greet the eager-eyed reporter.

'Come on, let's get this over with,' he muttered.

Latherfield nodded to the cameraman and began his normal, over-enunciated questioning. What had mildly irritated Gifford before was now incensing him. Everything about Latherfield was driving him mad, from his expensive-looking coat to his stupid grin.

'Well, Darren, it wasn't the result we were after today. How big of a setback is that for the team?'

Gifford grunted a reply and stayed glaring at the reporter, 'Yeah, it's obviously a terrible result and performance. In terms of how big a setback it is, we'll only know that after the next game.'

'To suffer a defeat like that to a team that is likely to be in the play-offs, does that raise any doubts about whether your side are good enough to be there?'

That was a further stab at Gifford's mindset, so he gritted his teeth and replied, 'Well, we can't worry about that now, we're not even in the play-offs yet.'

Latherfield's eyes briefly flashed with surprise. He knew he was getting nothing from the manager and stuttered through his next question, 'Do you still believe that you will make the play-offs, Darren?'

Gifford gave up and spat out a bitingly sarcastic response, 'No. Let's just give up now.'

Latherfield had lost his grin and was physically leaning further away from Gifford, 'Well, Darren. There were boos at half-time and full-time. Clearly the fans weren't happy with that performance, have you not got anything to say to them?'

'I respect our fans and I want to give them better performances than that. What I don't respect is a jumped-up reporter who knows nothing about the game asking me stupid questions. I don't need to justify myself to anyone, least of all you.'

Gifford walked away from Latherfield before he even had a chance to respond. He had worked himself up into a storm of anger and his head was spinning as he strutted along the grass. He wasn't sure if he was about to throw a punch or burst into tears.

Final score: Bucknall 0 Dagenham & Redbridge 4

37

Gifford returned home that evening with his head still in a storm. He made his way into the kitchen and went to wash up a bowl, so he could have some cereal. The bowl slipped in his hand as he turned the tap on and he caught the rim of it with the water, sending it rapidly splashing upwards into his face and chest. He cursed furiously and threw the bowl across the kitchen, smashing it into small pieces of ceramic. There was no noise in the house, which meant he was alone, so he swept up the pieces discretely, masking his embarrassment.

Once he had calmed slightly and made himself a cup of tea, he took a seat in the living room. There was an evening Premier League game on, but Gifford couldn't bring himself to reach the remote control to switch it on. He wanted to hide from football for the evening at least. After a few moments of peaceful silence, his phone buzzed in his pocket. It was Lee Chugwell. Gifford tentatively raised it to his ear.

'What the fuck were you doing, Giff?!' came Chugwell's voice, belting down the phone. 'Snapping at Latherfield like that. He showed me the interview, we can't put that out! It's our in-house fucking channel, not some hotshot reporter from Sky or BT! You can't talk to him like that. It makes you, and the whole club, look terrible.'

'He's had it coming,' replied Gifford sternly. 'I don't know why you even employ that prick, he wouldn't know a thing about football if one hit him in the face.'

'He's the son of one of Steve's mates, he's doing him a favour. Which means that Steve's gonna go absolutely ballistic when he finds out what happened.'

Gifford began to feel the first pangs of shame, 'OK, well I'm sorry. I'll apologise to him when I see him next.'

'No shit! I know it was a bad result today but you can't lose your head like that, we need you to be the calmest man around, steering us towards the play-offs. You've got to keep it together, mate.'

'Yes, OK, Chuggy. I will,' Gifford said, wishing the conversation to an end.

'And what was with the performance by the way? Are the players tired or something? It could have been a lot worse than 4-0.'

The first reminder of the game was the final straw for Gifford, 'I don't want to discuss the game any further. It's gone. I'm the fucking manager, Chuggy. I'll sort it. You worry about your job and I'll worry about mine. Goodbye.'

With that, he ended the call and half tossed the phone across the sofa, so it was at least out of his reach. He heard the front door open and the commotion of Keira and the kids returning. He stayed where he was sat and waited for them to find him. Keira popped her head round the door, still wearing her jacket.

'I saw the result. You OK, Darren?'

'Yeah. Fine,' was all he could muster in response.

'You want to help me with dinner?'

'Sure.'

The rest of the evening passed by in an uncomfortable silence. Gifford barely listened to Orla telling nonsensical stories or Danny giving them the lowdown on his friends. Keira had told him that Danny Golding had gone to try and patch things up with his girlfriend. Gifford still barely said a word until after the kids had gone to bed and him and Keira were left alone in the living room.

Keira muted the television and turned to her husband. 'Darren.' His name was said in a tone that he recognised as pre-empting a serious conversation or a telling-off.

'What?'

'You've got to get better at putting the game behind you. It's just a football match. It's not the end of the world to lose.'

'It's my job, Keira! "Just a football match" is what puts food on the fucking table for you and the kids.'

'Yeah, a table where you barely even looked at your kids tonight.'

The accusation against his parenting bristled Gifford, 'Look, I warned you what we were getting into when I took the job. You talked me into it, remember?'

'Yeah, but I didn't sign up for having an absent husband every time you lose a game!'

Gifford looked at her. Her brow was furrowed and her face was turning red, her eyes wide and bright, staring him down. He hadn't seen her this angry for a long time.

'I think that's bit of an over-reaction, I'm still there when you and the kids need me. The job is not dominating our lives.'

'Are you kidding?' she cut him off. 'There's probably an hour a week where football isn't on the telly; when you're not at training, you're planning and researching things; when you lose, it's like there's a cloud that hangs over the household and let's not forget, one of your players is currently living in our spare room!'

'You said you were fine with that!' yelled Gifford, the loudness of his voice surprising him.

'What else could I do? Of course, we needed to take him in, but it's just a classic sign that you can't separate work and home life.'

'OK, fine, it's difficult. But I can't help caring about my team and how they do, I'd be a pretty shit manager if that was the case.'

'I understand that, but then you need to try harder to relax and decompress after games. Have you even tried that neck pillow I got you?'

'Oh, fuck your neck pillow!'

That caused the first pause in the exchange. Keira's face took on a shocked, offended expression, her eyes briefly flashing from anger to upset. Gifford suddenly became aware of his movement, his body having shifted forward and his arms stretched out in front of him. He could feel his muscles vibrating with tension and he gritted his teeth together to try and loosen his jaw.

Keira had in contrast withdrawn back into her chair, in a more defensive, vulnerable pose. It helped to soothe Gifford's temper slightly.

'I'm sorry, sweetheart. I didn't mean to shout at you.'

'Look at yourself, Darren. The loss today didn't ultimately mean anything. Yes, I know it was bad. I get that. But it hasn't ruled you out of anything. What on earth are you going to be like if you don't make the play-offs? Or lose a final? I'm terrified to find out.'

Gifford began to realise that she was right, a gradual awareness spreading over him. This only served to incense him further. He felt like he had come too far and wasn't about to backtrack now. He pushed the guilt and sense back down, shaking his head furiously as a reflex to the concoction of emotions overwhelming him.

'Maybe if you were more supportive, I wouldn't feel like I was doing this on my own.'

He regretted the words as soon as they had left his mouth. He had wanted to hurt Keira, wanted to wound her as she had wounded him, but it immediately felt a cruel and unnecessary response. Her mouth fell open before she tensed her face and snapped back at him.

'Fuck off, Darren. Just fuck off.'

Gifford could count the amount of times his wife had sworn on one hand since they had been together. He had brought her to a rare level of anger and hurt. She stared at him, barely blinking, straining to preserve the stoic expression.

'Fine,' said Gifford, as he strode past her. He walked into the hallway and hurriedly jammed his feet into his shoes, not even bothering to do the laces. He muttered and swore under his breath. He heard Keira's first sob through the wall, just as he was slamming the front door.

It was only after he had steered the car off the driveway and angrily accelerated down their lane that rational thought returned to him. What was he doing? Where was he going? One hand slipped off the steering wheel and went to his forehead, roughly rubbing his skin.

He drove around aimlessly for another ten minutes, barely registering the roads he was driving on or the scenery around them. He finally stopped when a small service station came into view. It was late enough that no pump was being used, but Gifford pulled past them and stopped the car in the corner of the turn-in space. He sighed as the lights faded and he fell into darkness.

It was there he remained for a long, empty period of time. Unmoved, frozen to the leather of the seat, eyes out of focus. How had he let it come to this? It had felt that for a while his pursuit for the team's success had become an unstoppable, relentless force that he could no longer control. And he had swept up his family in the wreckage of it. Eventually, he began to take deep breaths as the sensation of pins and needles began to attack his limbs, finally signalling the slowing of his heart rate. He succumbed to resting his head against the frame of the steering wheel.

A series of thoughts ran through his mind, one following another like a set of dominoes falling in unison. He considered resigning but knew he would never be able to live with leaving the season unfinished. New methods of motivation, an overhauling of tactics and formation or dropping players all occurred to him, none seeming to ease his uncertainty. And then he thought of Keira, imagining her crying in their armchair, of his lack of connection with Danny in recent months; he thought of Orla and her jumping on to his lap, more excited than anyone in the world to see him. Gut-wrenching guilt enveloped him and he forced tears back from his eyes.

Gifford finally drove back to the house. The lights were all off as he arrived, meaning Keira had retreated to bed. He slipped inside quietly and headed back for the living room. Shifting some cushions around, he made himself a makeshift bed on the sofa and laid down his heavy head.

38

Bucknall vs Torquay United
Yewtree Lane
22 April

Torquay United were up next in another potentially decisive fixture in the run-in. If the Gulls were victorious at the Lane, they would leapfrog Bucknall into the play-off places. Since the defeat at home to Dagenham & Redbridge, the mood among the players and around the club had been sombre. The Bucks badly needed a win.

In the continued absence of Danny Golding, Gifford had switched to more of a 5-2-3 formation, pushing Archie Lewitt up to play as a left-winger and reinstating Nick Wrenshaw behind him at left wing-back.

		Finch (GK)		
Caldwell	Brook	Adomako	Warren-Smith	Wrenshaw
	D'Amato		Harrison	
	Pearce	Dunne	Lewitt	

There was a sense of expectation in the air. The game was another sell-out; Steve Rosser was in attendance and there were notably more faces in the press room. Gifford tried to block out all that exterior noise and keep the players focused purely on the game. He gathered them in a huddle,

'Torquay were our first opponents when I took over this job. We went there in hope, not knowing what was going to happen. And when they beat us, it was taken as a given. And here we are now, above them in the table and looking to stay there. Don't ever forget that. Don't forget how far you've come. But equally let's go out there today and prove to them and to everybody else that our journey isn't over just yet. It's only just beginning.'

The players broke away in determined applause, slapping each other on the backs and yelling so loud it echoed around the dressing room area and down the tunnel. They burst out on to the turf. It seemed as if every player had gained extra energy as the game began.

And then Torquay scored less than three minutes in.

It was their first venture into the Bucknall half, working the ball down the left-hand side. It was a hopeful cross that was half-cleared by Brook and returned into space by the Torquay midfield. It broke to one of them in space, with neither Stefon Harrison nor Sebastian D'Amato seemingly anywhere near them. The player steadied himself and got his foot over the ball, hitting a low and bobbling shot that seemed to take forever to make its way towards Matt Finch's far right-corner and then eventually off the post and in; 1-0.

Gifford closed his eyes, shutting out the moment as if that could prevent it from happening. The best-laid schemes and all that, he thought wistfully, Torquay had got in front in the game, and above Bucknall in the table, and the match had barely kicked off. Gifford saw that his defence was struggling badly. Their previous organisation and timing was nowhere to be seen as time and time again Torquay players made runs in the gaps between the three centre-halves.

The second came in abysmal fashion. It was a counterattack that came from a horribly mishit D'Amato corner. It was cleared and Lewitt lost a 50/50 in midfield and suddenly Torquay were four on two. The remaining two defenders, Conor Caldwell and Wrenshaw, tried valiantly to block off the space as best they could but the ball was eventually slipped to the winger who took one touch, faked to shoot and then returned it to the striker to roll it into the unguarded net. It reminded Gifford of a few of Germany's goals in their infamous 7-1 destruction of hosts Brazil in the World Cup. As if shooting with power seemed easy and unfair, so the better team chose to walk it in instead; 2-0.

The Bucknall fans were restless. That was now six unanswered goals conceded at Yewtree Lane in the last couple of games and against direct rivals as well. Gifford could feel some choice words being thrown at his direction. He knew that Rosser's icy glare would be lasered in on his back from above. He stayed as still as he could, internally pleading with the referee for half-time.

He had tried the crazed, fired-up motivation. He had tried the softer, simpler approach. It was as if he had run out of cards and was still somehow in the hand. As he trudged down the tunnel, he heard the boos ring out once more. The thought had become cemented in his mind, that if they lost the game, their season was finished.

When the players were sat in the dressing room, Gifford had already written three words on the white board and placed it front and centre for them all to see. In large, emboldened letters, the board simply read 'Get One Goal'.

'One goal, boys. That's all I'm asking for. I don't know what will happen after that. I don't really care. That's all I want, get that next goal for me.'

He switched the formation, taking off a struggling Max Warren-Smith and introducing Manny Orize. This left him with a four-man defence, two central midfielders, two out-and-out wingers and two strikers. At his most desperate moment, he was resorting to the simplest and most traditional thing he knew, a good, old-fashioned 4-4-2.

As he headed back to the pitch, for the second half, Gifford mentally returned to the empty, isolated garage off the A-road where he had sat in his car a few nights previously. He broke it down simply in his mind. That was your low point, Giff. Whatever happens now, it's not going to get any worse than that. He swallowed hard and emerged into the light with a smile on his face.

Bucknall finally woke up. The full-backs played high, supporting their wingers tirelessly to create a series of two-on-ones on the flanks. A succession of corners were won by Orize and Caldwell on the far side, which earned generous applause from the crowd. They could feel their team needed them. And then no more than five minutes later, Lewitt ran beyond Wrenshaw and wrapped his foot around the ball to pull it back across the area. It beat the stretching first man and Kieran Dunne arrived to slam it in at the near post; 2-1. Game on.

The touch paper had been lit. The boos had turned into manic screams of optimism. Songs began to ring out of the terraces, sweeping around the creaky old stadium and striking it into life once more. There was an expression that was widely banded around football circles – that of the crowd sucking the ball into the net. Gifford had felt it as a player and as a fan. It was a phenomenon impossible to explain or describe. It often transcended good sense, logic and all statistics. It could make a bad team look like world-beaters and a good team suddenly fall apart.

Bucknall were now camped in the Torquay second half, with Ryan Brook and Ardie Adomako holding their position on their halfway line. Once more, the barrage of crosses were continually swept into the box with Bucknall players throwing themselves at every deflection or ricochet. It felt like five players from either side had been sucked into a central zone in and around the penalty area, with the latest ball looping over all their heads. One player had not been drawn into the melee and had waited patiently in the space at the back post. Tommy Pearce took one touch to kill the cross and then smashed the ball into the pitch, beating the goalkeeper with the masterful connection he mustered; 2-2.

Gifford leapt into the air, yelling at the top of his lungs. A mixture of coaches and substitutes joined him and the heat generated by the friction of tracksuits rubbing together stayed on his skin after he was released. He could feel a mixture of sweat and tears stinging in his eyes. The crowd bayed the players on, sensing they could even win it now.

Torquay aimed their restart aimlessly into the Bucknall half, their players looking tired and shell-shocked at the chaos that was engulfing them. However, Brook and D'Amato, both bursting with adrenaline, sprinted to meet the ball at the same time and collided, leaving it to bounce through to the Torquay winger. There still seemed to be no danger as the winger had a long way to go and Adomako still to beat. He shimmied and worked the ball on to his right foot before curling a shot into the far corner; 3-2 Torquay.

Gifford dropped to his knees. He couldn't believe it. It was as if the bubble that had formed around the stadium was immediately punctured. It must have been the only time Torquay had been near the Bucknall goal for the entire half. The Bucks had pulled themselves back from the brink, only to throw it away once again. After a moment or two he found all he could do was laugh to himself. This was football at its anarchic best.

He threw Sajja Gujar on to the pitch, withdrawing Wrenshaw to create a 2-4-4, his tactics now becoming so retro that they had resorted to the early 1900s. At this point, playing Gujar was not so much in expectation of him scoring a goal but just having yet another body to cause chaos in the box. Again, Bucknall rallied and started to create chances, but Torquay had gained extra energy by their surprise lead and defended valiantly. The clock on the scoreboard on the old Batter's End ticked into the last five minutes.

D'Amato smashed in another corner; what seemed to be about his 30th of the match. Yet again, a Torquay head got there first and it was headed back towards him. Caldwell raced over to the corner to offer an option and D'Amato rolled the ball towards him. Gifford wasn't even looking and instead kept his eyes on the box, as he watched Ryan Brook make his way out of the six-yard box and towards the back post.

'Look for Brooky!' he screamed.

Whether Caldwell heard him or not, Gifford didn't know. What he saw was the full-back's foot going under the ball and sending it deep and high into the air. Brook was off his feet before it had even dropped, his stocky frame leaning on the Torquay centre-halves' shoulders. He got his forehead on the ball and it somehow squeezed in between the minute space between the goalkeeper and the post; 3-3.

The players jumped all over one another in the corner, creating a heaving mass of bodies that seeped off the pitch and into the advertising boards and first rows of the stands. Gifford darted down the touchline after them. He didn't join in the bundle and instead began pulling players to their feet, dragging them back to their half for the restart.

'There's still time! We can win this!'

When he returned to his technical area, his throat hurt and his voice was hoarse. His heart was thumping in his chest and the soft burn of moisture had returned to his eyelids. The final few minutes seemed to take place outside of real time. The noise of the crowd was so loud that Gifford didn't bother shouting instructions and he couldn't hear it if Gough and Haines were attempting to either. The images he witnessed played out like the montage in a film, slightly distorted and otherworldly.

With the clock now stuck on 90 and the allotted additional time now also coming to an end, Bucknall won yet another corner. Yet again it was half cleared and Pearce picked it up a few yards outside of the box. There wasn't time for him to do anything but return it as quick as he could and he clipped one more cross into the mix. Gifford didn't see what happened, but he would never forget the part when the ball somehow went past the Torquay goalkeeper and into the net; 4-3 Bucknall.

The next thing Gifford felt was the scent and taste of the grass as his face was pressed towards it, Gough having rugby tackled him from behind. He lifted his chin and saw fans running along the sides of the pitch, beer spray coating the air, children being thrown up their parents. He saw Matt Finch do a cartwheel and Pearce take his shirt off and wave it furiously as he did a lap of the pitch.

In all this, Gifford managed to stutter out the words, 'Who scored?'

The answer was revealed to him by the image of the rest of his team carrying one player on their shoulders as the game was finally brought to an end by the referee. Gifford felt like he had seen most things since taking over the Bucknall job, but he wasn't sure he had seen Sajja Gujar smile until that moment. The much-maligned striker was now being paraded like a Greek god around the pitch. The slightest flick off his head had turned Bucknall's season around once more.

Final score: Bucknall 4 Torquay United 3

39

Gifford stole a private moment in his office, long after the fans and most of the players and staff had gone home. He poured himself a drink and sat back with his legs on the desk and his head faced up towards the ceiling, the whiskey in the glass swirling softly in his right hand. He replayed the events of the game over and over in his mind and found himself smiling widely when he remembered the celebrations after Sajja Gujar's winner.

A voice from the doorway shattered his illusion and caused him to stumble in the chair. He caught himself and managed to keep the whiskey in the glass. It was only then that he had a chance to look at the figure who had surprised him.

'I see it hasn't taken you long to get on the old manager fuel,' said Martin Williams, Bucknall's greatest ever manager and Gifford's former boss.

Gifford hadn't seen him in years. Williams had always been a fairly short and plump man but had managed to maintain an authoritative, imposing presence. The deep, harsh sounds of his voice were simultaneously friendly and stern, while the words he spoke were always delivered in the same calm and slow tone. His face had aged, with grey whiskers visible around his chin and mouth while his cheeks were more flushed. He greeted Gifford with a trademark smirk he had seen hundreds of times before.

'Gaffer. What are you doing here?' said Gifford, getting off his chair to shake Williams's hand.

'Can't a man visit his old house once in a while, if only to check how it's holding up?'

'No, of course. Can I offer you a drink or anything?'

'Good lad, I see you've learned your manners early. Pour me whatever you're having.'

Gifford walked over to the shelf and splashed some whiskey in his only other tumbler. Williams sat in the chair adjacent to his own, which immediately felt strange. It felt that they were seated the wrong way around.

Gifford handed Williams the glass and settled into the conversation, asking the first question that occurred to him, 'Did you watch the game?'

Williams smiled, 'I did. Congratulations. The late wins are always the best.'

Gifford tried to contain the delight the comment incited in him. It was difficult not to feel like a schoolchild getting praise from their favourite teacher.

'No one told me you were coming. Were you in the stands?'

'Of course. I don't need anyone making a fuss over me in the press box or anything.'

'I used to do the same thing when I retired.'

Williams leaned forwards in the chair, resting the tumbler back on the desk, 'And yet here you are. In the hot seat.'

'Yeah. And what about you?'

'Oh, I'm enjoying my retirement. Maggie's been urging me to pack it in for years and now I think she's fed up of having me in the house, but it's good. I'm not going to be pulled back in. I've had my run.'

'Cheers to that,' said Gifford, raising his glass.

'Besides, I didn't pop my head in here to talk about me. I wanted to see how you were finding it, seems like you've taken to it remarkably well from what I've seen.'

'I'm glad it appears like that. Trust me, it feels very much like I'm making it up as I go along.'

Williams leaned in and muttered under his breath, 'I'll save you some time son, it never stops feeling like that. The best advice I can give you is no matter how uncertain you may be of a decision, make it seem like it's the surest thing in the world.'

Gifford nodded. The combination of the summer air, the burn of the whiskey and basking in the win had served to make him feel as relaxed and content as he had in weeks. He and Williams continued to catch up, his former manager listening intently as he told his tales of the season so far, only interrupting to offer a line about a particular manager or team that he had some distant connection to. They finished their glasses of whiskey and after putting up some feigned reluctance, Williams allowed Gifford to pour them one more. It was as he nursed the second glance that he made the first mention of the past.

'It's funny to think how much has changed. Feels like only yesterday we were in that damned penalty shoot-out.'

'Do you still think about it, Gaffer?'

'Of course I do. Don't get me wrong, I've come to terms with it now. It just wasn't meant to be. But you can't help thinking about what might have been I suppose. How would we have done in the Championship? Would it have convinced that dickhead owner to stick it out a bit longer? Would the club still have slipped back; would it be where is it now?'

Williams spoke out into the room, barely looking at Gifford until he had finished his rhetorical questioning. Gifford shrugged in response, privately wondering the exact same things.

'Never mind. That's football I suppose. You've got one world on one side, full of hope and maybes, and then you've got a different, gloomier reality. And the only thing that separates one from the other is a fucking penalty kick,' said Williams, with a wistful finality to his voice.

Gifford stared at his former manager as he tried to collect his thoughts once more. Williams seemed to be taking in his familiar surroundings, studying every inch of the room, from the dents in the wall to the dust that lingered on the shelves.

'Can I ask you a question, Gaffer?' asked Gifford. 'Did you ever manage to get away from it? The game I mean. It just feels that no matter what I do or where I am, I can't switch it off in my head.'

Williams took a second to answer, smiling to himself in a knowing fashion, 'I was like that at the beginning. Maggie would tell you I never grew out of it, but the truth is I did in my own way. We're competitors, Giff. It's fucking seared into us and we can't escape it. And that's a good thing. But you can't make it your whole fucking reason for existing. Trust me, it's not enjoyable enough to make it worth it. You know Carlo Ancelotti? I met him once at an LMA event, got to shake his hand. Didn't know who the fuck I was of course. He said, "Football is the most important of the less important things in the world." And I think that's probably about right. It's more important than your average job or hobby for sure, because most plumbers don't have a whole town's hopes and dreams hanging on whether they'll make a fucking tap stop leaking when they go to work. But it's not more important than your friends, your family and your general wellbeing. What I'm saying is: work out how much you're prepared to give to the game and make sure you give nothing more or nothing less than that.'

'Thanks, Gaffer,' said Gifford.

'Besides, at the end of it, all you'll be left with is a few decent memories and the chance to occasionally watch a team you could once call your own. And often you'll see that the bloke standing where you used to is doing it much better than you did anyway.'

Williams gave Gifford a wink and finished the last of his drink. Gifford watched him leave, his muscles moving noticeably slower than they used to as his frame disappeared out of the doorway. He reflected on their conversation; there had been a part of him that worried Williams had disapproved of his taking over of the Bucknall job, his previous radio silence a sign that he felt it was beyond Gifford. Instead, he had simply picked the perfect moment, just as he had when he was the manager. Never the loudest or most frequent voice, but the one that always seemed to say the right thing.

40

Maidenhead United vs Bucknall
York Road
11 May

The final game of the season arrived. Bucknall entered the fixture hanging on to their play-off position, but with a total of three teams all capable of replacing them. They travelled to Maidenhead knowing that a point would be enough to ensure their season went on for another few weeks at least. The team coach was deathly quiet as it pulled away from Yewtree Lane, Gifford seeing row after row of his players staring out the window, a mixture of focus and nerves settling in.

Gifford endured the near-silence for a while, before deciding he needed to do something to take his players' minds off the game. He slipped into the aisle and projected his voice down the length of the coach.

'Right, I'm not having us travel all the way there like this. Everybody is going to come to the front of the coach and you are going to entertain your team-mates for a couple of minutes. Entertain how? You might ask. Well I suggest you figure that out. Sing a song, or if you can't sing, then tell us a joke. If you can't think of a joke, well you can stand there in silence as we all abuse you instead.'

He pointed at Ryan Brook, 'Skip, you're first up. No pressure.'

And so the onboard entertainment began. Brook was always game and kicked things off with a series of woeful-cum-hilarious one-liners,

'Did you hear about the Italian chef who died? He pasta-way!'

Stefon Harrison and Manny Orize executed an impressive freestyle rap which drew genuine applause. Max Warren-Smith did a series of basic card tricks and Gough even got up to belt out Frank Sinatra's 'Come Fly With Me'. And then Kieran Dunne stood up. Dunne was a man who was always comfortable in the spotlight and while using a banana as a makeshift microphone, he executed a roast of his team-mates.

'I think we're all looking forward to Caldwell's turn up here. If he has to speak for two minutes, that'll be the most he's said all season! In fact, I reckon Con has said less words than Saj has scored goals! What are you laughing at, Seba? Haven't you got some face cream to apply or something? Honestly mate, you take longer in the mirror than my missus, and you're probably prettier than her and all. And now Pearcey. Pearcey, Pearcey, Pearcey. The man with the magic feet. Do you know why he's got such quick feet, lads? Makes it easier when he's running to his next club. You know, the only club Pearcey's stayed at for a while is his prison side, and that's because he literally couldn't get out!'

At that, Tommy Pearce leapt from his chair and started throwing pulled punches at Dunne's chest. The rest of the coach burst into a chorus of laughter that continued to rise and fall for a while after. Eventually, the two of them sat down and there was a discussion about who was next. The coach burst into a chorus of 'We want Seba' and Sebastian D'Amato was pushed to his feet, eventually singing his cover of 'Wonderwall' that had proved so popular at Christmas. They were still yelling 'I said maybe!' as the coach pulled off the M4.

Gifford's idea seemed to have worked, with spirits lifted ahead of the match. The players stayed in their boisterous mood when they reached the dressing room and he didn't need to offer many words of motivation before they made their way on to the pitch. There was an extra factor in the experience of the game, with all other fixtures taking place at the same time. Haines was left in charge of keeping an eye on the other scores, with Woking travelling to Harrogate, Torquay hosting Altrincham and Sutton heading down to Dover. It was the kind of afternoon Gifford loved watching on television, with the permutations changing in every game and with every goal, but it was one he was dreading to be a part of.

'We just need a point,' he told himself, while nervously chomping his way through a pack of gum.

Maidenhead were comfortably mid-table and so in theory were as good opponents as Bucknall could hope for, with little riding on the game for the hosts. This feeling of apathy as reflected in the early stages, with very little pace in the play. Gifford could tell his own team were playing with no risks, with absolutely no chances being taken at the back. Matt Finch launched the ball as far as he could every time it was passed back to him.

After 20 minutes, the pressure was amplified further. Both Torquay and Sutton were in front. There was no margin of error whatsoever. Gifford decided not to pass the message on to the pitch, instead just urging concentration whenever one of his players came close to him. There was a peaceful, quiet atmosphere within the stadium, with large stretches of possession playing out to near silence. For teams that knew their season was coming to a close, the last games played out like the last day of school: no one trying their hardest, just waiting for the final bell to ring.

There was another twist just before half-time, Haines walking over and muttering to Gifford that Woking had scored at Harrogate, knocking them out of the play-off places. Again, it didn't affect Bucknall directly, but it was a reminder of just how high the stakes were.

It prompted Gifford to stride forwards and bark further instruction, 'Don't you dare fucking coast, lads! Intensity, keep up the intensity!'

There was barely even a murmur from the crowd at half-time. Gifford breathed out deeply. They were halfway there. As they all packed back into the dressing room, the players were asking after the other scores.

'Torquay and Sutton are winning, Torquay by a couple, so we can't afford a slip. Harrogate are behind so at the moment they're dropping out. We are nearly there, boys. Don't blow it now, you will kick yourselves forever if you do. These are there for the taking, I'm telling you. Half of them are off on their holidays already. Let's do this in style.'

It didn't work out that way. Bucknall were caught in the knowledge that 0-0 was enough for them and proceeded to play as lifelessly as they had all season. It was Maidenhead who started to gain encouragement and motivation and began to up the tempo. Despite Gifford's pleas, his wing-backs didn't dare push past the halfway line and the Bucks were starting to play with a flat five in defence.

A couple of Maidenhead corners caused havoc in the box, with Bucknall players desperately swinging their legs to hack it clear. Gifford was sweating profusely now and took off his jacket. He felt he had no control of his side. To make matters worse, Torquay were battering Altrincham and Sutton still led at Dover. Gifford knew his team needed to push out and try and at least pose a threat on the counterattack and yet he resisted the temptation to make an attacking change. It felt like too much of an unnecessary risk. He asked the fourth official how long was left on two separate occasions.

With ten minutes to go, Maidenhead created the best chance of the game. A midfielder came short and played a nice one-two with the winger, who broke the line of the defence. He crossed first time, before the centre-halves could drop back in line with the ball. The ball was whipped perfectly and the Maidenhead striker was free as a bird in the centre of the box. Gifford closed his eyes, sensing the inevitable.

There was an initial cheer from the crowd that transformed into a gasp at the last second. Gifford opened his eyes just in time to see Matt Finch dive down to his left, the opposite direction to where his feet had been moving. The keeper stuck out one of his large hands and flicked his fingers towards the ball, shifting it just enough to guide it on to the post. Brook smashed it out of the ground as it came back to him and then picked Finch off the floor, engulfing him in a bear hug.

'What a fucking save that is,' Gifford heard the opposing manager say, smirking in his direction.

Gifford could feel goosebumps running up and down his body. He looked up at the sky on several occasions, as if pleading with above. He had never enjoyed a game of football less than this. Again, Maidenhead poured forward. Their nothing-to-lose mentality which had previously seemed an advantage was now proving a nightmare, with their players trying ambitious passes and skills, which was surprising Bucknall. Another player burst into the box and put his foot through the ball. Max Warren-Smith slid in at the last moment and blocked it for another corner. Gifford and the whole side instinctively burst into applause. He checked his watch again.

'Full time in the other games. We're there as it stands,' said Haines.

Gifford didn't even react, his eyes still glued to the ball. A through pass trickled through and Finch collapsed on to it, to another huge sigh of relief. He took a good minute or so to get back to his feet, as if waking up in the morning, and when he eventually smashed the ball high into the clouds, Gifford heard the sweet sound of the whistle pierce through the air. They had done it.

The players dropped to their knees, some even laying down with sheer exhaustion. Gifford tried his best to shake hands with all the Maidenhead staff but he was interrupted by members of his team and staff jumping all over his back. The subs burst on to the pitch, mobbing the rest of the team. Gifford eventually made his way over to the away end, where hundreds of Bucks fans were waiting.

The players and staff linked hands and approached the fans, like a Roman army advancing on the battlefield. They raised their arms in unison, each time accompanied by a gleeful cry from the stands. Gough and Haines pushed Gifford forwards, ahead of the rest of them, and he clapped his adoring supporters. He allowed himself to soak it in for a while, but he knew that they had not yet achieved their goal. The players eagerly enjoyed a beer in the dressing room but in among the sweat, joy and anticipation, Gifford issued a final address,

'We've made the play-off lads, now let's go and fucking win them!'

Final score: Maidenhead United 0 Bucknall 0

		Played	Points
5.	Yeovil Town	46	72
6.	Bucknall	46	70
7.	Torquay United	46	69
8.	Sutton United	46	69
9.	Harrogate Town	46	68

41

Gifford gave the players four days off after the Maidenhead game, but really he was giving himself a break. He decided he needed to take his mind completely off football for a little while, so that he could recharge for the play-off campaign. In one of those days, Danny Golding phoned him as he was sat playing with Orla in the living room. Gifford instinctively felt a pang of dread when Golding's name flashed up, given the recent history, but all the player wanted was to come and retrieve the last of his things.

Gifford packed them together and cleared their guest room, putting everything he could find into a large sports bag. When Golding arrived, he headed upstairs to meet Gifford. The two men stood in the empty room and Gifford began to feel sentimental. Golding may have only stayed with them for a few weeks but standing there with his belongings made it feel like a much more significant farewell.

'I think that's everything. If there's the odd thing that we find, I can always give it to you at training.'

'Cheers Gaffer.'

Gifford handed him the bag and they shared a brief moment of silence.

'What will you do now then?'

'I've patched things up with Zoey, so I'm going to move back into the apartment. We had a really good talk about everything and now she understands just how much I struggle with it, she's going to help me going forward. And I've got support from the PFA and everything now. It's going to take a while but I'm in a better place.'

'Good,' said Gifford, smiling.

Golding was carrying a paper bag in his hand and he removed some items from it. The first was a bottle of wine.

'This is for you and Keira. I know it's not enough to thank you for what you've done for me, but I hope it's a start at least.'

'It's very kind, mate.'

Golding returned to the bag once more, 'And can you give these to Danny?' He displayed a pair of Adidas football boots, in the classic Predator style. 'They're a bit small for me now and I know he likes them.'

'Sure. Thank you.'

Now that Gifford had his hands full with the wine and boots, he couldn't reach out to Golding in the manner he wanted. Instead, he nodded and gestured for the door. It was as Golding was heading down the stairs that he spoke again.

'Oh one more thing. I suggest you get your fitness back up over the time off and that you start staying behind after training again. I'm starting you against Yeovil.'

Golding turned so that Gifford could see the beaming smile that had settled on his face. He muttered a few words of thanks and then finally left the house for good. Gifford watched his car pull away through the front window, still clutching the gifts he had left behind.

That night, he and Keira went out for dinner. There was a very limited selection of restaurants in their village and so they tended to frequent the local curry house, The Tandoori Tale. They had arranged a babysitter for the kids and Gifford had made an extra effort with his appearance, wearing a smart jumper over a shirt that had long been left at the bottom of his drawer. As they drove the short journey up the road, he felt nervous in a way he hadn't since they had first started dating. They had a lot to talk about and this was their chance to do it.

They were welcomed into the restaurant with the kind of friendliness only reserved for regular guests and taken to their table. They had an empty conversation about the food before more or less ordering exactly as they always did. It was only once the waiter had departed again that Gifford felt the courage to address the more serious topics at hand. He cleared his throat and began to stutter out an opening.

'I wanted to apologise to you, Keira. I've let you down recently.'

'Oh, don't be ridiculous, Darren.'

'No, I have. You've been so understanding of me throughout our entire relationship, and I have let the job get on top of me. I got angry at you because you were telling me things I already knew and I just didn't want to hear them.'

Keira's face softened with his words. Her eyes looked extra beautiful with the makeup that she delicately adorned them with and Gifford found himself unable to avoid them.

'Well I want to apologise too. I don't know if I've ever seen you so occupied, even when you were playing, and that can only be because you're doing something you love and that you're brilliant at. I'm so proud of you, and I don't think I've said that enough.'

Gifford took a sip of his beer before he spoke again, swallowing down the emotions that were bubbling up, 'I do love the job, but if it's not the best thing for the family, I would drop it in a heartbeat. I'm going to take the play-off games and then make a decision. I'll arrange to have a meeting with Chuggy and Rosser, whatever happens from now.'

Keira leaned forwards and took his hands in hers, stroking the top of his fingers. 'OK, but that decision is completely up to you.'

Gifford chuckled, 'No advice from my agent this time?'

'I'm afraid not. I believe our working relationship has been compromised.'

She rolled her tongue over her bottom lip after she spoke and Gifford felt excitement run throughout his body. Keira could still completely enchant him whenever she wanted.

'Danny Golding came by to get the last of his stuff earlier. He's moving back in with his girlfriend.'

'That's great. He was a sweet boy, fragile but with a really good heart.'

'I know. He left us a bottle of wine as well. We can drink that when we get back if you like.'

'Sure.'

Keira sat back in her chair and looked up at the ceiling, clearly contemplating something. Gifford returned to his beer, pleased with how the conversation had gone. Keira spoke again after a brief pause, as if she were continuing her thoughts out loud.

'You know, Darren. All my friends think I went for you because you were a footballer. They say that to me all the time. "Oh, Keira likes a footballer." But that's really not the case. I never thought I'd live a life where football was this prominent. And I guess even now I don't see it that way. I married you because I could see past that completely. I married you because you are a decent man. A kind man. And whatever you did in your playing career didn't matter to me and whatever you might achieve as manager won't matter either. You'll always be a decent man, first and foremost. You should remember that.'

42

Yeovil Town vs Bucknall
Huish Park
28 May
Play-off quarter-final

The play-offs arrived. The way the National League structured their competition to determine which team would gain promotion to the promised land of the EFL was complicated and unique. The champions would go up automatically, then the teams that finished second and third were put through to home semi-finals while the four remaining teams, who placed fourth to seventh, would battle it out to determine who would advance to play them. This meant that Bucknall were handed an away match against Yeovil, who finished a place above them, with a one-off tie and the possibility of extra time and penalties lying in wait for them.

Going to Huish Park for the midweek evening game gave Gifford the feeling that he and the club had come full circle through the season. He had watched the Glovers come to Yewtree Lane and demolish the Bucks back when he was only a spectator. The chance to beat them to advance in the play-offs was a sign of how far the team had come.

When the Bucknall players arrived at the rickety old stadium, they were aware of the extra attention they were getting. Yeovil supporters booed them off their coach and there were cameramen positioned to film their walk into the dressing room. The National League suddenly felt rather box-office. The players gathered themselves and began to get changed and adhere to their pre-match rituals, while Gifford mentally rehearsed what he was going to say to them.

'OK, lads. There is no point in me hyping up this match any more than it has been already. We all know what this means. Now, we're the visitors here. They have 8,000 or so of their fans who are going to be cheering them on the entire game. We are here to stop their fucking party. Now, this fixture is a bonus game, OK? We've played our 46 league games this season already. You've earned yourselves one more. Which means I'm not fussed if we lose out there today, I'm already proud of what you've achieved. But I do care about how we play. If I see you shrink on the big occasion and play within themselves, that will piss me off. Play the game, lads. That's all.'

He turned and made sure he looked at each of them, staring sternly to generate some extra steel. He made sure to nod at Danny Golding, who he had restored to the line-up as he promised. Ryan Brook shouted a few more words of encouragement and led the team on to the pitch.

During the final few minutes before kick-off, Gifford could feel the hairs on his arms standing on edge. There was a raucous atmosphere in the stadium, as he expected. The stakes of the match coupled with the unfamiliar sunset backdrop gave it a different feel. It felt like they were now in a separate universe to the tough monotony of the rest of the season. He wanted to stay there for a while longer.

Yeovil began the game at a frantic pace, every challenge celebrated like a goal by the home fans. Bucknall barely strung two passes together as the Glovers pressed and harassed them, flying into every interception or tackle. They won three corners in a row and each one caused a scramble in the box. Gifford stepped out towards the touchline immediately, telling his players to calm down and taking a series of deep breaths himself. He knew they just needed to get through this early onslaught without conceding.

And then with the ball finally at the other end of the pitch, something bizarre happened. It was passed into the Yeovil midfield and the player took a heavy touch, running into trouble. Stefon Harrison sensed the opportunity and ran in to nick it. The players collided and the ball span off them back towards the goal where Kieran Dunne was retreating after closing down the goalkeeper. He let the ball run past him, took few looks around at the linesman and referee, and then took a touch and slotted it past the goalkeeper. Gifford didn't even celebrate. He was so unsure of what happened. A few terribly uncertain seconds passed before the referee pointed to the centre-circle and gave the goal; 1-0.

The Yeovil bench were incensed, furiously screaming and gesturing at the fourth official and referee. The game didn't immediately restart as the ref trotted over to speak to the Yeovil manager. Gifford made sure he lingered just close enough so he could hear.

'We believe the last touch has come off the Yeovil player so the Bucknall player can therefore not be offside. That's why the goal stands.'

He ran back to the centre circle and restarted the game. The Yeovil manager exploded into abuse.

'How the fuck can you give that? He's half a mile offside and their player has definitely got something on the ball. Fucking hell.' He then spotted Gifford still looking at him and aimed words in his direction, 'And you can fuck off as well. Fucking cheats.'

Gifford turned away and caught Gough's eye. He couldn't stop his mouth from curling into a smile and Gough burst out laughing. Somehow, the football gods had decided to shine on Bucknall in a crucial moment. They had the lead.

Yeovil wilted in their own frustration. The fans now protested every single decision given against them, from a throw-in to a free kick, and the players continued to get in the referee's face. Bucknall found some rhythm finally. They started to utilise Conor Caldwell and Archie Lewitt in wide positions and Tommy Pearce got some more time on the ball. He turned away from his marker with typical guile and won another free kick, a few metres inside the Yeovil half and just in front of Gifford's eye line.

Sebastian D'Amato jogged over to take it. Gifford muttered to him to aim for the back post, where the centre-backs were gathering. D'Amato got good purchase on the ball and lofted it where his manager had directed. Brook was marked tightly but managed to wriggle into enough space to get his head to the ball first. It bounced straight into a defender's midriff, but the keeper had dived in the direction it was heading and when it dropped loose, Ardie Adomako was free to pass it in the empty net; 2-0. Bucknall were flying.

Now Gifford celebrated, wildly jumping all over Gough and Haines. Adomako ran around the goal with a delighted and stunned expression on his face. He hadn't scored all season; in fact, Gifford wasn't sure he'd even seen him score in training. Again, this was a surefire sign that everything was going Bucknall's way. They kept their two-goal lead going into the break.

Gifford kept his message short and sweet, 'They're going to throw everything at you, lads. They've got nothing to lose now. So, we need to make sure we kill the pace of the game as much as possible. Take your time over every set piece but don't go getting yourselves booked. I promise you, they will over-commit eventually and leave space in behind where we can kill this off. So be patient. We do not need to force this now.'

The players executed it perfectly. Yeovil created some half chances, but none that looked like leading to a goal. Bucknall threw their bodies on the line as they had done at

Mansfield and against Doncaster in the FA Cup, putting in another admirable, backs-to-the-wall display. And with a little over ten minutes to go they did get their break. Dunne released down the channel by an incisive pass by Lewitt. He waited and held the ball up as best he could before pulling it back for Pearce to sweep home; 3-0.

It was a goal that finally silenced the stadium. Apart from the goals, it was the only time Gifford had heard the Bucks fans all game. Now there were loud 'oles' for every pass and an emphatic cry of 'you're not singing any more!' Gifford was able to enjoy the last few minutes, watching his team on with a joyous smile on his face. Pearce entered showboat mode and threw in as many step-overs and chops as he could manage. Lewitt made a determined run beyond him and Pearce slipped the pass on the inside of the full-back. Lewitt composed himself and sent the goalkeeper the wrong way, sending a slightly scruffy shot trickling into the far corner; 4-0. The match had gone better than anyone could possibly have imagined.

Final score: Yeovil Town 0 Bucknall 4

Chester FC vs Bucknall
Deva Stadium
4 June
Play-off semi-final

The build-up to the Chester game was far more focused and tactical. Gifford knew that his side had been taken apart by the Seals on their last visit to the Deva Stadium. He worked tirelessly on an unusual tactical plan. He instructed Kieran Dunne and Tommy Pearce to act as wide players when Bucknall didn't have the ball and to follow the Chester full-backs as they attacked. This would stop them from always being the free men and limit the amount of time they'd have on the ball and therefore the amount of crosses they could put in. It was defensive, with Gifford basically instructing his entire side to come back and defend, but he knew if they had any chance it would be to keep the scoring low and try and nick the first goal.

He could tell that the team had got their momentum back. They had basically scrapped their way into the play-offs in the end, never really hitting the heights of performance they had managed in the middle of the season. And yet with one controversial and fortunate goal, they had suddenly clicked back into groove and had defeated an accomplished Yeovil team in style. He could sense there was genuine belief among his players again; there was a buzz at training and a confidence in the way they interacted with each other.

When the game arrived, Gifford found himself in a calmer mood. If they were slight underdogs against Yeovil, they were massive outsiders against Chester, who were frankly very unlucky not to be promoted automatically. He took a sharp intake of breath, knowing he was in for a tense evening where his side would surrender practically all control of the game.

His plan was executed well. Dunne and Pearce did their job diligently, tracking the full-backs every time they came forward. At one point, Dunne, the team's striker, was deeper than Max Warren-Smith and Archie Lewitt on their side. Chester were still good enough on the ball to work little corridors of space in the midfield and they had a couple of shots from outside the box that Matt Finch saved comfortably. Gifford found himself looking constantly at the clock in the far corner of the stadium. They got through ten minutes. Then 20. Then they had a spell of possession that led up to the half-hour mark. The home fans began to get reckless.

Bucknall hadn't even had a shot at this point, until D'Amato finally found a pass into Pearce's feet, out on the far-right touchline. Pearce went to pass the ball infield but cut the ball back, digging his ankle into the turf to send the approaching defender sliding into space as he turned away from him. He stuck out his left leg to poke the ball forwards, just keeping it on the pitch. For the first time in the game, he had open space in front of him. Dunne was the only player in the attacking half and was on the other side of the pitch so Pearce advanced, keeping the ball close to his feet. Another player approached and Pearce rolled the ball under his studs to slip it between his legs. The player grabbed at him, trying to save his embarrassment by physically nudging him off the ball. Pearce got his body in front and emerged, still moving forwards.

Gifford instinctively stepped forwards, his eyes fixed on the ball. Pearce was now approaching the edge of the penalty area as a Chester centre-half came out to close him down. Pearce faked to shoot a few times, making the defender flinch and freeze for a split second. He continued to move inside him, controlling the ball with the edge of his toe to keep it just out of reach. The defender lunged in and Pearce shifted it away at the last moment. Now he could shoot. Gifford was practically on the pitch, screaming at his player. Pearce dummied one more time, allowing the ball to run past the other centre-half before he finally put his foot through the ball. The last dummy had also wrong-footed the goalkeeper and he was powerless as it went high into the back of the net; 1-0.

Gifford let out a loud, guttural roar and threw his arms in the air, before breaking out into hysterical laughter. It was the goal of the season. Pearce had just done a Maradona. The striker knew it too, dodging his team-mates' crazed dives at him and shaking his hand with lips pursed and an arrogant grin on his face. He eventually made his way to the away fans and simply outstretched his arms in front of them, allowing himself to bask in their adoration. A few of them began to bow in front of him and a few of the Bucknall players joined in. Gifford's mind flashed back to the moment he and Lee Chugwell had arrived at Pearce's house in the autumn. His gamble had been repaid tenfold.

The goal was such a rare one that it caused a strange vacuum in the stadium. Gifford was certain he had even heard a few claps from the Chester fans behind him. It was as if everyone, from players to fans, couldn't believe what they had just seen. When the half-time whistle sounded, there were no boos or cheers, just a general stunned whimper around the ground.

When Gifford got back to the dressing room, he saw Kieran Dunne and Stefon Harrison asking Pearce questions about the goal, Pearce sat back leaning against the lockers, enjoying the attention of his audience.

Gifford yelled at them, making half the room jump, 'Oi! You two! What the fuck are you doing?! Talking to him like he's your idol. The game isn't over! I don't want to hear any mention of the goal until the game is finished, do you understand me? We are not there yet. We've got a lead to defend and the focus should on be nothing else.'

Gifford was deliberately raising his voice and stressing the words harder than he needed to. He wasn't mad. In fact, he wanted to tell Pearce of his brilliance himself, but he knew he needed to shake the team up. They would lose if they got too comfortable, even for a second. He continued to criticise their first-half performance, ignoring the confused and shocked expressions of the players. He needed to keep them on edge.

He sent them out early as well, ensuring they were properly warmed up for the second half. His mind was fighting its own battle, thoughts of the final and Wembley flashed through it like a series of photos, but he shrugged them away, refusing to get carried away. Chester had clearly been given a rollocking of their own at the break and upped the tempo even further when the game restarted.

In the end, their pressure was too much. They kept recycling the ball into the box and as Bucknall's players tired, they began to stop tracking the runs in the wide areas. After a ball was flicked on a few times in the box, it eventually fell to the back post, where the Chester winger smashed it into the back of the net, amid the entire Bucknall defence throwing themselves to the floor in unison, trying to block it; 1-1. Gifford sighed and looked briefly to the sky, but he had known it was coming. He called Conor Caldwell over to him and whispered as discretely as he could, 'Just get to extra time. Don't over-commit.'

In the end, Chester settled for that as well. The final five minutes ebbed away as was always the case when both teams could sense that the extra period was coming. The pressing from both sides stopped, with neither daring to break away from their shape, even for a second. Gifford didn't sit down for a moment, manically ordering his players around and urging them on until the final whistle. He breathed a sigh of relief when it arrived.

He gathered the staff, substitutes and players in a large huddle in their half of the pitch, breaking into the middle of it to offer instructions. This was the first time they had played past the allotted 90 minutes all season and Gifford felt in uncharted territory. There were thoughts of Alf Ramsey's 'You've won it once, go and win it again' in his mind, but he knew that wasn't necessary here. His players looked exhausted. There was heavy breathing and pale, gaunt faces all around the circle. Gifford opted for a simple message, taking a huge punt with his words.

'I wanted it to go to extra time, because I knew we'd win it. They've put too much into getting back into the game, they're more shattered than you are. We're going to win this, I know it.'

He made one more big gamble, withdrawing Pearce for Sajja Gujar. It was always a risk as Pearce was perhaps Bucknall's only player capable of scoring from nothing, as he had displayed earlier in the game, but he had barely been able to run in the closing stages and Gifford decided they couldn't afford a passenger for the next half an hour. Gujar would bring energy and enthusiasm and that could never be knocked.

Chester thew another attacker on themselves, so Gifford adapted the formation a final time, finally relinquishing the strikers of their defensive duties and putting an extra full-back on to essentially revert to a back six, with Golding and Harrison patrolling the midfield in front of them and Dunne and Gujar allowed to stay upfront to pose a counter threat. Chester continued to miss chances. A centre-half badly mistimed a free header in the box, shouldering it over. Their striker worked a yard of space but Brook's studs stopped the pace of the ball and sent it bouncing up harmlessly into Finch's gloves. They had a free kick that beat the wall and missed the near post by an inch. Bucknall got through one half and into the final 15 minutes.

Gifford was praying for one moment, knowing that general football logic would dictate that they would get at least one. Gujar put pressure on the tired centre-half and his pass was deflected to Golding. Gujar ran in behind immediately and Golding measured his pass perfectly, sliding it down the channel with the side of his foot. The bench all rose to their feet. Gujar ran on to it as the Chester goalkeeper approached. It was going to be a difficult chance. He stuck out his right leg and got his foot on the ball, slipping it under the goalkeeper. There was no pace on it and it seemed to take an age as it trickled towards the goal line. Gifford found himself willing the ball on, moving his hand forwards as if he could somehow push it in. A defender dived in, but it was too late. The ball gently brushed against the back of the net; 2-1.

The whole team came together in a writhing cacophony of bodies. There were screams and shrieks and sobs. It was impossible to know whose limb belonged to who as they meshed together, intertwining and interlocking. Gifford's ears began to throb and he could feel a ringing in them for the final few minutes of the game. Any instructions he tried to give got caught in his throat. He didn't even hear the whistle, but Haines grabbing him by the waist and grappling him on to the pitch was enough confirmation.

Once more, he and his team came together in front of their away fans. Gifford found a moment to find Tommy Pearce and mutter in his ear,

'That was one of the greatest goals I've ever seen by the way.'

The Chester fans dissipated away as it was only Bucknall voices and figures left in the stadium. The players suddenly found adrenaline that had deserted them for most of the previous hour and were bouncing with delight. They joined the supporters in their songs and hugged each other tightly. Gifford stayed out of it as best he could, but he couldn't resist one particular tune.

He joined in with the hundreds of other hoarse, hearty voices that broke out into the evening breeze and belted out the words at the top of his lungs, 'Que sera, sera. Whatever will be, will be! We're going to Wembley!'

Final score: Chester FC 1 Bucknall 2 (after extra time)

43

On the Friday before the weekend of the play-off final, Darren Gifford headed to the Goose on the Water to meet up with Gough and Haines and a few other members of the Bucknall staff. A final drink before the battle began were Lee Chugwell's words in the WhatsApp group when arranging the event.

As Gifford pulled into the familiar pebbled car park, he was taken back to the time he had retreated there after watching the Yeovil game earlier in the season. The decision to escape the traffic and get as far as he could out of town had indirectly set in motion a series of events that had led him to Wembley Stadium as manager of his beloved team. He stayed sitting in the Golf as he pulled up, even after he had switched the engine off, collecting his thoughts. He watched the stream flow gently, following it bend and loop around the pub. Some calm before the storm, he mused, and opened the car door.

He found the other inside and they gathered around a large table in the corner, with drinks being ordered en masse.

Chugwell raised his glass and kicked proceedings off with a toast.

'I'd just to like to say that I'm incredibly proud of everyone at this table. We have achieved an incredible feat this season, regardless of whether a win or loss awaits us this weekend. Cheers to that.'

The sentiment echoed around the table in a series of clangs and clinks. There were half-assed attempts to make casual conversation, asking after each others' families and other issues outside of football, but it was clear there was only one thing anyone wanted to talk about. Gough slumped back and said into space,

'Bloody hell. Wembley hey?'

And thus began a great sharing of memories; a commune on what made football people fall in love with football. They took it in turns recounting their favourite Wembley moments, going around the table like a kind of 'Football Fans Anonymous' meeting.

'The first one I remember is the Ricky Villa goal. Weaving in and out of the City players, as if the game was suddenly being played in slow motion. He didn't even need to run, the ball was that under his spell,' said Haines.

'A poor man's Tommy Pearce, you could say!' said Nick, the commercial exec, to enthused laughter.

'For me, it's the Wimbledon final. The Crazy Gang have beaten the Culture Club!' said Gough, dramatically doing his best John Motson impression. 'And that Vinnie Jones tackle on Steve McMahon. Back in the days of proper football!'

'Oh, I've got one,' said Chugwell, chiming in. 'The Liverpool suits. At the – what was it – '95 final. No, it was '96. I can tell you with absolute certainty we will not be doing that!'

'You sure? I've always fancied myself in a bit of cream!' exclaimed Gough.

'The Gazza goal,' said Nick, and there was a chorus of noises bordering on arousal. 'The flick on from Darren Anderton, the whoopsy over poor old Colin Hendry's head and then he leathers it past Jim Leighton. And then he tops it all off with the best celebration in history. That's the moment I fell in love with football right there, I'm telling you.'

'What about you, Giff?' asked Chugwell.

There was a brief silence for the first time as everybody's eyes flickered in Gifford's direction. Gifford paused. He knew what his answer was, but wasn't sure it was in keeping with the nostalgic mood of the conversation. Eventually, he cleared his throat and spoke.

'Well, for me I only think of the play-off final I played in myself. I still consider it the highlight of my career probably, even though we lost. You just know that you're in the same dressing rooms as so many legends that have become more. You can feel the ghosts of greatness, you know what I mean? And then when you step out on to that pitch. It's like you're writing your own little line in the history of football.'

'You're talking about the Dion Mackie final, right?' asked Nick, eagerly leaning forward in his chair.

'Yeah.'

'To think, we were that close to the Championship. If only Dion Mackie could take a fucking penalty, hey?'

'Well, Dion was brilliant for us. He had basically got us there in the first place with his goals that season.'

'I know, but just you think about where the club might be.'

'Well, I doubt any of us would be sat here at this table, with our own Wembley final to go to, that's for sure.'

'That's true. To Dion Mackie then,' said Chugwell.

'To Dion Mackie!' cried the ensemble.

Another round was ordered. The drinks helped to ease their tongues even further and the questions that had been restrained at the start of their gathering could now not be held back any longer.

'What do you reckon then, Giff. Are we going to do it?' asked Nick.

'It's impossible to tell, mate. I would say that I don't think the players could possibly be in a better place. I think they've found their second wind at exactly the right time. But Dagenham & Redbridge are a top team, as we well know.'

'Yeah, let's hope it's not 4-0 again!' said Chugwell.

'It won't be,' said Gifford sternly, fixing Chugwell with an icy glare. 'I can say with some certainty it's going to be tight. We've just got to hope we come out on top in the crucial moments.'

'Imagine if we do manage it though. We started the season trying to stay in the bleeding National League and now we might be back in the EFL!' said Nick, his excitement nearly causing him to spill his pint.

'Well that's all down to our manager. Didn't I say, Nick, last time we were in this pub in fact, you never know what you're gonna get with managers at this level. We just happened to find a Guardiola.'

Gifford shrugged away the compliment instantly, 'I am no Guardiola, let me tell you.'

'All I'm saying is that if we do happen to end the weekend on the right side of things, with a trophy in our grasp, I know we've got the right man to lead us into League Two and beyond.'

Gifford went silent and withdrew into himself. He let the laughter and discussion continue in muted murmurs around him but was occupied purely with his own thoughts. He had pushed all thoughts of what lay ahead after the final completely from his mind. It was just as a final should be: an ending; the sporting equivalent of a curtain call. What came next could wait until after he had taken his final bow at least.

44

Bucknall vs Dagenham & Redbridge
11 June
Wembley
Play-off final

Darren Gifford stepped into the dressing room. The space was five times larger than Bucknall's own home dressing room, with immaculate silver walls and bright lights illuminating the space. It bordered on a spiritual space, closer to a yoga studio than a place for football boots and shin pads. The players' shirts were already hung up for them, all lined up on pegs, numbers and surnames facing out into the room. The squad sat on the benches, curved around in the oval shape, with Gifford stepping out into the smooth, tiled surface to address his team one more time.

He held his arms out, chewing his lip slightly, rehearsing a speech he had planned over and over for the whole of the previous week. This was the last time he could really make a difference to his side and he wasn't going to waste it.

'Well. We're here. Take it all in, lads. It's a special day,' he began, making sure to enunciate and stress each word. 'Now, we've all seen a thousand of these. Finals will always lead to a winner and a loser. And in every game, there is a different story. Sometimes the better team wins comfortably and asserts their supremacy, sometimes the underdog defends valiantly and rides their luck to a famous win, sometimes it's a scrap between two sides who are so evenly matched, it takes the narrowest of margins to separate them. The only pattern I can possibly find between all of these finals is that the team who wins is always the one who handles the occasion better. The team that gets the closest to playing their best. Make sure that that's you today.'

He continued, but started to walk around the room, addressing individual players with specific remarks, a tactic he had never used before, 'Think about what you're playing for. Be sure to find your individual inspiration. Brooky, you've got the chance to lift that trophy above your head as a winning captain. Con, Archie, both of you are good enough to be playing in the EFL, so let's make that happen. Stef, Ardie, the way that you two have dealt with what happened earlier this season already makes you heroes in my eyes, so you can play without fear. Goldo, the same with you, you've already overcome your demons, this game is nothing compared to that. Pearcey, you've proven to everybody that you're the best player in this entire division, now is your chance to complete the perfect redemption.'

Gifford paused, finding that he needed to swallow to hold his emotions in check. He offered one final message, 'Don't forget, I've been in your shoes boys. I've played in a final at this magnificent stadium. And I came up short. I don't think I can cope with coming up short again.'

The players lined up in the tunnel, Gifford standing at the front, dressed in his best suit. He could hear the noise of the crowd funnelling through the open doors in front of them. Looking back at his team, there was nothing but pride filling his body. He looked across at the Dagenham team, the red and blue of their kit juxtaposed with the grey and black of the Bucknall strip. They got the nod and began to make their way through the doors, the light and warmth of the sun gradually stretching over them with every step they took. The grey banks of the stands either side of them curved up as the first fans came into view, peeking over the bannisters to get a glimpse at the teams. He hadn't heard of a single Bucknall supporter who wasn't attending but the smaller size of both clubs meant there were still empty seats in view in the top tiers of the giant stands, the bright red patches acting like a party banner around the stadium.

There were still plenty of fans to see. Decked out in their respective teams' colours, they bellowed and applauded with all the energy they could muster as they came out into the open. It was a noise completely removed from any other atmosphere Gifford had experienced all season. The sheer vastness of Wembley meant that the noise seemed to go on for miles. It was as if they had ten Yewtree Lanes lined up in a row, all echoing the same call. The grandeur of the stage was overwhelming. It was all so vast and bright and vibrant; a colosseum welcoming its champions to the field. The shadow of the roof left one half of the pitch in shadow, the other in blazing sunlight. The curve of the arch hanging over them like a great, distant halo.

His body was shaking with adrenaline, as if programming him to run on the pitch himself. He greeted the Dagenham staff warmly, being sure to offer extra kindness than normal. It was a day to show your best side, after all. In the moments before the match began, Gifford looked high up into the stands, darting his eyes around until he found the Bucknall box. There he saw Lee Chugwell, wearing a pristine suit of his own standing next to Steven Rosser, marked by his permanent weary frown. And then nearby, he saw his family, all wearing their Bucknall kits. Keira with her arm around Orla, who was tucked in at her mother's side, staring out in wonder. Danny stood next to them, looking much tenser. He was his father's son after all.

Gifford had named his best 11 and he looked at them as they stood in their formation; the formation he had championed and prepared.

		Finch (GK)		
Caldwell	Brook	Adomako	Warren-Smith	Lewitt
	Golding	D'Amato	Harrison	
	Pearce		Dunne	

And finally – almost mercifully – the game began. The noise level rose once more as Bucknall began to pass the ball around, each player taking as much care as possible with every single touch, eyes fixed to the ball as it rolled their way. There were fluctuations in the noise as the sides took it in turns to play passes deep into the opposite half, making the respective defences turn and retreat for the first time. There were a few signs of nerves, with a goal kick from each goalkeeper being scuffed into midfield rather than towards the strikers. Free kicks were won for trips and scuffles and the minutes ticked on.

Gifford yelled at his players for width, gesturing for Conor Caldwell to pull out right to the near touch-line. When he did, Sebastian D'Amato found him with a nice lofted pass. Caldwell had time to advance into space and played a smooth one-two with Danny Golding, taking the nearest marker out of the game. He looked up to assess his options for an early cross but saw Tommy Pearce drop off instead and pull into space on the edge of the box. The pass to him was crisp and Pearce could look up before he received it. Kieran Dunne made a run off the left-hand side of the centre-half so he was on the edge of the penalty area, creating a few yards of space. Pearce took one touch out of his feet and crunched a pass towards Dunne, with plenty of pace. Dunne prepared in advance and turned his body to open up the angle for the shot. The defender wasn't going to get there in time. Just as the ball approached, it took the slightest bobble off the turf, skipping up wonderfully, like a golf ball off a tee. Dunne connected with the side of his foot and curled the ball round. The ball drifted in and nestled into the far corner of the net; 1-0 Bucknall.

Cue the celebrations. The Bucks were off to the perfect start. Gifford swung his fist in delight, but went no further than that, knowing there was still a long way to go. The players and staff were jumping around in delight and the Bucknall end of the stadium exploded into mayhem, a frantic flurry of noise and colour. It was a glorious moment.

Dagenham immediately fought back. The rest of the half was undeniably theirs, with their twin strikers causing the Bucknall defence problems as they had in their previous meetings. In the minutes before half-time, they found their equaliser. It was played into the striker's feet and he played a first-time ball around the corner, into the gap between Ardie Adomako and Max Warren-Smith. Their midfielder ran on to it and half volleyed it past Matt Finch; 1-1. A goal as good as Bucknall's; a moment of quality apiece. It was the Dagenham fans' turn to celebrate wildly and Gifford felt a familiar tension in his stomach. He gritted his teeth and breathed through it.

Gifford couldn't believe how fast the game was moving. The moments before kick-off had felt like an eternity and yet the first half had gone by in an instant. He had planned a series of inspirational half-time team talks in case of various catastrophic scenarios but none were needed. Of the kinds of final he had known, it was the tight, nothing-in-it kind. The worst one to go through as a manager.

The game started to become a series of sensations, as much as passages of play. When Bucknall had comfortable possession, Gifford found he could think clearly. When Dagenham had the ball in open play, his muscles tightened but he still felt comfortable, as the players stayed disciplined in their shape and the ball wasn't making it into dangerous areas. It was the scruffy moments that he found he hated the most, the uncontrollable periods that lay out of his tactical reach. Deflections that bounced the wrong way in the midfield or free kicks that didn't need to be conceded in dangerous areas. These were the moments where he could feel his heart thumping and his throat and mouth getting dryer.

His worries were proven correct. A poor corner was headed away comfortably by a Bucknall head but as the players pushed, both Lewitt and Harrison went to press the player who received it, meaning the corner taker could make a run into the space behind them. It happened before Gifford could yell the words of warning and the Dagenham man had the ball on the touchline in the box. He pulled the ball across, driving his foot through it. It seemed to evade everyone until the Dagenham striker and leant back and dug his foot behind it, stumbling over as he did so. Finch had thrown himself down to make the save, but the ball spooned up and evaded him. A horribly untidy goal, and yet the one that might have finally killed their dream; 2-1 Dagenham & Redbridge.

Gifford responded immediately, taking off Warren-Smith for Sajja Gujar and switching to a 4-1-2-1-2. He wanted Pearce to drop into the half spaces between midfield and attack and outnumber them in those key areas. Bucknall had 15 minutes to save themselves. That was more than enough time, Gifford said to himself. The formation had the desired effect and Bucknall gained further control as Dagenham inevitably sat back more. Their defence marshalled their penalty area brilliantly, clearing anything that came their way. Gifford knew the Bucks were going to need to do something different to score. The traditional routes weren't available to them.

More minutes ticked by. Pearce got frustrated and tried a shot from distance that went horribly high into the stands, to loud jeers. Gifford kept muttering 'patience' to any player who came within earshot of him, but he was struggling to come up with any new solutions himself. Archie Lewitt courageously took on three defenders who crowded him in the corner and kicked it off their shins. D'Amato prepared to swing the ball in. Gifford's head dropped as it was another Dagenham head that got there first, sending the ball into space before it dropped towards the edge of the box. Pearce was setting himself for a volley but Gifford loudly shouted for him not to shoot.

Pearce, at the last second, let the ball drop on to the top of his foot and he cushioned it to the side of him, evading the two closing defenders. It set up beautifully for Stefon Harrison to come on to and he did have time to get a shot away. He waited and drilled the ball with his left foot, hitting it downwards so it spun off the turf. It went through a crowd of players. Gifford heard the roar of the crowd before he saw that the ball had settled in the bottom corner; 2-2.

The game petered out after that; 2-2, extra time once more. Gifford checked in with all of his players to asses their fitness and energy levels. Every single one of them reassured him they were good to stay on the pitch. He discussed potential changes with Gough and Haines as the referee called the players back once more.

'You know what we have to think about, don't you?' said Haines.

'What?'

'Making sure we finish with our best penalty takers.'

The mention of the word penalty sent a brief shiver trickling down Gifford's back. It was a looming shadow that hung over the entirety of the extra 30 minutes. Unlike the Chester game, it was a disjointed affair which was mainly dominated by players going down for cramp and confrontations as the tempers began to flare. It was as if both sides had accepted they weren't going to break down the other in open play and so started to play for set pieces and long throw-ins. Gifford screamed at the fourth official for a red card after Pearce was cynically brought down on a rare counterattack. He knew that it was only worthy of a yellow and offered an apology a few minutes afterwards, desperate to retain some class amid the chaos. Ryan Brook went down after Bucknall had used all their subs and, after a brief conversation with Gifford and the physio, limped back on to the pitch. Gifford wasn't sure if Brook could actually kick the ball any longer, but he still continued to head it clear.

It was during the 119th minute of the final when the realisation occurred. It was going to go to penalties. Gifford stopped focusing on the game and started picking names in his mind. When the whistle finally sounded, he knew the players who he was going to trust to win them promotion with five uncontested shots at goal. Just like his own play-off final, it was 2-2 again. Penalties. Again.

The team gathered in a huddle by their dugout as Gifford revealed who he had chosen. Dunne was their regular taker so he would shoot first. The first penalty set the tone, so you wanted your best for that. D'Amato and Pearce were the best technical players at the club so they were two and three. Gifford picked Gujar at four, though this was the first default choice as he was the only other attacker left on the pitch. And at five, Gifford had chosen Golding.

The referee tossed a coin. He pointed to the end where the Bucknall fans were mainly congregated. That was good. Dagenham & Redbridge were going to kick first. That was not.

Both teams formed separate lines on each side of the pitch, arms around each other, gripping their shoulders tightly. Gifford and his staff did the same as they watched on. It was very welcome as it helped hold in and restrain the tension that was circulating in his body. He clenched his face, trying to mask the suffocating emotions he was experiencing.

Dagenham's first kick. Strode up and side-footed high to Finch's left. It clattered off the post! Miss; 0-0.

Kieran Dunne. Puffing out his cheeks, a sideways run-up, sent the keeper the wrong way and smashed into the bottom right. Goal; 0-1.

Dagenham's second. Left-footer. Did Finch with his eyes. Goal; 1-1.

Sebastian D'Amato. Too weak. Saved comfortably by the keeper. Miss; 1-1.

Dagenham's third. Finch went the right way but beaten by pace. Goal; 2-1.

Tommy Pearce. Short run-up. Panenka down the middle. Typical. Goal; 2-2.

Dagenham's fourth. Straight down the middle. Goal; 3-2.

Sajja Gujar. The best of the lot. High into the top left. Goal; 3-3.

Dagenham's fifth. Struck to the keeper's right. Finch sticking out a right hand to palm it clear. Miss; 3-3.

And so it all came down to the last kick. Danny Golding stepped out of the line and made his walk towards the goal. He picked the ball up and bounced it a few times. Gifford dug his fingers in Gough's collar bone. His mind was clicking at a rate he had never known, thought after thought filling his mind. The Goose on the Water. His first game. The crowd singing his song. His first award. The FA Cup run. The Christmas party. The Trosley incident. His talk with John Williams. Danny Golding. His Danny. Keira. Orla. Dion fucking Mackie.

Golding settled over the ball and stayed looking at it. He took a few steps back and started his run-up. He put the side of the foot behind the ball and angled it towards the right of the goal. The keeper dived and stretched out a long arm. The ball skidded along and hit the base of the post. Gifford froze. It bounced back and sneaked back across the goal line, before kissing the back of the net. Goal; 3-4.

Bucknall had won.

Final score: Bucknall 2 Dagenham & Redbridge 2 (after extra time, Bucknall won 4-3 on penalties

45

The players made their way up the famous steps. Darren Gifford's suit was now soaked through, his tie abandoned in his pocket and his shirt opened at the top. He shook hands with as many people as he could as he made the ascent, a series of hands outstretched, clinging to him as he passed them. There were various things shouted at him, ranging from words of congratulation to declarations of love. His body was totally exhausted and he could feel each step in his knees. The smell of sweat tinged with body spray and Deep Heat wafted down the line of the players in front of him.

They turned the corner, taking them out on to the viewing tier, where a series of people were waiting for them, as well as the shining silver trophy. A bulky base and then a delicate thin spine that ballooned out into the mouth of the cup, curving around before branching into its two coiled arms. The grey and black ribbons hanging down from the lid, with a small, thin spiral sitting on its top.

Lee Chugwell and Steven Rosser were among those who had made their way to greet them. Chugwell gave Gifford a delighted wink. Rosser nodded in his direction before breaking out into a smile. There were other dignitaries of the league who offered polite words as the entirety of the squad and staff emerged out, with the whole majesty of the stadium in front of them. Ryan Brook was handed the trophy, which he greeted with a kiss, before raising it high above his head. The Bucknall fans jumped and applauded. Pyro was fired in the stadium and confetti rained down from the roof. Gifford stood and watched every one of his players have their turn with the cup, thinking of each of their contributions towards it as they did so.

Eventually, it found its way to him. He gripped the metal tightly, feeling it give slightly as his hands adjusted to the weight. Before he raised it, he once more looked out into the stadium and found the frames of the people he most wanted to see. His family looked back at him, waving madly. Even across half the stadium, Gifford felt he was meeting Keira's eyes. He raised the trophy into the air and they cheered back at him. There was one phrase that formed in his mind as he let the euphoria engulf him.

Football, he thought. Bloody hell.

ND - #0320 - 270225 - C0 - 234/156/11 - PB - 9781780916545 - Gloss Lamination